Salvation
at
Rio Feo

STEVEN LANE SMITH

outskirtspress

DENVER, COLORADO

Outskirts Press, Inc.
http://www.outskirtspress.com

ISBN: 978-1-4787-5994-2

Outskirts Press and the "OP" logo are trademarks belonging to Outskirts Press, Inc.

For Luke and Edie

Chapter 1
TOMMY GUNN

TOMMY GUNN WAS a towheaded American boy born in the South by the grace of God in Kegg County near the town of Toxic Lick, Kentucky. An only child, he became the sole survivor of his family at the age of two when his parents were gunned down in Detroit. Choate and Diane Gunn had left Tommy in the care of Choate's father, Pop Gunn, so Choate and Diane could find employment on an auto assembly line in Michigan.

"At the time," as Pop told the story, "the job of takin' money from working people to give to people who wouldn't work lay mostly in the hands of the Government. That wasn't enough for some in Detroit, however, so a few fellers with a hankering for action were stealing wallets and handbags from people stuck in traffic jams. Well, one feller broke Choate's windows with a chain, and Choate decapitated him with his sawed-off twelve gauge. Shortly after that, Choate had eight bullets in him and Diane had four. They bled out before the traffic light turned green."

Pop always told the story the same matter-of-fact way to

hide how gravely the loss of Choate had wounded him. Pop lost his tolerance for confrontation after that, so he kept the truth from Tommy. Tommy turned eight still believing his parents had died making Ford Mustangs.

That wasn't Pop's first brush with misfortune. Several years before Choate's death, Pop's passions had migrated from his wife to whiskey. Pop's drinking had been Mrs. Gunn's main justification for running away, out of the blue, with an auctioneer from Louisiana.

"I woulda appreciated a heads-up that she was runnin' off with that fast-talking Coon-ass so I wouldna looked like such a fool driving around lookin' for her like she was a lost puppy," Pop said.

Some men drown their sorrows in booze, but Pop's sorrows were already well-marinated in shine and legal stuff, too. From the day of Mrs. Gunn's departure, moderation ruled Pop's drinking, eating, judgments, opinions, and sense of discipline. Usually.

"Moderation in all things," Pop used to say, "including moderation."

Pop was a gentle man. He never raised a hand against Tommy. On the other hand, he didn't make a show of public affection, either. The words *I love you* never passed Pop's lips. Pop sometimes regretted that he had never uttered those three intimate words to Choate. The closest he ever got was, *When it comes to lovin' your son, I reckon I do.* That's what Pop said at Choate's funeral when it was too late to do Choate any good. To make up for these failings, Pop doted on Tommy.

Tommy had spent the previous night with the Tolliver Family so Pop could prepare *the surprise* for his grandson's eighth birthday. Early in the afternoon, the three Tollivers arrived at Pop's trailer with Tommy, blindfolded Iranian-hostage style.

"That's a fine looking pony," Mr. Tolliver dissembled. About thirty, he was sun-tanned from working in tobacco fields. He wore a cotton plaid shirt, overalls, beat-up boots, and a blue University of Kentucky baseball cap. He stood beside Pop's mobile home with a big grin on his face and a can of Budweiser in hand.

"Nothing as pleasing as a new lawn mower," Mrs. Tolliver said. She was dressed in culottes, a gingham blouse, and sandals. Her eyes were the same sky blue color as all the Tollivers and the Gunns. Blue was the default eye color in the hollows of Kegg County.

Eight-year-old Lori Tolliver, Tommy's best friend, said nothing. Her hair was as pale as corn silk. She was barefoot, and she wore cotton shorts and a blue tee shirt with white letters that read "KENTUCKY".

Pop Gunn was a spry man of fifty-four years. He was dressed in a white tee shirt, worn overalls, and brown boots. He used one hand to hold his Budweiser and the other to aim Tommy toward *the surprise*.

Dressed in a white tee shirt and a pair of cut-off jeans, Tommy sniffed to guess the origin of the tar smell.

When Pop lowered the bandanna from Tommy's eyes, the Birthday Boy's knees buckled, because *the surprise* exceeded all his expectations. A new backboard post was set into a freshly laid square of asphalt measuring thirty by thirty feet. The adjustable rim had been installed at eight feet above the surface of the court. Pop flipped a brand new basketball to Tommy.

"Your future ain't in them tobacco fields yonder," Pop said. "This here's your future."

Tommy dribbled the ball on the court. He felt the heat of the freshly-laid asphalt on the soles of his bare feet. He launched a jump shot that went through the hoop and nested briefly in the tight new nylon net.

"I've done some calculating," Pop said, "and if you shoot two hundred and seventy-four shots ever' day, by the time you're eighteen, you'll have a million shots under your belt. Yes, sir, that there's your future."

Pop pressed the fingertips and palm of Tommy's right hand onto the moist underside of the lid of a can of Wildcat Blue exterior paint. He got Tommy to jump as high as he could to leave a hand print on the post. Pop painted an "8" beside the fresh hand print.

Tommy was no genius, but he wasn't a dunce, either. Pop's permissive hand and liberal praise, however, had cultivated a sense of superiority in Tommy. Like his father Choate, Tommy thought he was smarter than everyone else, so he seldom sought advice and he shunned collaboration. When he got an idea, he ran with it.

Within twenty minutes of cleaning the blue paint from his hand, Tommy dragged his mini-trampoline onto the court in front of the rim. He gave a lot of thought to the takeoff but almost none to the landing. He got a running start, bounced on the trampoline, soared into the air, slam-dunked his new basketball, and fell to the asphalt, breaking both ankles. Tommy had taken off with twenty-six bones in each foot, but, after landing, he had more than that. You could hear bones cracking all the way to the picnic table in the front lawn where the Tollivers sat chatting with Pop. Lori screamed bloody murder and ran to comfort the grounded high-flyer.

"What the hell's that young'un gone and done now?" Pop asked.

Tommy writhed in pain on the asphalt and wished he had tested his theory before implementing it.

Many people might have chosen a new pastime, but not Tommy. While he was still on crutches, both feet immobilized in plaster, he was out shooting baskets on his new court. He rehabilitated quickly, often shooting hoops with Lori for hours at a time. As soon as the casts came off his feet, Tommy constructed a home-made leg press machine using wood scraps, hay-bailing twine, a three-inch iron pipe, and cinderblocks. A decade of leg presses and shooting jump shots gave Tommy the legs of a kangaroo. As the annual hand prints on the goal post recorded, Tommy jumped higher every year. By the time he took his one-millionth jump shot, he was eighteen years old, six feet tall, and the apex of his hand print reached almost to twelve feet. His *vertical* measured fifty-inches. Even a person who didn't know a *vertical* from a *ventricle* understood that fifty inches was a lot of *vertical*.

"That boy's got hang time like a space shot," Pop told the men down at the general store.

Tommy and Lori became star shooting guards on the Toxic Lick high school boys' and girls' basketball teams. After graduation, the only college that offered them both full basketball scholarships was Kentucky Barber College, a small Methodist school located in downtown Toxic Lick.

KBC's name was as deceiving as Stetson, Rice, and Colgate. Students didn't attend Stetson University to make hats or Rice University to become farmers or Colgate University to make toothpaste, and students didn't go to Kentucky Barber to learn how to cut hair. KBC had been founded as a school for boys by the Reverend Jedediah Barber in 1822, two years after he had established a boutique sect of Methodists called Barberians.

The Barberians' signature doctrine was based on Genesis 17:14. "Any uncircumcised male, who has not been circumcised in the flesh, will be cut off from his people." The Barberians became known as *Cutters*. Methodists on the other side of the theological divide cited Romans 2:29, "Circumcision is circumcision of the heart," and First Corinthians 7:18, "Circumcision is nothing". The rift was so irreparable that the Barberians broke away from Methodism, and Reverend Barber donated everything he owned to found a college where the critical need for penis modification could be taught into perpetuity.

So, KBC and the Barberians had nothing to do with cutting hair and everything to do with flaying foreskins. As an example of the power of sectarianism in modern times, however, girls now attended KBC, people assumed KBC was a school for hair stylists, the school mascot was a Barber Pole, and varsity sports teams followed a firmly-entrenched tradition of getting haircuts before every game. Revisionist poppycock had taken root.

When the mayor of Toxic Lick made inflammatory remarks on the subject, Pop wrote a letter to the editor of the

Kegg County Independent.

"Things change over time. Harvard University was started by Puritans, but look at 'em now; they're a gaggle of godless Yankee socialist pinheads." Pop had never met anyone from Harvard, but he had reliable sources.

Pop wrote lots of letters to the editor, and the editor printed a few after a rigorous cleansing of syntax. Pop's most recent essay was a celebration of Kentucky Barber College's inclusion in the NCAA Tournament field.

"The fifteenth state to join the Union, Kentucky has always been the pick of the litter. We're famous for our thoroughbred horses, our tobacco, our whiskey — and — most of all – our basketball. The University of Kentucky has won the NCAA basketball title eight times, and the University of Louisville has won it three times. Now Kentucky Barber College has a shot. I thank the Lord for being born in Kentucky and for living to see this day."

During her four years as a Lady Cutter, Lori made an average of 56.3% of the field goals she attempted. Tommy's average was 52.7%. "In the words of Helen Reddy," Lori said, "I am woman, hear me roar." More than fourteen years had passed since their birthday-cake-eating, ankle-smashing introduction to basketball. During those years, they had transitioned from friends, to going steady, to secret lovers.

Lori's senior season with the Lady Cutters was too mediocre to earn a post-season tournament spot, but Tommy's

Cutters team had a remarkable year, advancing to the NCAA tournament for the first time in school history as a sixteen seed. The Cutters traveled by bus to Saint Louis for the opening round of the Midwest Regional where they were expected to get whipped and sent home by the number one seed from Columbia, Missouri, the Tigers of the University of Missouri.

Then, something unprecedented happened: the sixteenth-seeded Cutters moved through the tournament bracket like a runaway pair of hair clippers. The Cutters upset the University of Missouri and then went on to sneak by Arizona, Texas, Kentucky, and Kansas. This most talked-about subject on sports radio and TV was causing financial devastation among bookies from Connecticut to Las Vegas. Probabilities were out of whack. The Pendulum had swung in one direction too long. Something had to give when KBC played the Brut University Hyenas for the championship on the coming Monday night, the climax of March Madness.

CHAPTER 2

RIO FEO, NEW MEXICO

FIVE DECADES AGO, Rio Feo's phosphate mines had lured miners from as far away as North Dakota. The town grew quickly and without the benefit of zoning, so it was a visually offensive hodge-podge of adobe and wooden-frame structures. There was token diversification: two oil wells, a cotton gin, three cattle ranches, and a small pottery factory. Mesquite bushes grew sparsely on the desert sand that sprawled on all sides of Rio Feo to the horizon defined by mountains to the west.

A dry ravine split the town like a jagged incision. Old timers remembered torrential rainfall occasionally roiling through the ravine, hence the name *Rio Feo*. During such gully-washers, dormant miniature shrimp came alive for a day to be eaten by coyotes and vermin as the water receded and the arroyo baked in the sun until it was as dry as it had been the day the rains had come. The shrimp and the deluge were almost folk lore, because it hadn't rained in a serious way for over twenty years.

The phosphate mines played out and the mining companies closed down. The pottery factory closed for lack of water. The irrigated cotton fields grew less productive every year. Despite the arid conditions, rust covered the walking beams, horse heads, and counter weights of the two pump jacks that sucked oil up from deposits beneath the town. Whether you called them nodding donkeys, rocking horses, thirsty birds, or Big Texans, the pump jacks creaked around the clock, pulling up ever decreasing amounts of oil per stroke. In summary, Rio Feo was poor and getting poorer.

Inside a tired-looking adobe high school building, five serious souls met in a small conference room. The Rio Feo School Board was convened to hear another depressing report from the high school principal. Principal Charles Bradley, aged forty-five, always wore a bolo tie for these meetings, because it made him look like a local instead of the Wisconsin blow-in that he was. A misunderstanding over discretionary funding had sent him into exile to Rio Feo. Principal Bradley's tufts of hair spiked up like stunted corn stalks in a drought-stricken field. No one had the *cajones* to tell him to shave the wisps of hair away. He was a graduate of the Elmer Fudd School of Diction, and his life-time battle with the letter *R* made even serious statements sound comical.

"We're *dwopping* football and *westling*. We don't have enough students and we sure don't have the money."

The faces of the board members were morose masks, their eyes dulled by his dismal report.

"We'll keep basketball and baseball for as long as the football equipment budget will *cawwy* them."

"How will you find coaches?" one member asked.

"*Twust* me," Principal Bradley said.

The mood of the board matched the appearance of the town – tired, worn-out, hopeless.

"We are not without *attwactive attwibutes*," Principal Bradley lied to lift morale. "We have lots of sunshine, low humidity, and a low cost of living." Rio Feo had attributes, but, really, they weren't attractive.

Chapter 3

THE BRIEFCASE

TOMMY'S FIRST GLIMPSE of the stacks of money made his heart fibrillate. It was the same high-octane kick-in-the-heart he had felt on a roller coaster up in Louisville. Still, Caution remained ahead of Greed. Call it Caution 4 – Greed 2. Tommy stood up to evacuate the diner booth.

"*No hablo Ingles*," he said to the fat man named Puff Conducci.

"Sit down." Puff's lips were shiny with grease from his plate of all-you-can-eat fried chicken. His stubby fingers made oily prints on the briefcase when he opened it for Tommy to take another peek at the money.

Greed surged ahead. Greed 10 – Caution 4. Almost in slow motion, Tommy started yielding to temptation. He initiated negotiations with God.

Dear Heavenly Father, he prayed, *let me have the hundred thousand dollars and I'll pay off Pop's trailer and buy Lori a diamond ring and I'll walk the straight-and-narrow forever and ever, amen.* Tommy added a kicker to make the deal irresistible to God: *I'll put a hundred dollars in the Sunday offering.*

No, make it two.

Tommy didn't take money for granted, because he'd never had any. The prospect of so much money made him giddy. He knew that a hundred thousand dollars, a *hundo K*, a hundred large could turn a *nobody* into a *somebody* in a Kegg County nano-second. And, as Tommy had told Lori dozens of times, what he wanted more than anything was to be *somebody*.

Puff explained the agreement in a cartoonish Chicago accent.

"My boss, The Smelt . . . forget I said that . . . wants ya so friggin' motivated ya could eat a basketball like okra or whatever crap it is you hicks eat down here."

Down here was a fast-food joint on Broadway in Lexington. Puff wouldn't stop talking, as though he was nervous or was hiding something. He even complained about his nickname. Was he trying to be pals?

"They name ya, and that's it. *Puff*? You're thinking *Puff-the-Magic-friggin'-Dragon*, right? Do you see green scales or flames shooting out of my mouth? No."

Tommy shook his head. Why piss off the man with the money? Indeed, Tommy did *not* see scales or fire. What he *did* see was a three-hundred-pound bucket of guts dressed in a stained white shirt, brown suit, polyester tie, and tartan suspenders that would have made a Salvation Army volunteer blush. Puff reeked of garlic and stale tobacco. Puff's face couldn't have been more pock-marked if he had been blasted with buckshot. The birthmark on his right cheek was the shape of West Virginia.

"No. They call me Puff because I'm a friggin' chain-smoker.

That solves that mystery. Enough about me, let's talk business. You schmucks have upset Mizzou, Arizona, Texas, Kentucky, and Kansas in the N-C-double-friggin'-A tournament. There's a lot of interest in ya in the gaming community. All ya gotta do to keep the friggin' *hundo K* is beat Brut Monday night. I'm paying ya to win. If ya lose, ya give the money back to me."

A *hundo K* was a term-of-art not previously known to Tommy. A *stiff* was a corpse. A *heater* was a gun. But who knew that a *hundo K* was a hundred thousand dollars?

Puff sensed that the kid didn't know *finance* from *phinance*, so he kept talking. "It's like a no-collateral loan. Banks have been doing it forever, but it's the new wave in the gaming industry. We're Beta Testing it. We're leaders in the industry." Puff never came up for air. "It's all about trust. Why should ya trust me – a complete stranger? What if I promise to pay ya, and ya do your part, and then I run away without paying up? That's no good. So, turn it around. I lend ya the money in advance so ya know you've got it in your hands. If ya don't deliver the goods, ya give the loan – the money — back to me or I hunt ya down and crush your nuts. It's all about trust."

Tommy tried to keep an open mind about new ideas. He had heard of being paid to *lose* a game – like the Chicago "Black Sox" in 1919, for example. His own great-great-great-great grandfather had accepted a thousand dollars to throw the heavyweight fight between an Englishman, Bob *The Freckled Wonder* Fitzsimmons, and an Irishman named *Sailor* Sharkey in 1896. That San Francisco fight refereed by Wyatt Earp was a prominent landmark in Gunn family history.

Being paid to win was edgy, counter-intuitive. Tommy needed time to grasp it.

"It's Win Insurance," Puff said. "It guarantees that you
bring your friggin' *A* game."

"And you'll pay me *before* the game for sure?"

Puff nodded, lit up, and waved for the check.

"There's one more thing."

Tommy's shoulders sagged. "What?" he asked.

"You know that Brut point guard, D'Treeus Jones?"

"I know who he is."

"Take him out before the start of the second half."

"Take him out?"

"I don't care how ya do it. We don't want to see him
on the floor when the second half starts. Promise me that
and I'll give ya the money tonight. If ya lose or Jones is still
standing after the first half, bring it back to the same place at
midnight after the game. It all depends on trust."

It was a blow-out, Greed 32 – Caution 4. Tommy made
up his mind. "I'll do it."

"You're a bright kid. Ya pick up complex stuff fast."
Flattery cost nothing.

Puff paid the bill in cash and dropped a five-dollar tip
before waddling toward the left exit. Tommy wedged a dollar bill under his plate. He could afford it. In a few hours, he
would be wealthy. He would be *somebody*.

Chapter 4

BRIBES

TOMMY HAD LIVED FOR twenty-two years in tranquil Toxic Lick without laying eyes on a gangster. But in one day, this Sunday, the day before the championship game, he was about to meet a second thug in the space of three hours. Tommy's emotions were a mixture of anxiety, hope, fear, and greed. He hadn't gone looking for the gangsters; they had reached out to him, first Puff the Italian and then Igor the Russian, whose accent on the phone was almost unintelligible to Tommy. Tommy spotted Igor across the park from a hundred yards away. Igor's fashion statement comprised a black winter coat, furry Russian *ushanka*, sunglasses, and black rubber-soled shoes. The mysterious slender man walked right up to Tommy and looked over both of his shoulders in turn.

"You got light?" Igor asked.

Tommy shook his head.

"Me neither," Igor said.

Igor pointed to a park bench and removed his sunglasses. His bony face was as glum and his eyes as dead as Vladimir Putin's.

"You smoke?"

Tommy shook his head again.

"Me neither. Very dirty habit." Igor's *R*s sounded like Pop's irrigation pump.

Tommy guessed Igor's age at about fifty. Igor's beady eyes darted around like the eyes of a weasel. His black shoes hadn't seen polish in a long time. His brown socks sagged on his ankles. A fly shot touch-and-goes on the furry surface of Igor's *ushanka*.

"Very dirty," Igor said as he continued his nervous survey of the park. "Open your jacket."

Tommy unzipped his jacket and Igor's bony hands flashed inside the fleece to grope his back, ribs, stomach, chest, and neck.

"No wire?"

Tommy shook his head. He was flattered by the question. Frisking was big-time stuff.

"You'll pay me fifty thousand up front, right?" Tommy asked.

Igor nodded. "You must lose by more than three points. Our book way out of balance and my boss can't lay off action."

"No problem."

"Very big," Igor continued. "Boss cover at two-thousand-to-one. Could lose ten million. He will blow up nuclear bomb before he pay ten million."

Tommy looked confused. He had never considered bombs and basketball in the same context before.

"You miss jumping shots. You miss free shots. You drop ball into crowd. Whatever it take to lose game by more than three points."

"No problem."

Igor slipped a bundle of bills to Tommy, who nestled the money into an interior pocket of his jacket.

"You know what happen if you don't do?"

"I know."

"You can't imagine."

"I can imagine," Tommy said.

This irritated Igor. "If you don't lose by more than three, you bring money here noon next day." Worried that he hadn't made clear the terrifying consequences of failure, Igor added, "If you don't do — very bad." Igor jumped up off the bench. He took three paces then turned back toward Tommy. "Very, very bad."

Tommy exited the park in the opposite direction. He was elated. Without any effort on his part, the Italian mob had promised him a *hundo K* to win (and to sideline D'Treeus) and the Russians had promised him half as much to lose by more than three. What a racket! Tommy had no intention of returning a dime to either one of these ignorant pud-knockers no matter how the game turned out. Neither did he have any intention of crippling D'Treeus who was a sure bet to move on to the NBA. Tommy happily would have raked in more no-collateral loans, because he was going to keep it all. He couldn't wait to tell Lori.

Chapter 5

THE MOP CLOSET

TOMMY'S PREMEDITATED MOVE looked like abduction to the Guatemalan-American maid who saw Tommy pushing Lori into a small janitor's closet. Confronting a kidnapper was small potatoes to a woman who had traversed three thousand harrowing miles to reach Kentucky, so she opened the door.

"*Puedo ayudarle?*" she asked.

Tommy could wrestle with the Spanish language as well as the next guy with a year of high school Spanish, but, truly, he had no idea what she had said. He pointed to Lori and replied to the maid in Tommy Spanish.

"*Te quiero.*"

Lori and the maid made eye contact. Lori saw a well-meaning woman, and the maid saw a pretty girl who was not in distress.

"*Oy, perdoname,*" the maid said patiently. It was no skin off her nose if these crazy Gringos wanted to mess around in the company of brooms and vacuum cleaners.

"*Yo compro una manzana en el museo,*" Tommy said.

(Translation: *I buy an apple in the museum.*) Tommy believed that a second language could open doors. In this case, it closed one. The maid left them alone.

Tommy had chosen the broom closet for its privacy, not for its ambience. He needed to be alone with his beloved Lori. Lori had been the object of his desires since his first erection, a symptom he had misdiagnosed as *cancer of the thing*. Lori's angelic face was a joy to behold, even in the harsh glare of a bare one-hundred-watt light bulb in a small room marinated in Lysol. He ran his hands over her breasts, down her tight bottom, around her narrow waist, up along her spine, and through her flowing blonde hair. Lori had beautiful inner qualities, too. She was non-judgmental and forgiving. She saw the best in people. She never bragged. Lori had dozens of wonderful intangible qualities, but Tommy was fixated on her wonderful *tangible* qualities at the moment.

Of course, he would have preferred to take Lori to his hotel room. That was ill-advised, however, because his roommate was Tananga — seven-foot-six-inch Tananga — the giant center of the Kentucky Barber College basketball team — Tananga of the horrifying face, scarred by ceremonial etching common in his native Zuzuland. The thick keloid scars that covered his cheeks and forehead glistened like ebony night-crawlers, an effect sufficiently frightening to make even the stout-hearted cringe. The other Zuzulander, the power forward, a relative midget at seven-feet-three-inches, had once confided in Tommy that cannibalism was prevalent in parts of Zuzuland. Cannibalism! No, with roommate Tananga indulging in eight-thousand-calories-a-day room service orgies while bingeing on children's television, the hotel room was no place for Lori, the love of Tommy's life.

"Lord, it stinks in here." Lori seldom complained. She took the Lord's name in vain even less often.

Tommy propped a vacuum filter over the solitary light bulb to create a more romantic milieu. Judging by smell, the filter could burst into flames at any moment, but Tommy didn't intend to spend the whole day there. He snagged one of her blouse buttons with the gold ring on his right pinky finger. That gold ring, passed down from Tommy's mother, was a symbol of their love. Tommy had presented the ring to Lori on her most recent birthday, and then, while fooling around in the back seat of his clunker, had slipped it onto his pinky. No amount of silicon spray or ice would get the ring off his finger. He planned to have the ring removed by an expert when basketball season was over. Then, Tommy planned to present the ring to Lori again so she could keep it and treasure it forever.

"I'm not making out in a mop closet," Lori said.

"We're not here to make out." Tommy lowered his voice to build suspense. "Tonight, a guy's going to give me a *hundo K*, a hundred large."

"Large what?"

"A hundred . . . thousand . . . dollars."

Lori was stunned, jolted, astounded by the number of zeros. "Like a scholarship?"

"More like a . . . like a . . ."

"Bribe?"

"No . . . like a bonus."

"No, Tommy, it's a bribe. Come on, I'm not Bonnie . . . and you're not Clyde . . . ."

"This isn't stealing. That's not it. This is *monetizing* . . . it's like an insurance policy. I'll never see this much money again . . . ."

"You're all over the place. You wanted to be a famous player until you figured out you're not John Stockton. Now you want to be a famous coach . . . ."

"I just want to be somebody. This is a shortcut. Another guy's already given me fifty grand to lose by more than three points."

Lori was incredulous. "You took money to win *and* to lose?" She ran some numbers in her head. "What if you lose by two points? Both gangsters will kill you."

"They have to find me to kill me." Tommy had considered every angle.

"Oh, they'll find you. This is insane, Tommy." Lori gazed into his blue eyes, touched his face with her fingertips, and then rubbed the muscles in his back, a massage that normally settled him down. "Tommy, I wish you'd say you love me. I wish that was enough for you, just you and me living a simple life, no large."

Tommy decoded Lori's message and side-stepped the *I love you* part, because he found the expression as terrifying as he found the practice pleasurable. Gunns didn't say *I love you.* Also, it was bad form for athletes to use language like *I love you.* The sentiment reflected weakness and vulnerability.

"Lori, you already know how I feel about you. When a windfall comes, you gotta be quick . . . you gotta be smart enough to grab it and not let it get away."

"None of this makes sense to me . . . ."

"Don't go looking for sense in a windfall."

Lori caressed Tommy to sooth his passion.

"You said we might be poor, but we'll be happy."

"Well, now, we can be *rich* and happy."

Tommy played with the ring on his right pinky. Lori rested her head on his chest to listen to his heart. She could tell him that he already was somebody, but he would just rattle off his list of risk-takers, men who had become somebodies – Rockefeller, Hilton, Carnegie, Buffet, Jobs.

"Why do you always take shortcuts?"

"I do want to be a great coach like John Wooden or Dean Smith or Mike Sshh – that Duke guy."

"You're not going to be happy until you stop concentrating on what you want all the time and start thinking about what other people need."

"Lori, this is going to be a fantastic journey."

Chapter 6

THE BOMB

PUFF PACKED THE RUST-RED Semtex carefully, taping the bomb and the detonating device to the briefcase interior. Puff's hands were coarse; his nails were split and dirty, and the tip of his right thumb had been sacrificed on a table saw long ago. Puff's senior partner Banjo Dulcini covered his groin with both hands — a precaution as effective as a helmet on a Kamikaze pilot — until Puff was finished. Puff soaped the mononitrotoluene tagging vapor off his hands, and Banjo lit up a post-operative cigar.

Banjo was almost as huge as Puff, who, in turn, was almost as huge as their boss, The Smelt, who favored big men in his selection of employees. He liked them ugly, too, ugly like Banjo. If you threaded banjo strings through Banjo's lips and tightened them over his forehead, sure enough, his face would look like a banjo. Banjo was missing his left front tooth. His remaining front tooth was discolored, and, to see it was to wish it were missing, too. As tough as Banjo was, however, he was not a complete stranger to sentimentality.

"Ya got a nice touch." Banjo's voice sounded like he'd

been horsing around with helium-filled balloons. Banjo's pitch was as high as The Smelt's was low.

"Workin' with my hands feeds my soul."

Puff thrived on compliments.

Banjo loaded stacks of newly-printed one-hundred-dollar bills into the briefcase well away from the bomb. A premature detonation could be such a heart-breaker.

Puff pondered the waste of blowing up money, real or bogus. "What a crying shame," he said.

"Don't get emotional. It's counterfeit," Banjo said

"Phony bucks spend just as good as the real ones."

"Don't be greedy. The counterfeit money is a proxy. Ya know what that is?"

Puff admitted that he did not.

"It means, if the bomb goes off, the bogus money turns into confetti and The Smelt thinks the real dough is gone. If the kid runs with the bogus money, The Smelt goes after him, and we keep the real dough. It's a proxy."

"So, the one bad thing that can happen is if the kid brings the money back, we gotta replace the counterfeit with the real money and give it back to The Smelt."

"The Smelt ain't getting his money back," Banjo said with a satisfied grin on his kisser. "Either the kid gets to keep the counterfeit dough or we blow it up. Ya think the kid's going to complain? Where does he go to complain that his point-shaving money was make-believe?"

"Ya thought of everything," Puff said. "It's an honor to work with ya."

Chapter 7
PRE-GAME

TOMMY'S ROOMMATE TANANGA was a seven-foot-six-inch genetic freak. He had devoured six room service trays laden with food since the semi-final Kansas game. He ate the rinds of lemon and orange garnish. He sucked the marrow out of meat bones. He heaped bare plates on stacked trays like trophies. If the NBA didn't work out, Tananga would be gone in the first round of the draft for bus boys. He pushed the clean cutlery to the side, because he preferred eating with traditional *dlętŭkę*, implements carved out of warthog tusks and used like chopsticks. (The suffix *-ŭkę* formed the plural of masculine and feminine nouns in Tananga's dialect.)

Tananga was fascinated by all manner of Western hotel amenities not available in his native land. He stayed in frequent contact with the concierge, ordering dry cleaning, extra towels, and an in-room massage. He sent out his *tzákŭd-ndzę*, a multi-colored tribal garment shaped like a sheet, for laundering every night before retiring. Each morning he asked the front desk for a new tooth brush, specifying the color to round out his collection. On the day after the Cutters upset of Kansas, a young man carrying a folding massage table knocked on the door.

"*Ndzá-klüt-pnę-tszę*," Tananga said as he opened the door. He was showing off, having seen how enchanted some Americans are by the sound of a foreign tongue.

"I am Phillip," the masseuse said, his eyes sparkling as he took in the full measure of giant Tananga. Tommy asked Phillip if he charged by the inch, which convulsed Phillip. As Phillip's laughter trailed off to giggles, Tommy sensed it was time for him to take a long walk. Tommy returned from his walkabout grateful to find Tananga snoring soundly. Tommy plugged his headset into the television so he could watch TV sports news without disturbing his roommate, the least-hungry, least-stressed Zuzulander on the planet.

The TV screen was filled with the image of a huge young man in a letter jacket dwarfing everyone in the crowded lobby of Rupp Arena. An analyst said, "Dozens of high school stars are here in Lexington to see the Final Four. Here's the number one high school recruit in the land, Rocky *Mountain* High out of Seminole, Texas."

Replacing Rocky on the screen was a female reporter named Edwina Yonk, best known for leading the fight to allow women reporters in men's locker rooms for post-game interviews. *Veracity* magazine's piece on Edwina revealed that it had taken a village to get Edwina into Harvard. Her mother had written her application essays. A cousin had taken her SAT exams for her. She had fabricated many hours of volunteer community service at a non-existent Brooklyn abortion clinic. Killing innocent babies and protecting mass murderers from capital punishment made perfect sense to Edwina, so, according to *Veracity*, she had blended in with the Harvard faculty and student body. She was popular as a television sports reporter, because the way she squinted at cameras and stage-whispered into microphones mesmerized audiences like no one since Donald Trump.

"Until Kentucky Barber College beat Mizzou in the first round," Edwina said, "no sixteen seed had ever advanced in the tournament . . . ever."

The nude figures of Tananga and his sky-scraper team-mates cavorted in the background.

"The Cutters' unlikely run has bookies chewing aspirin and chugging Drano." Edwina lowered her voice to an even more sincere pitch. "The Cutters start four players taller than seven feet recruited from Zuzuland, Latvia, and Croatia. The last guy's from Montenegro, but that's too controversial for this network."

Tananga cracked a towel hard against the buttocks of the Latvian power forward and cackled with glee. The privacy dots hiding the genitals of the giant athletes were the largest ever used by the network.

"I've never seen them this big," Edwina confided. "And, get this, six-foot point guard Tommy Gunn, a local Toxic Lick boy, has a vertical leap of fifty inches. That's a lot of inches." A video showed Tommy levitating to drill a jump shot from twenty-five feet.

"Coach Gillette has the Cutters hitting on all cylinders. His rigid discipline is paying off. Every player gets a haircut before each game. They put on fresh uniforms at half time. They wear garters to keep their socks up and their jersey tails in."

An x-ray image of a garter filled the screen for the benefit of viewers too young to remember a time when men wore garters, suspenders, and fedoras.

"Can the Brut University Hyenas stop the juggernaut from the Bluegrass State?"

Tommy turned off the television for fear of incubating over-confidence. How many times had his grandfather, Pop Gunn, quoted Scripture to warn him against pride and arrogance? Pop often paraphrased the prophets and the apostles.

"Better to show what you got than make a claim on it." That was Pop's executive summary of Saint Paul's letter to the Corinthians, a group of early Christians who had gotten too big for their britches.

Tommy unplugged his headphone cord and lay on his bed, leaving the sound-canceling headphones over his ears to calm his nerves on the eve of the most unexpected thrill of his life – the chance to play for the national title. Tommy daydreamed about the money. Then he dreamed about Lori. He dreamed about wearing an expensive suit, brand new Italian loafers, and a silk tie coaching an imaginary team from the sideline of an imaginary court nestled in an imaginary arena. In his dreams, Tommy made Rick Pitino look like a pauper.

Fearless in his sleep, Tommy dared to dream about wealth, love, and fame with no premonition of the penalty he would have to pay for his avarice.

Chapter 8

THE CORRIDOR

AT AN HOUR BEFORE MIDNIGHT, Tommy rode the hotel service elevator to the basement floor, where he passed a storage room, a maintenance workshop, and a laundry before opening a metal door that accessed a dark corridor leading to a parking garage. As motivated as he was to get his hands on the *hundo K*, he was reluctant to see Puff again in this dank subterranean vault. Puff's appearance was revolting in broad daylight, so Tommy could guess what a heart-stopper Puff would be in this unwelcoming domain of cobwebs and dust. Tommy spotted a point of amber light down the corridor.

Although Puff stood in shadow, his cigarette tip shone like a beacon. As Tommy approached the corpulent mobster, Puff exhaled a cloud of smoke that obscured a *NO SMOKING* sign mounted on the wall behind his head. A lifetime of compliance with product safety labels to prevent drowning, suffocation, and lung cancer moved Tommy to point at the sign. The amiable gesture offended Puff.

"Signs aren't part of my belief system, ya deep-fried dip stick," Puff growled.

So, that's how it was going to be? Puff's hostile attitude was an irritant Tommy had to tolerate if he was to score the *hundo K*. Puff shoved the briefcase into Tommy's hands.

"Three things will make the bomb go off . . . ."

Bomb? Tommy tried to return the briefcase, but Puff refused it. Tommy had seen enough movies to know not to get into a shoving match with a gangster, especially when a bomb was involved. Jiggling nitroglycerin, for example, could transport a person to a faraway place.

"First, if ya try to open the case before game time, you're bacon bits." Puff allowed time for Point One to sink in. "Second, if ya lose the game and try to open the case, boom. Third, if ya lose the game and don't return the case by midnight tomorrow night, the bomb will blow the money and your pecker off the face of the earth."

Realizing he was stuck with the briefcase, with its sundry positives and negatives, Tommy nodded to assure the big man that he understood the rules of detonation.

Puff said, "Don't even think about losing. Put D'Treeus in the hospital. The Smelt is counting on you."

"The Smelt?"

"My boss. Forget I said that." As an afterthought, he said, "If ya don't make it, it's been nice knowing you."

Tommy knew he didn't mean it. All Tommy could think about was the bomb in the briefcase. His fantastic journey had taken a detour. Tommy took his cue and he left Puff, the smoke, and the garlic vapor cloud in the shadows. Tommy's plan required modification.

He retraced his route out of the basement, past the laundry room, past the maintenance workshop, and past the storage room. Just before he pressed the elevator button, an idea popped into Tommy's mind. He turned around and entered the open doorway to the unoccupied workshop.

Power tools, door hardware, and bathroom fixtures were scattered on work benches around the circumference of the room. Tommy sat on an old couch away from the doorway and waited long enough to ensure that Puff wasn't following him. He divided his problem into two parts: first, he had to think of a way to get the money out of the briefcase and then he had to dispose of the bomb. Puff had warned him that opening the briefcase would detonate the bomb. *What if,* he thought, *instead of opening it conventionally, I cut away a panel from the side of the case? I could then extract the money, leaving only the bomb in the briefcase.* Pressurized moments like these were the times Tommy did his clearest thinking.

He balanced the briefcase in his hands and determined that the bomb was secured to the bottom of the case. He could cut the panel out of the top third of the case and stay well away from the explosives. He could start by drilling a one-inch hole in the side of the case. Then, he could use the hole as a port for feeling around the inside the case with a finger before proceeding. The unexpected challenge made Tommy grateful for years of Pop's handyman instruction and for two years of shop class in the Toxic Lick school system. *You could never predict,* Tommy thought, *when education would pay off.*

Tommy donned welding goggles and giant ear protectors and inspected his image in a workshop mirror. For a moment, he considered leaving a will, but the *sound mind and body* requirement might not stand up to a legal challenge if he were to blow himself up. He decided a better course was to think positively and to concentrate.

The one-inch drill bit made a clean hole in the plastic. By probing with his index finger through the hole, he determined that the area within two-and-a-half inches of the center of the hole was free of impediments. He used a Dremel cutting tool to enlarge the hole to a square that measured four inches on a side. He repeated the probing action with his index finger and, again, found no obstructions of any kind. He enlarged the square panel size to six inches on a side. Using a mag light and a miniature mirror, he surveyed the interior of the briefcase. He used soldering tongs to remove bundles of money one-at-a-time until the ten stacks of money lay on the workbench.

Tommy searched the room for a container. He found a small yellow gym bag to his liking. Stealing a ten-dollar gym bag seemed a trivial offense in the grand scheme of things. It was all about proportion. With gloved hands, he emptied the bag of its contents — an anti-deodorant stick, a vial of cologne, a tube of athlete's foot cream, and a tube of hair gel. The stacks of money fit so nicely into the yellow bag that it seemed preordained.

Tommy lowered a mag light into the interior of the briefcase to illuminate the contents. Manipulating the mirror, he shuddered at the sight of blinking light-emitting diodes on the fuse timing unit. It would be immoral to leave the bomb in the workshop or in a dumpster in the rear of the hotel. He considered hand-printing a warning label, affixing it to the briefcase, and leaving the briefcase like an abandoned baby at the front desk. He knew that all of these disposal methods were unsatisfactory. He was a man of conscience, especially when money wasn't involved. Then, he thought of the fish tank.

At the top of the stairs that opened onto the lobby, Tommy scanned the reception area to make certain it was clear of potential witnesses. Confident he was alone, Tommy approached the fish tank. Under different circumstances, he could have gazed at the multi-colored fish for hours. He remembered from physics class that liquids were not compressible. He pictured a fish's tiny ear drums and spleen being compressed by the shock wave. *Live in the moment, Little Ones*, he thought. He submerged the briefcase into the immense fish tank and watched the briefcase settle to the bottom. The tropical fish, ignorant of the fragility of life, swam into and out of the hole in the side of the briefcase. He regretted that his windfall should be their downfall, but they were, after all, only fish. Was it Darwin who called the world a zero-sum-game? Tommy's mind was as sharp as a knife edge honed on adrenalin and intelligence. He detoured around security cameras by using the fire escape stairwell to return to his hotel room.

Tommy was relieved to hear Tananga's Harley-Davidson snore. Tommy had dodged another evening of Tananga's boasting about his courageous father, *Chief Mndzgę* or about his seven mothers or about hunting wildebeest. Tommy couldn't reciprocate with stories of his own, because he had no memories of his parents. The largest animal Tommy had ever shot was a deer, hardly in the class of slaying a wildebeest with a spear. Tommy believed that cultural exchanges were overrated.

Tommy added the Russian bribe to the Italian bribe in the yellow gym bag and hid it under his own bed. After tiptoeing to the bathroom, he sat clothed on the toilet seat and placed a towel over his head for an extra layer of privacy. He placed a cell phone call to Lori. She was as good-natured after midnight as she was in the daytime.

"The team will be waiting for the bus in the lobby at three," he said in a low voice muffled by the towel. "The money will be in a yellow gym bag. Hide the bag in the trunk of my car and hide the keys in the gas cap recess. You'll have to catch a bus back to the Lick." The precision and sheer daring of the operation made his hands tremble.

Tananga burst into the bathroom wearing a huge pair of pajama bottoms festooned with the image of Zuzuland's equivalent of Bart Simpson brandishing a machete. Tananga was startled by the towel-draped figure straddling the toilet, and he withdrew promptly, smacking his head on the overhead door jamb. The only part of Tommy's conversation Tananga overheard was, "Wear a disguise."

Chapter 9

THE BUREAU

THE FBI COMMAND CENTER was set up in a vacant warehouse in an industrial park near the Lexington Airport. Agents arrived early in a swarm of no-frills black sedans and they worked late so they could pad their overtime hours and expense reports. Out of view of the public, agents peeled off their dark suit jackets for that working-my-ass-off look, validated by conservative ties loosely knotted and pistols in shoulder harnesses. The partition walls around them were decorated with mug shots, girlie centerfolds, and March Madness brackets.

Anyone could see that Agent Bogart was in charge. His rolled-up sleeves exposed hairy forearms, so vital for advancement in the Bureau. He alone had whiteboard marker privileges, and his penmanship was first-rate. His gun was bigger than the guns of other agents. He didn't have to say *sir* to anyone in the center, and only he could utter expletives beginning with the letter *F*. Agent Bogart was one tough cookie.

Agent Bogart had been promoted after suggesting that the Bureau use a single world-wide time benchmark

— Newfoundland Standard Time, which was Greenwich Mean Time minus three-and-one-half hours. Agent Bogart's suggestion never got traction, but his ornate writing style and heavy use of words like *utilize* were enough to get the job done. He was a smart cookie, too.

He was also good at saying, *Yes, sir, yes, sir, three bags full.* At last, he was commander of his little chunk of the FBI universe, and he could say anything he wanted to say. He copied the style of his cinematic namesake as he briefed his team of gallant agents.

"This is dirty stuff. Dirty, I tell you. Kentucky Barber College? Never heard of them." He pointed his finger at his favorite agent. "You ever heard of 'em?"

"Never heard of 'em," the agent said.

"I never heard of Brut University," said his least favorite agent, a Brown graduate who knew about only Ivy schools — Dartmouth, Cornell, Penn, Columbia, Princeton, Yale, Brown, and . . . oh, yeah, Harvard.

"There's a lot of crap you never heard of," Agent Bogart said. Pressures to shut down illegal gambling during March Madness made him grumpy. "Millions of dollars is corrupting the tournament, see? We're going to bust it wide open, wide open, I tell you." He gestured toward a tournament bracket taped to the whiteboard. "Turn in your money and your brackets by seventeen hundred." Probably local Eastern Standard Time, not Newfoundland Standard or Greenwich Mean Time.

Agent Bogart had won the tournament pool two years running. March Madness was his favorite time of year.

Chapter 10

THE TRANSFER

GAWKERS IN THE HOTEL lobby *oohed* and *aahed* at the impeccably-groomed Cutters as Tommy led them past the fish tank where the briefcase lay on the bottom like a giant clam, unnoticed by everyone but Tommy. Why would anyone look for a briefcase in a fish tank when he could gape at a seven-foot-six-inch tall Zuzulander with a nightmare for a face? Despite his massage, Tananga had slept fitfully with his size twenty hooves hanging off his bed. He was in a surly mood, and he brushed aside even the most brazen autograph-seekers.

"*Ndzę-ná-tük-mŭn-sŭrd-kę,*" he growled.

No one but Tananga and his kinsman knew what that meant, but the Zuzuland trash talk and Tananga's visage was enough to clear a ten-foot radius around him.

While sitting on a couch on the fringe of Tananga's circle of discontent, Tommy recognized Lori's athletic figure the moment she glided into the lobby. Tommy wasn't fooled by Lori's rust-colored wig, Lucille Ball sunglasses, earpiece, and boom mike. He knew her every move, her aroma, her feel, and, sometimes, her thoughts. Lori sat on the same couch as Tommy, but she looked away from him when she transmitted her secret coded greeting.

"Bavarian biscuits and butter are best."

Yep. It was Lori all right. If Tommy had been vibrating from excitement any worse, his fillings would have popped out. He, too, looked away deceptively as he spoke lowly into the boom mike attached to his earpiece.

"Is that a new blouse? You bought a new blouse for this?"

"It was on sale. Vertical stripes are thinning."

"You're thin enough."

Tommy was all business, concentrating on the upcoming battle with the Brut University Hyenas, looking good in his Cutters blazer, and ripping the Russians and the Italians off for a hundred, fifty thousand dollars. He didn't have time for banter.

"Stash the bag in the trunk, hide the keys like I said, and catch the first bus back to Toxic Lick. Oh, scalp your game ticket and take a couple of *Benjamins* for yourself." Ah, such beneficence from a man who had never before in his life seen a hundred-dollar bill. "Take four or five."

Lori inserted a parking lot voucher between two cushions of the couch. Tommy gathered the voucher with his fingertips. For a moment, their eyes locked.

"Lori, look away, don't let . . . ."

"I can't look away. Tommy, you're so handsome. I could look at you all day."

Flattered but flustered, Tommy shifted his gaze, but, eventually, he looked back at Lori.

"You're crying . . . why?"

Lori raised her sunglasses to wipe tears away. Tommy loved the sight of her face, so guileless, so free of make-up, so full of trust even in distress. During their pre-pubescent years, he had prattled about marriage. Years later, common sense had quashed such talk, but he still thought about it. Lori was his core, his inspiration for striving to be special.

"Tommy, when we're together, it's so wonderful. It's like the Garden of Eden. But, now, I feel like you're making me eat the apple, and I'm scared."

Tommy forced himself to look away. It was a time to be resolute.

"That bag is our Garden of Eden. Take it and go."

Lori grabbed the yellow gym bag and got up from the couch in one motion. As Tommy watched her go, he noticed Tananga's dark, foreboding eyes frozen on him. The keloid scars across Tananga's forehead and down his cheeks glistened like black tree roots pressing to burst out from his ebony skin. Tommy shivered and looked away.

Chapter 11
THE BIG DANCE

LEXINGTON'S RUPP ARENA was bedlam. Only five-point-five seconds of playing time remained on the clock, and the Hyenas were ahead of the Cutters, 71–70. Perennial powerhouse Brut University's avid following barked like hyenas for victory and a fifth national title. A small contingent of Cutters fans was joined by Kansas and Kentucky faithful in cheering for the upstart Kentucky Barber College squad. The teams huddled beside their benches. A television cameraman focused on the Cutters' Barber Pole mascot whacking the Brut Hyena on the head with a noodle, all in good fun. Another cameraman aimed his equipment at the Cutters' cheerleaders romping about with boundless enthusiasm, perfect sets of teeth, flawless smiles, toned legs, and marvelous cleavage.

Igor, dressed in a bushy *ushanka* and a trench coat, looked out-of-place among the teeming crowd of collegiate sports fans. He contemplated the disaster looming should KBC win or lose by three points or fewer. Across Rupp Arena from Igor, Puff and Banjo were squeezed in on all sides by maniacal fans. Their two ugly faces were distorted by extreme discomfort, knowing that, barring a miracle, one of them was going to have to call The Smelt with news that KBC had lost.

TV announcers near the scorers' table babbled phrases about *student athletes* and *diaper dandies* and the pageantry of college athletics to kill time until play resumed. The timekeeper's horn bleated, the teams took to the court, and a referee handed the basketball to a Brut player out-of-bounds beneath the Brut basket.

Enormous athletes in Hyena uniforms cut and set screens trying to free a player to receive the inbound pass. The inbound pass was a long one, arching toward a Brut player at mid-court. Tommy dashed toward the receiver, leaped incredibly high, and tipped the ball down-court toward the Cutters' basket. Bedlam turned into certified insanity with Brut supporters screaming in despair and Cutters fans rejoicing at their pending good fortune. Tommy spun away from the Brut player, reached the tipped ball, dribbled twice, and leaped into the air. He spun three-hundred-sixty degrees, and attempted a right-handed slam dunk in a spectacular feat of athleticism, balance, and art. It was a move for the ages, fourteen years in the making.

Tommy's violent dunk attempt slammed into the rim. The ring on his right pinky caught on the rim, cutting into the skin all around, dislocating the joint, and spraying blood in all directions as he fell awkwardly onto the court. The final buzzer sounded. Half of the Rupp Arena crowd groaned in dismay while Brut fans shouted hysterically and jumped up and down like lunatics. Igor looked like a man who had just received a death sentence; KBC had not lost by more than three points. His Russian Boss was ruined. Puff and Banjo looked at one another in dismay. KBC had lost and The Smelt's net worth had taken a beating. At the epicenter of the chaos, Tommy sprawled on the court in pain holding his bleeding finger. Brut partisans rushed the court. Balloons fell from the ceiling. Tommy struggled to his feet among the stampede of spectators and ran for the exit tunnel past hundreds of Brut celebrants.

———— ((○)) ————

Sitting behind a littered desk in a disheveled office on the second floor of a decrepit warehouse in Chicago, a huge man named *The Smelt* was on the phone with Banjo, who was thankful to be in Lexington, three-hundred-seventy miles away from his ruthless, mean, unforgiving mob boss. Warts on The Smelt's forehead looked like miniature bumpers in a pin-ball game. An angry scar ran down the left side of his face. According to mob lore, The Smelt had picked up the scar by being dragged by a chain fastened to the chassis of a Mercury Cougar down in Joliet. It was hard to know which came first, the bleakness of his soul or his dragging. His scar was a rudimentary blood-pressure indicator, and, as he talked on the telephone, his scar turned as red as an ambulance beacon. The Smelt's voice was so deep that dogs couldn't hear it.

"I'm losing millions. I'm bleeding. I'm sick. I'm dying." The Smelt exaggerated when under stress.

"Kids, today," Banjo said. "Ya gotta buy the whole friggin' team."

"This friggin' Tommy Gunn dick-head, all the dumb cracker had to do was lay the friggin' ball in the friggin' basket," The Smelt howled. "It's not the friggin' shot put in the friggin' Olympics. I mean it's friggin' basketball, not platform diving!"

Banjo remained quiet. He had learned from experience that nothing good came from his attempts to explain, mitigate, or console. He wasn't a gifted quipster. Banjo's snappiest repartee lagged conversations by hours.

"I'm so depressed I wanna kill everybody, including myself," The Smelt groaned. "It's getting hard to make a living."

"Ya want I should waste the Gunn kid if he don't return the money?"

"Yeah. Search every emergency room within two hundred miles of Lexington. If I don't get the dough, he don't get the dough. Cut off his arms and legs. Give him a zero-inch vertical."

You had to give credit to The Smelt. He knew his basketball lingo.

<hr />

A clock struck twelve midnight. Outside Rupp Arena, Banjo pulled a garage door opener from his trench coat pocket and poised his thumb over the red activator button. He speed-dialed Puff, who was on the lookout for Tommy and the briefcase in the hotel basement. Puff looked like a

North Korean Nuke Inspector; he was wearing ear protection and goggles so an untimely explosion wouldn't deafen or blind him. He planned to witness Tommy's death and the destruction of the counterfeit money and then join up with Banjo for the getaway. Such moments before a hit invigorated him.

"The Smelt's pissed," Banjo said.

"That ain't news." Puff's voice echoed in the basement.

"I mean . . . *really* pissed."

"The kid ain't here."

"Come on up," Banjo said. "I'm blowing the bag. We're outta here."

Banjo pressed his thumb down on the red button. At residences in the background, two garage doors opened.

In the lobby in the hotel, in the fish tank in the lobby, in the briefcase in the fish tank, light emitting diodes turned solid green a millisecond before blowing up like a World War Two depth charge. The glass didn't break, but, when the bubbles cleared, the fish of many colors were floating on the surface and the briefcase was shredded.

Chapter 12
THE GETAWAY

ROCK MUSIC BLARED on Tommy's car radio, drowning out the hum of the engine, the rumble of a leaking muffler, and the drone of worn tires. Static sounded between radio stations as Tommy searched for sports news.

". . . standing on a corner in Winslow, Arizona."

". . . I've seen fire and I've seen rain."

". . . and a low of thirty-four in the Queen City."

". . . final — Brut 71, Kentucky Barber College 70."

Tommy listened to a country number titled *If I'd Shot You Then, I'd Be Out By Now*. His bloody right pinky was wrapped in a torn tee shirt. The throbbing of his dislocated pinky was as bad as the pain he had endured when he'd had all four impacted wisdom teeth extracted on the same morning on the advice of a quack in Toxic Lick.

——— «O» ———

Lori curled up in a seat near the back of a nearly empty

bus rolling through the night toward Toxic Lick. She broke Tommy's secret communications protocol by calling his cell phone. She replayed a video clip of his near-amputation twice. The quantity of blood squirting in all directions like Bloody Mary mix in a blender shocked her. She told Tommy to lie low because of the first rioting in Toxic Lick since the bread shortage of 1931.

"They burned a cross at Pop's trailer," Lori said.

"I can't get through to his phone," Tommy said. "I 'spect he ran away through the tobacco field the minute that cross lit up. He's a peace-loving man."

"I'll keep trying to call him while you *reposition*." Lori didn't want to say *skip the country* for fear their conversation might be monitored.

"Tell him I'll get home to him as soon as I can."

"Don't get his hopes too high. Kentucky fans forget real slow."

Tommy wished he could undo his decision, snuggle close to Lori, and end the nightmare. Lori wished she could comfort the boy she loved. Those wishes weren't coming true. Tommy had to go undercover and Lori had to be strong. They had already talked too long. A snoop could be listening. They had seen enough conspiracy TV to know that you couldn't hiccup without the government finding out. Someone had to be the adult and end the conversation before their locations were compromised.

"I love you, Tommy."

Tommy longed to see Lori's lips swell with his kiss, to see her bright blue eyes go all dreamy, to hear her sigh.

"Me, too." He crossed the bridge to Cincinnati.

The way he said *me, too* like he was allergic to *I love you* irritated Lori. But, love being patient and love being kind, she waited and waited some more.

———— ⊛ ————

The Veterinarian's framed certificate was so ornate Tommy couldn't read it. Was it *Mississippi*? How many words have four *S*s? *Sassafras. Senseless. Stressfulness. Sessions. Sissies. Susurruses.* Had to be *Mississippi.* The morphine was working. The Vet was a scrawny, elderly black man displeased to be woken in the middle of the night, notwithstanding his Hippocratic Oath. The Vet's office was decorated in 1950s garage sale furniture accented with cobwebs and peeling wall paint.

"I don't reset things as much as I cut 'em off."

"Well, I need you to push this thing back into joint right now, because I'm near to fainting with the pain."

"It'll cost you."

"How much?"

"Five or six hundred."

"Make it six," Tommy said. The largesse made him feel better as the morphine started to kick in for real.

"You've bled a lot. What's your type?"

"I can be moody . . . ."

The Vet chalked it up to anemia.

"Your blood type . . . ." When it was obvious Tommy didn't know the answer, the Vet grabbed a packet of Type O plasma and rigged an intravenous feeding tube. "Let's hook you up. Something's better than nothing."

"Is it human?"

The Vet ignored Tommy's question. He was busy laying out sterile stainless steel implements.

"You do horses?" Tommy was feeling chatty and eager to get on the Vet's good side. Pop's advice was *never cross a man with a sharp object in hand.*

"Naw, sir. I'm a cat and dog man."

Tommy faked nonchalance. "I reckon we're distant cousins of cats and dogs." The morphine was fabulous.

"Speak for yourself. Let's get me paid in advance."

Tommy handed the Vet six stiff one-hundred-dollar bills, and the elderly man pocketed them. The Vet placed a plastic mask on Tommy's face.

"Breathe on this for a spell. I'll spin the bottle."

At the time, it seemed like the funniest thing Tommy had ever heard.

———— ((◉)) ————

When Tommy woke up from anesthesia, the tired Vet was completing the casting of Tommy's right hand.

"Where am I?" Tommy asked.

"Ohio. You're out of the piano-playing business."

Tommy took a critical look at the cast on his right hand while his wits coagulated and his memory rebooted.

"Son, I know who you are. I saw the end of the game. I've never seen a white boy jump as high as you."

"You're stereotyping." Tommy felt pious shedding the

light of impartiality on discrimination of all kinds.

"Stereotypes save a lot of time and effort. That's the problem with your generation, you don't know how to draw inferences, how to discriminate. You gotta learn general rules from specific experiences. You've forgotten simple logic. You call *up . . . down*. You call *good . . . bad*. You hide behind definitions – *that depends on what the definition of is is* – you know, like that cracker from down in Arkansas."

Tommy could afford to be feisty now that the Vet was disarmed. "I can be as logical as the next guy."

"If you're so logical, why didn't you just lay the ball in?"

Remorse burrowed its way back into Tommy's consciousness. "I knew I'd never have an audience like that again in my life."

"Well, you screwed up royal on national TV," the Vet said. "I believe I'd stay away from Kentucky . . . ."

"I might change my identity."

"I would."

The Vet had cut Tommy's pinky ring from his finger and strung it onto a thin, gold-plated chain that he lowered over Tommy's head. "You just about cut off that pinky. You'd be a terror at circumcisions."

"I'll pay extra for the chain and for the whole bottle of Oxycodone," Tommy said. He was feeling expansive because his pain was dulled and because he was rich. "I like you, Doc."

"I don't care," the Vet said.

Tommy stopped feeling rich the next morning when he tried to pay his motel bill and breakfast charge with one of his ill-gotten hundred-dollar bills. The desk clerk was no beauty queen, but she was as quick as a fox, and she stopped the transaction cold.

"Uh, oh," she said. "You've got a bum note here."

Tommy looked surprised. Then flabbergasted. Then appalled.

"I've been had," he said.

"You *certainly* have." She was itching to display her knowledge on the subject and to point out as many printing flaws as possible. "See how blurred the scrollwork is here at the bottom? And the serial numbers are printed in a different color of green from the Treasury seal."

"Blow me down," Tommy said. His Popeye impersonation was a way to feign interest while his mind raced to resolve his fiscal setback.

"And notice Franklin's left eye. *Certainly* a dead giveaway. And look at this hologram."

"I'll run to my bank and withdraw cash," Tommy suggested. He didn't want to hear any more ways in which his bogus bill was deficient.

"We can *certainly* take a debit or credit card."

"Good. Can you take a personal check?"

"*Certainly*," she said.

Tommy didn't have a personal check. He didn't have a debit card. His credit card balance had spiked with the purchase of his roundtrip ticket to Paris. He disengaged from the amateur numismatist to search his bag for a stack of Russian bribe money. Luckily, the Russian money was legit. He faced the truth: he didn't have $150,000; he had only $50,000. With several hours to kill, Tommy set out to convert counterfeit bills into legal tender. Over the next four hours, he managed to hustle among Kentucky yard sales, Covington pawn shops, and a Keyser County swap meet to convert more than two thousand dollars of counterfeit bills into five hundred dollars of legitimate cash. He taped the $50,000 in legitimate bills to the insides of his thighs. He taped banded bogus bills worth twenty thousand dollars to his torso for distribution in Europe. The other seventy-odd thousand counterfeit dollars he hid underneath the rear seat of his clunker, which he had parked in a long-term lot in Kentucky.

His finger was throbbing by the time he had paid his hotel bill, and so was his head. It was time for another Oxycodone. One thing Tommy had figured out about life: it was always more complicated than it looked.

Chapter 13

CROSSING THE POND

THE CINCINNATI INTERNATIONAL Airport was a tolerable place to wait for a flight departure unless, like Tommy, you doubled the prescribed dosage of Oxycodone; then, it was sensational. The overdose stopped pain in its tracks, enhanced humor, dulled memory, and made time fly. Tommy's whimsical smile combined with his bulky black sweater, wig, and sunglasses gave him the look of a slightly daft lobsterman on shore leave. Suspended in this artificial state of euphoria, Tommy watched a TV news reporter compare the Toxic Lick rioting to wartime Aleppo. The broken liquor store window serving as a backdrop for the reporter's view of the apocalypse was well known to Tommy. It had always looked as rundown as it did at that moment. The journalist was so distraught he looked constipated. This was his biggest story since the Jim Beam warehouse fire on August 4, 2003, when 19,000 barrels of whiskey went up in flames and grown men throughout the Bluegrass wept openly.

"Police in Toxic Lick estimate the damage done by looters and rioters at over ten thousand dollars. Calm has been restored, and only a faint smell of tear gas remains to remind local residents of this night of terror."

At a time when he should have been buried by guilt, regret, and remorse, Tommy, with the help of pain medication, was grinning like a nit-wit. His grin began to fade the moment he acknowledged to himself that he was, at least indirectly, responsible for the unrest and for a whole procession of events bound to follow.

A mug shot of a hideous bloated man flashed onto the TV screen. In a left profile shot, an angry scar ran in a jagged line from his earlobe to his chin. A script banner at the bottom of the screen read, "Francis Frantupo". While the repulsive image stayed on the TV screen, Edwina Yonk's voice droned from off-screen.

"Chicago's Francis *The Smelt* Frantupo."

Tommy's grin morphed to a portrait of fright when he recognized the name dropped by Puff – *The Smelt*.

"Frantupo is being investigated by Chicago Police on suspicion of fixing games in the recent NCAA basketball tournament. The FBI has begun interviewing college players to testify against the notorious bookie."

A video of The Smelt being escorted by his slick lawyer appeared on the screen. The Smelt straight-armed a cameraman and his voice sounded like thunder when he said, "I didn't do nuttin'."

—((●))—

In the smoky warehouse loft that served as The Smelt's

reception room in Chicago, Banjo coached Puff while the two portly gangsters waited nervously, sweating like whores in church. They knew better than to play eight ball on the beat-up pool table at the far end of the room. That privilege was reserved for more agreeable occasions. The table didn't get much play.

"Deny everything," Banjo said, "stick with the story — the clodhopper took the money and ran."

"*Mendacem memorem esse oportet*," Puff said just above a whisper.

Banjo, who thought he had heard everything from the lips of his partner stared at Puff in bewilderment.

"What?"

"*Mendacem* . . . ."

"What does it mean?"

"It means, *A liar needs a good memory*," Puff said.

"We're not friggin' lying," Banjo hissed. "The kid ran with the money."

"The kid ran with the counterfeit mon . . . ."

Banjo clamped his beefy hand over Puff's mouth to muffle the kind of speech he feared most – the truth.

"Don't say friggin' nothin' in here," Banjo whispered. "He's probably bugged the spider webs."

Puff saw wisdom in Banjo's caution.

"What were ya talkin'?" Banjo asked. "Greek?"

"No. Greeks are haughty. It was Latin."

"Sounded Greek. How do ya know from Latin?"

"Catholic School," Puff told him. "I learned all about the Latins. They invented civilization."

"You mean the Romans."

"The Latins. They spoke Latin," Puff insisted. "The Latins were very influential under Caesar. They invented roads . . . aqueducts . . . baths . . . orgies."

Their nerves were frayed. Banjo's color was rising, and his vocal pitch shot even higher than normal.

"It was the friggin' Romans who invented friggin' aqueducts. Latins are from Mexico. Ya never heard of Latin-Americans? They're Mexicans. And Mexicans never invented diddly-squat any more than you did!"

The insult stung. Puff kept Latin and English comments to himself for a while. Finally he broke the ice that had encrusted their conversation.

"When we go out West to spend the money, I'm buying ya a history book."

Banjo just glared at his partner, too frustrated and too weary to discuss it any further.

A deep-pitched growl issued from the office, then a shout like thunder.

"Banjo, you and Puff the Magic . . . friggin' whatever, get in here."

The Smelt, never a sight for sore eyes, looked awful. His hair was matted. His eyeballs were red. His inflamed facial scar made his left jaw seem poised to secede from his face. His two mobster henchmen weren't winning any prizes, either. Banjo's hairy hands were shaking like mohair mittens in a breeze. Puff looked faint.

"Put out those cigarettes," The Smelt bellowed. "I got enough problems without passive lung cancer." The two gangsters complied meekly. "Let's keep this simple," The Smelt continued, "I get my money or it's your ass!"

"I told ya . . . I blew up the money . . . ." Banjo's high-pitched voice was less confident in the presence of The Smelt than it had been in the reception room.

"There wasn't no friggin' money in the fish tank!" The Smelt bawled.

"Then the hayseed musta ran with it!"

"I don't care if *he's* got it, *you* got it, or the *Pope's* got it, *I* want it, so *get* it!" He regained control over his passions. "We gotta eliminate witnesses, because the FBI is asking questions about bribes and point-shaving. These smart-ass college boys talk tough, but the rattle of jail cell keys makes 'em sing like birds. So, kill the kid. And, if I don't get my money back, you'll wish ya never met me."

You could always count on The Smelt to keep it brief and on-point. Banjo and Puff knew that The Smelt's office was as stockpiled with weapons as an armory. There were lots of ways to die in that office, so the less time they spent there, the better. They were elated to hear The Smelt tell them to get out of his sight. They had survived.

————)((•)) ————

Tommy scanned the airport men's room to make sure he was alone before hiking up his sweater to inspect the money bands duct-taped to his stomach. His image in the mirror bore a strong resemblance to a suicide bomber. He needed a suitable fiction to explain the bundles of money, both legitimate and illegitimate. Pop always said that the fleeting benefit of a lie wasn't worth the high cost of maintenance. *Take the easy road and always tell the truth* was Pop's advice. Of course, Pop had never crossed the mob and been on the run that Tommy knew of. Tommy's present chemical state wasn't conducive to inventing cover stories, so he trusted that the crack security employees guarding the borders of the United States and France wouldn't question an injured person like him. His faith was powered by Oxycodone, a tablet of which, by golly, he thought he would swallow another before boarding the jet. Thus fortified, Tommy found solitude in a deserted waiting area, where he broke his own strict communications protocol by calling Lori on his cell phone.

"They keep showing your finger exploding in slow motion with a *viewer's discretion* warning on account of your finger and the blood . . . ."

"I got that sucker fixed," Tommy informed her. Damn, he was smooth. Honestly, he felt like James Bond.

"You poor thing . . . it's awful. Did you know that the Lick was on fire when my bus got in?"

"They'll build it back better than ever . . . like Nagasaki."

"I 'spect so."

"I got some bad news at breakfast this morning. The Italian money is counterfeit."

"No!" Lori exclaimed. "I wish you'd never laid eyes on that cursed bag of money."

"I guess I short-changed the doc, but I reckon he'll get over it. I'd bet he's seen disappointment more than once in the past. I was able to convert some bills over in Kentucky. They're not as particular in the Bluegrass."

"Tommy, forget the money and come back to the Lick." Lori's voice pulled at his heart. Lori had always been incapable of deceit. She was honest, tender, and pure.

"I can't come back. That bomb in the hotel lobby was intended for me. I'm on the run, Sweetheart. My car's in a lot on Petersburg Road . . . so come pick it up if you're inclined. The key's in the gas cap flap and some phony you-know-what's under the rear seat. I bled a lot, so it looks like a hog got butchered in the front seat."

"This isn't right, Tommy."

Tommy maintained his course. "I'll buy French dollars soon as I get to Paris. Frogs don't know shit from shinola about American money." All Tommy could think about was his money. All Lori could think about was getting Tommy back home.

"Please come back and face up to the haters . . . just apologize."

"The mob won't let me live long enough to face up to any-body." He felt stoic, brave. He braced himself to deliver the lines he'd practiced a dozen times since his fifth Oxycodone. In a normal state-of-mind, he would have preferred to dislo-cate and delaminate another finger than to say what he was about to say. "Forget me, Lori. For your own sake, pretend I never existed. Our life together was a dream. Now, get on with your life."

Tommy heard Lori crying. His eyes were moist, too. He felt a stabbing ache in his heart. Then, Oxycodone dulled that, too.

Tommy elevated his finger cast in a bid for sympathy while being searched by a bored TSA employee who ran her hands over the lumpy bundles of cash without notice. She was cute from the chin up. Next she probed his junk so thoroughly that he tipped her ten real dollars.

He removed the wig and glasses for the boarding process, during which an employee compared his face to his passport photo. His passport was practically new. The only time he had ever traveled on it was when the Cutters had played in a Christmas tournament in Halifax, Nova Scotia. Tommy slept through most of the flight, courtesy of his new pal — Oxycodone. He noticed some side effects — itching, cold sweats, and confusion — but they were only three of eighty-eight listed symptoms, so he felt fortunate. He reread the warning label and found a couple of more side effects he was experiencing. He had heard Doctor Denny opine on television that it was silly for a patient in this day and age to endure pain when so many modern analgesic agents were available. Tommy couldn't agree with Doctor Denny more.

<hr />

The French girl selling train tickets spoke good English, but she had a difficult time understanding English as it was spoken by Tommy. He had to speak loudly and slowly for her to understand.

"I whanja gozha Swizgherlun."

His lips felt numb, but his mind was razor sharp, so he patiently spoke his request again . . . and again. Finally the girl understood.

"*Genève?*"

"Thazghit. Bud therzgha *va* at the end. Zgha-knee-*va*."

"Ge-ne-va," the girl said.

"Thazghit. Practizghit everday zsheven timezun you'll geddid."

On the Paris-to-Geneva train, Tommy stayed conscious long enough to scan a *Herald Tribune* account of the game between Kentucky Barber College and Brut. He drank a small bottle of wine with his pill, further narrowing the line between confusion and profound freedom from pain. The last sentence he read before passing out was, "Three terrorist groups have claimed responsibility for an explosion in a fish tank in the lobby of a Lexington hotel." He had never been part of history before.

———◉———

Coincidentally, Tommy's grandfather and former guardian was availing of public transportation at the same time. Pop Gun was in remarkable condition for a man of sixty-eight when his history of whiskey consumption and tobacco use were figured in. He was riding in the back of an interstate bus wearing overalls, scuffed boots, a cotton shirt, and a John Deere baseball cap. The single modern thing on his body was the cell phone he was using to call Lori Tolliver.

Lori was bottle-feeding an adorable calf down by the barn on her parents' Kegg County farm outside Toxic Lick. Observing Lori dressed in Daisy Mae attire might inspire any man to take up agriculture. The calf didn't miss a lick feeding when Pop's call came through, because, according to Maslow's hierarchy of needs, food trumped cell phone ring tones every time.

"Howdy, Miss Lori."

"Pop, I've been worried about you since they burned down your mobile home."

"Don't fret about me. I'm on a bus to anywhere but Kegg County. I'm worried sick about Tommy."

"He's lying low on account of some dangerous men who want to do him harm. I'm praying he'll come back soon."

"I 'spect he'll come back to you 'fore he comes back to me. You all right?"

"I'm awful lonely," Lori sighed. "Aristotle. . . ."

"Who?"

"Aristotle."

"Don't rightly know if . . . ."

"He was a Greek philosopher."

"Then I probably run across him sometime or other. Them Greeks are a haughty bunch."

"Aristotle wrote that love is one soul inhabiting two bodies. Well, only one of 'em's here."

"Tommy's saved up a lot of love from not having a momma or daddy . . . and I believe he wants to give it to you."

"He never was much for expressing it."

"That's because he's a Gunn. He'll be back — but the Bluegrass ain't a forgiving place when it comes to basketball, so it'll be a while."

Chapter 14

CRASH

ONE-HUNDRED-DOLLAR BILLS LAY scattered around the interior of the Fiat at the bottom of a rock slide. Within moments of the car coming to rest two hundred meters below the point where it had skidded off the road, a bicyclist, clambering over rocks to reach the wreck from a switchback below, finished collecting the bills from where they lay, some on Tommy's body, one stuck to the blood on his forehead. A few bills had fluttered out of the broken windscreen and had been carried by the wind up the slope to where the girl lay. The bicyclist collected almost fifty of the uncirculated bills. He stuffed them into his belly pack, descended over rocks to his bicycle beside the road in the lower switchback, and coasted downhill to his village in the valley. The dead girl and the unconscious boy had nothing to do with him. He anonymously reported the accident to police. He was jubilant over his stroke of luck until he noticed that each bill had the same serial number.

Tommy was admitted to a hospital in Mies. Police impounded almost thirteen thousand counterfeit American dollars found in an inside pocket of Tommy's jacket. They also found nearly fifty thousand dollars in bona fide currency. They were confident that the injured American had broken some laws.

⸺⸺◈⸺⸺

In a matter of days, independent Internet searches by Igor and Banjo yielded details about Tommy's accident.

Tommy's money was in police custody and Tommy lay incapacitated in a Mies hospital bed. Without The Smelt's knowledge, Banjo dispatched Puff to Switzerland to snuff out Tommy's flame. Across town, Igor promised his boss that he would somehow claim the money and terminate Tommy's life. *Kill* in Igor-speak was *keel*. "I *keel theese dubiina*." Igor sounded clownish, but he was deadly serious about assassinations. If Igor was on the case, you could kiss off his intended victim.

At Chicago O'Hare, Igor waited for the same Lufthansa flight as Puff. Igor glanced at Puff and thought, *fat ass*. Igor admired his own figure reflected in a pane of glass and thought, *not bad*. Puff noticed Igor preening at the window and thought two conflicting things: *I need to lose a couple of pounds* and *I've got time for another doughnut*. The two assassins – one who ate no fat and one who ate no lean – had more in common than they could suppose. They had been assigned to hit the same target.

Chapter 15
THE HUNT

THE SWISS HOSPITAL was so aseptic that any bacterium worth its cytoplasm had long since migrated along with virulent viruses and vagrant germs to less stringent environs in France and Italy. Dirt, it seemed, had been outlawed in Switzerland. Had obesity been outlawed, too? Slender doctors, lithe nurses, and svelte orderlies populated the corridors. Of course, heavies existed in Switzerland on account of spectacular Swiss cheeses and chocolates, but the chunkers were shunted to back rooms where they couldn't degrade the unspoiled image of a healthy, spotless confederation of health and vigor.

Tommy lay motionless in a sanitized state-of-the-art bed in Room Seven. His head and right hand were wrapped in spotless white gauze. Privacy screens surrounded his bed. Swiss catheters were color-coded. Tommy's was blue (large). With all that had gone wrong recently, the knowledge that he had a large catheter would have raised his spirits, but he didn't know that blue meant large and, almost all of the time, he didn't know who he was. Three intravenous tubes were stuck into various sites. The IV pouches were colored, too, but for decorative purposes, not for size or content. Good taste would prohibit a green bag being suspended next to an orange bag, for example. Twenty-seven electrical leads were snapped onto sticky blue discs attached to Tommy's limbs – ankles, calves, pelvic girdle, wrists, and forearms. Eight were stuck to his chest alone. Even his penis had a blue disc stuck to it with a yellow wire leading to the monitor, because, in Switzerland, you couldn't have too much information. Swiss researchers had discovered that men patients found immense peace of mind knowing their primary phalli were being monitored twenty-four by seven. Tommy's heartbeat and respiration as recorded on the vital signs monitor were not up to Swiss standards, but were not bad for an American.

A huge man in a plumber's uniform plodded down the corridor carrying a tool box. His blue jumpsuit comprised enough cotton to make a schooner mainsail. He didn't fit into this domain of slender Swiss persons. Nevertheless, the hospital staff ignored him. Puff, the portly plumber, entered Room Seven with authority. He set his tool box aside. He stretched an arm through a gap in the privacy screen, and his stubby forefinger and thumb turned all three IV stopcocks to the *OFF* position. He thought his plan brilliant for its simplicity and for its anonymity. Tommy's silent death would be blamed on medical malfeasance. Puff collected his tool box and departed the way he had come. As he passed by a linen closet, the door opened.

Igor closed the linen closet door behind him. He was dressed in scrubs, booties, hat, and a surgical mask. He followed the identical path Puff had taken into Room Seven and behind the privacy screen. He stretched an arm through a gap in the screen and rotated the three IV stopcock valves back to *ON*. Tommy tossed in his bed, causing the connection to the vital signs monitor to come undone. Digital symbols on the monitor flat-lined. No heartbeat. No respiration. A warning tone chimed. Lights out. Igor flitted out of the room.

On the following morning at the hospital ward nurses' station, Igor arrived wearing a cheap suit and carrying a selection of spring flowers.

"I express condolence for death of Mr. Gunn," Igor said. The nurse seemed surprised, confused.

"*Herr* Gunn is quite *alife*," the nurse said. "I *vill* give him *ze* flowers, if you *vish*."

"No. I don't wish it. I come back."

As Igor exited the ward, he passed Puff who was wearing an even cheaper-looking suit and carrying a fist-full of flowers. Like his fellow assassin, Puff soon learned of the inefficacy of his first attempt on Tommy's life, an attempt that turned out to be less brilliant than supposed.

An hour later, Puff showed up on Tommy's ward dressed as a nurse, the largest such professional ever seen in Mies. Puff's makeup was uneven. His West Virginia-shaped birthmark appeared to Swiss observers to be a likeness of a map of the Canton of Freiberg. His Latex gloves stretched to the limit to cover his pudgy hands. His starched white dress crinkled as he waddled into the private bathroom where Tommy reclined in a hot bath. Nurse Puff shunted aside the three IV tubes so he could place a small circulating fan on a shelf over the bath tub. He turned the fan on, and its vibration started it creeping ever closer to the edge of the shelf. Unaware of the danger, Tommy soaked in the hot water with his bandaged head and right arm protruding above the surface. Puff breezed out of the bathroom. The dimming of lights would announce Tommy's electrocution. No finger prints, no evidence to link Puff to Tommy's demise. The hit man had devised a devilish way to exterminate Tommy, or so he thought.

The fan vibrated off the shelf and fell toward the tub. The cord was too short to reach, however, and the plug jerked out of the socket before the fan splashed into the tub. Tommy awoke with a start. With his left hand, he salvaged the fan from the watery depths of the tub.

Nurse Puff plodded off the ward past a door held open by a clown clinging to a cluster of helium balloons. Only the keenest observer could recognize the man in the red nose, neck ruffles, and gaudy makeup as Igor. A clown bearing balloons is not what a patient expects to see while bathing, but Tommy was too busy putting the fan into dry dock to think about it. Igor injected the contents of a syringe into one of Tommy's IV lines. Igor didn't notice that he had inserted the needle all the way through the tubing, and, when he pressed the syringe, the deadly poison squirted onto the floor harmlessly. Igor made a quick exit and passed out balloons on his way off the ward.

Igor returned to the ward the next morning in a rumpled

suit and bearing the same flowers from the day before. The bouquet had not benefited from rough handling and the ravages of time.

"Sympathies for Mr. Gunn," Igor said.

"He's not in his room," the nurse said.

"Yes, I know. I mourn his death."

"*Herr* Gunn is quite *alife*. He is taking sunshine in *ze* garden. I *vill* give him *ze* flowers, if you *vish*."

Igor frowned. Was he losing his touch?

"No. I don't wish it. I come back."

On his way out, Igor passed Puff who was headed toward the nurses' station with his recycled bouquet from the previous day. Puff looked familiar, but Igor couldn't place him. Puff repeated his oral exchange with the ward nurse and discovered that, like a cat with nine lives, Tommy had survived his most recent encounter with death. Puff wasn't concerned. He had time on his side, and he knew a dozen diabolical ways to finish Tommy off.

Igor regrouped to plan his next attack on Tommy's longevity. Igor had trained for clandestine operations in Myanmar back during his youth in the Russian forces. He could field-strip a PLQ-63 in eight seconds. He could make bombs out of pancake mix and fingernail polish. He knew seventeen ways to kill a man with his hands, eighteen, if you counted the Mulrovian ankle kick. At the moment, Igor was prowling around the spa's extensive gardens. His movements went unnoticed by the hospital staff because of his stealth and the surplus Ninja outfit he had ordered online from a distributer in Belgrade. He reached the patio where Tommy napped in his wheelchair. Igor crouched and prepared his authentic pygmy blowpipe for the kill. He measured the poison onto the dart tip with precision. Too much poison or too little would induce only a temporary paralysis. Igor was looking for paralysis of a more permanent kind.

Puff roamed the gardens dressed in a monk's coarse brown gown. He looked like a super-sized version of Friar Tuck in need of a haircut. His forearms were inserted into the floppy sleeves of his robe. Concealed in one hand was a lethal wire garrote. In the other hand, he palmed a syringe full of fast-acting muscle-relaxer capable of paralyzing a rhino in three seconds. Puff was an ecclesiastical killing machine.

Ninja Igor aimed his blowpipe at the back of Tommy's head. He couldn't miss at this range. He inhaled deeply in preparation for shooting the poison-tipped dart. He blew into the pipe, making a sound like a needle being pulled out of a freshly-inflated basketball. At that precise moment, Friar Puff lunged into the path of the dart. Puff's right arm was raised to inject muscle relaxer into Tommy's chest from behind. Igor's dart stuck into the back of Puff's head, just below his *zucchetta*. Puff spun and fell head first into the bushes where Igor crouched. Puff's syringe impaled Igor's cheek. Both assassins quivered, stiffened, and passed out among the plants and bushes, Puff on top of Igor. Oblivious to the schemes that had just *gang aglay*, an alert nurse arrived to wheel Tommy back to his private room. Well away from the bushes where Puff rested in the arms of Igor, she called Security on her cell phone.

"I am not certain," she said discretely, "but I think a priest and a boy are up to no good in *ze* bushes beside *ze* sun patio."

The third morning of Puff's Swiss adventure arrived with Tommy still breathing and Puff suffering an epic headache. In his hotel, Puff nursed his sore head with an ice pack made of ice cubes crammed into a shower cap. Banjo's voice on the telephone stabbed Puff's eardrums.

"Stop farting around and kill the son-of-a-bitch," Banjo said.

"I've killed him three times already. He won't die."

"Do it right or I'll fly over there and do it myself."

In a hotel on the north side of Mies, Igor was soaking in a bath full of water so hot that it created a fog bank that enveloped the tiny bathroom. An uncapped bottle of pain medication sat on the rim of the tub like a sentinel.

"I tell you, this bastard not die," he moaned into a telephone.

"If he does not die, you will." Igor's boss was a plain-spoken man. "No one makes fool of me."

"I *keel* him. No more mess around."

Back on the hospital ward, a man with gauze wrapped around his head argued with a nurse. A body guard dressed in black tended the faceless man's wheel chair as the patient arrogantly scolded the nurse.

"I am paying top Euro for the best room, and I insist on having it."

"But it is occupied . . . by an American patient."

"All the more reason to move him out. Do not upset me. I want that room immediately."

The faceless man had done nothing but complain since his arrival. Tommy hadn't complained in over a week. The easiest thing to do was to take Tommy out of Room Seven and into Room Eleven and to insert the faceless man into Room Seven. The faceless man shooed his body guard and an orderly out of his cocoon inside the privacy screens in Room Seven. He dozed off.

Igor and Puff ambled side-by-side down the hospital corridor holding clutches of flowers that were well past a presentable state. The unmatched pair entered the screened portion of Room Seven to stand on either side of the mummy-like patient.

"He is great man," Igor said.

"One of a kind," Puff said.

Igor laid his half-dead flowers on a bedside table.

"I go now. My emotion very sad."

Puff followed Igor's lead, leaving his tawdry floral tribute on the other side of the bed.

The two men stepped outside the privacy screens on either side of the bed. Igor pushed the barrel of his silencer through a gap in the screen. He aimed at the faceless man's left temple. He didn't notice another silencer barrel protruding from the screen on the other side of the mummy's bed.

Puff concentrated so intently on lining up his shot on the faceless man's right temple, he didn't notice Igor's gun. The sound of Igor's silenced shot sounded like a sneeze.

"God bless you," Puff said.

A small black hole appeared in the left temple of the Faceless Man. It turned scarlet against the brilliant white gauze. The sound of Puff's shot also sounded like a sneeze.

"God bless you, also." Igor was an atheist, but theism was not an issue at the moment.

The faceless man had matching crimson dots, one on either side of his head. The untidy exit wounds of his bound head were hidden by his pillow, but the blood draining from his body was not. The bloody work of the two assassins was done. Puff believed his switch of the counterfeit bills for the real money was a secret known only to him and Banjo. Igor believed that Tommy Gunn no longer could testify against the Russian mob. Igor opened the door for Puff, and he followed Puff into the hallway.

"Is good hospital?" Igor asked.

"Good enough," Puff replied.

Chapter 16

REHABILITATION

AFTER TOMMY REGAINED his strength, he was transferred to a nearby plastic surgery clinic overlooking Lake Geneva. During occasional memory flashes that he mistook for dreams, he was in a Fiat skidding off a mountain road and tumbling to oblivion. His heart rate accelerated until the dreams ended with an after-taste of paranoia. Then fatigue. Finally, sleep. He slept a lot. During most of his waking hours, he drifted into and out of fantasies as though his memory couldn't gain traction.

A cosmetic surgeon named Doctor Fahr repaired Tommy's facial injuries. Tommy approved of Doctor Fahr the moment he met him, because Doctor Fahr was so good looking. Tommy had no more use for an ugly plastic surgeon than he had for a bald barber or a one-armed golf instructor.

Tommy's confidence in Doctor Fahr was fortified by the Doctor's frequent use of German nouns such as *Kreislaufstörüng*, for example, or *Krankenversicherung* or *Beruhigungsmittel*. Impressive stuff. It required a superior mind to keep all that straight. Tommy considered learning to speak German until he discovered that the German word for X-ray was *Röntgenaufnahme*. He concluded that life was too short.

The Doctor showed Tommy his repaired pinky. It was not a cause for euphoria at first sight. His pinky was stiff, swollen, and psychedelically colored in hues not normally associated with human flesh. Tommy couldn't feel it and he couldn't move it. Doctor Fahr's serene demeanor calmed Tommy's fears, however. Apparently, milky-blue with crusty purple fringes was par for the course when it came to mangled digits.

"I *haff* corrected *ze* botched procedure done in *Sinsin-ee-tee.*"

"Cincinnati."

"Yes." Doctor Fahr tweaked the pinky and smiled.

It was too early for Tommy to declare victory, however, because his face was still as shrouded in mystery as a mummy. If his finger looked like an albino Vienna sausage, who could guess at the condition of his face?

"Rehabilitation *vill* restore *ze* use of *ze* finger." Doctor Fahr pronounced *finger* like *zinger* with an *f* in place of the *z*. "Now . . . *ve* examine *ze* face."

The Doctor removed layers of gauze as though suspense were included in the price of the surgery. Tommy's eyes were glued to the mirror as bands of gauze fell away from his head. The removal of the last strip revealed a masterpiece of cosmetic surgery. In Tommy's opinion, his new face surpassed even Doctor Fahr's for sheer comeliness. Overlooking small pockets of bruising, the term *magnificent* barely scratched the surface. Tommy couldn't take his eyes off himself. Move over, Narcissus.

"Doctor Fahr, you're a genius!"

"You make me blush in *ze* face."

While Tommy worshipped his new image, Doctor Fahr pressed a button, and a woman he introduced as Sophie entered the office. Tommy diverted his eyes from adoring himself long enough to admire Sophie's face and trim body. She was a credit to her profession, whatever it might be. Doctor Fahr told Tommy that Sophie would assist him in his recovery. As rare as it might be for a man to fall in love twice in one day, Tommy had just done it, first with himself and, then, with Sophie.

Chapter 17
CONVALESCENCE

TOMMY WAS RECLINED on a couch beside a chair occupied by Sophie, who was wearing a snow-white smock. Sophie was a compassionate, intelligent woman in her late thirties. Beneath her smock, she was dressed conservatively, like a nanny or a teacher. When she smiled, a dimple appeared on her left cheek, and left cheek only. Sophie was a patient listener. Even when she took notes, Tommy knew she was listening attentively.

"Talk about *Pop*," Sophie said.

"My grandfather? He raised me after my mother and father . . . we already . . . ."

Tommy felt disoriented. He couldn't distinguish between reality and dreams. The chronology of his fragments of memories was jumbled. Sometimes he lapsed into silence. Sophie never rushed him. She waited patiently and wrote in her notebook.

"You were talking about visualization," she said. "What do you mean?"

"Take basketball. I could leg press six hundred pounds

for twenty reps, and, during each rep, I'd visualize jumping real high. Hovering. Hanging . . . ."

"And, then?"

"Then I'd go out and do it. I had this amazing hang time. My vertical was fifty inches."

Tommy could tell that the term puzzled Sophie.

"That's about a hundred and thirty, uh, kilograms."

"Kilograms?" Sophie was still puzzled.

"Meters? I'm fuzzy on how y'all do it over here."

"You jump high, but not because of the weights?"

"No, because of the visualization."

"And now you are visualizing . . . ."

"I'm visualizing being a model. I have the face for it. I'm changing my name, too. From now on, call me *Rance*." Tommy gazed dreamily at the clouds that skirted the lake. "That's how visualization works. I blew my chance to be a national champion, but I won't blow my chance to be a star."

He marveled at his face in a mirror, content in his cloud of faux grandiosity. During the following weeks, Tommy drifted into and out of his alternative ego state, starring in his own dreams that could last for days.

Chapter 18
WINNEMUCCA, NEVADA

POP'S SOCIAL SECURITY CHECK arrived in the nick of time after being forwarded from the Toxic Lick Post Office to Winnemucca General Delivery. He paid up rent on his trailer an extra month in advance. A recycler before recycling was cool, Pop used the back of the envelope to make a list of the pluses and minuses of his new home in the Nevada desert.

The heat of cloudless summer days was a *minus*. The broken compressor motor on the ancient window air-conditioner was a *plus* in Pop's system of evaluation, because he saved a bundle on electricity by leaving the unit unplugged. If it was ninety-five degrees in the afternoon, it would be fifty-five by midnight. If you averaged the two, you were close to perfect. The remote location of his trailer on the edge of town near the Humboldt River made both lists. *One man's loneliness is another man's solitude*, he used to say.

Pop didn't claim to be an intelligent man. Brilliant men don't live in ovens disguised as trailers. He had made a lot of wrong choices in his life, but he had learned from those mistakes, and he had passed along those lessons to Tommy in a series of autobiographical morality tales.

"I might've *tolt* you this before, but when I was sixteen, I took a hankerin' to make some spending money, so I commenced to makin' moonshine distribution runs in my old Studebaker. Boys over in McCreary County didn't take kindly to my Kegg County license plates on their turf and I had more than a few bullet holes in the old buggy to show for it. Well, one night runnin' out of Greenwood at a high rate of speed on U.S. Twenty-seven headed for Somerset, I saw some ol' boys up ahead comin' at me in two cars . . . lights on bright . . . a two-car convoy. I turned my lights off and kept my speed up . . . neighborhood of a hundred . . . and zipped right by them peckerwoods. Ended up makin' ruts in a soy bean field, but it's amazing the amount of mud you can plow through when you carry plenty of speed into a field. When I got back on U.S. Twenty-seven dragging some barbed wire and some fence posts, all I could see in my rear view mirror was two sets of lights tumblin' around behind me. I turned my headlights back on, 'cause I didn't know the road that good, and laughed all the way back to Kegg County." After chuckling for a minute and blotting his tears, Pop said, "That kinda' conduct is inexcusable, and the only reason I mention it is so you know to steer clear. Don't you have nothin' to do with them kinda' shenanigans."

Pop also tried to pass along common sense in the form of old-fashioned parables and colorful analogies. *Neither a lender nor a borrower be* was one of Pop's teachings. *Don't waste your time wishin' for stuff you could git if you didn't stand around wishin' all the time* was another. *If you do the right thing, you'll amaze somebody and puzzle the hell out everybody else* was one he stole from Mark Twain. *If doing the right thing is too painful, ask somebody for advice; maybe they know a shortcut.* Sometimes, he quoted Scripture verses like Exodus 23:19, "Do not cook a young goat in its mother's milk." He risked blasphemy to get a laugh on more than one occasion. Pop's many life lessons had made him a cautious man when sober. For example, maybe he could have stopped hiding from the whackos who had torched his trailer; maybe it was safe to go back to Kegg County, but, to be certain, he endured exile. For days on end, Pop spoke to no one. Pop had always said *there's worse company to keep than your own.* Now he was living proof.

"A spell in the desert ain't a big deal," he said. "Our Lord and Savior did it for forty days."

The greatest treat in Pop's secluded existence was his weekly telephone conversation with Lori Tolliver.

Several weeks had passed since Lori's season-ending Lady Cutters basketball game. She stayed away from the Kentucky Barber College gym, because she didn't want to deal with well-meaning or mal-intended inquiries about Tommy. Instead of working out on a basketball court, she lowered her caloric intake and jogged for miles on the back roads that spider-webbed around her parents' farm. She had stayed in close contact with the graduate placement office and had managed to schedule graduate assistant coaching interviews at Indiana University, Middle Tennessee State University, and Polo University, an up-and-coming rich kids' school down in Texas. Lori was on her parents' porch swing recovering from the effects of a three-mile run when Pop called.

"Still ain't heard a thing from Tommy," he said. "My nerves twang like a guitar string ever' time the phone rings. It's never Tommy. It's always some *yay-hoo* selling something. Course, I ain't buying. I know they invented time to keep everything from happening at once, but it'd please me to fast-forward." Pop came up for air. "How 'bout you?"

"Not a thing. I haven't got a job yet, but I got some interviews lined up."

"You just keep trying, young lady. You're going to make somebody a world class coach."

"They put what was left of your trailer in a dump truck last week. Then they scraped the ground flat with a bull dozer. I looked around for anything valuable."

"Nothin' to find less'n the foreman lost his wallet," Pop said. "I'm holed up in Winnemucca."

"What is that . . . a R.V.?"

"No, ma'am, it's a town in the middle of Nevada."

"Like Las Vegas?"

"Nothing like 'Vegas. I reckon they're still talkin' about Tommy there in the Lick, are they?"

"Here in the Lick," Lori said sadly, "the town clock's still stuck on five-fifty-five and they're still talking about the Civil War."

Chapter 19

HEALING

PSYCHIATRY APPEARED TO BE a good racket, judging by the wood paneling and the richly padded furniture in the Psychiatrist's office overlooking the lake. Tommy made a mental note to consider the profession if he ever tired of modeling. Tommy's days were dreamlike. Pain no longer tormented him, but he kept pounding Oxycodone because it helped him levitate above gritty cares such as blowing the national championship, nearly losing a finger, running from gangsters, abandoning the girl he loved, and deserting Pop.

A Swiss shrink tripped stiff-legged into the room hugging a clipboard. God had not treated her kindly when handing out looks, but He must have compensated for the slight when it came to brains, because four diplomas hung on her office walls. Tommy made small talk as the Shrink shuffled around the office as though her buttocks were nailed together. She seemed nervous, and Tommy wanted to make her feel more at ease.

"We must visit my cabin in the Alps or my cliff house in Slovenia some time," he said. His imagination and sophistication were in peak form again.

The Shrink pursed her lips as though she had just popped a sour ball and gazed at him like an owl through her round glasses. She did that a lot.

Tommy's emotions were unpredictable. He often laughed and cried at the wrong times. When he blamed it on drugs, Sophie and the Shrink both responded with impassive faces and silence, so Tommy didn't know whether they agreed with him or thought he was full of crap. Tommy stared at a chrome fob hanging from a chain. With the slightest twist of her wrist, the Shrink swung the pendulum in an arc ten centimeters wide.

"You are getting sleepy," she said.

Tommy realized that this skinny woman had a fat woman's voice. What an insight! Then he fell asleep.

"*Venn* you *avake*, you *vill* speak *vitt* an erotic French accent."

The world's thinnest psychiatrist snapped her fingers and Tommy's eyes popped open alertly. When he spoke, both doctor and patient recoiled.

"Blimey! A wee kip does a bloke good!" Was it Dick Van Dyke or Michael Caine?

"*Merde*," the Shrink whispered under her breath. The Cockney accent was a rasp drawn over the Shrink's nerve endings. She acted quickly before Tommy could break out in a verse of *chim-chiminey-chim-chiminey-chim-chim-charoo*.

She resumed swinging the chrome fob. Tommy locked onto it like a hungry cat watching a goldfish.

"You are getting sleepy." She hadn't lost her touch. Tommy conked out immediately. "You no longer *vill* speak *vitt* your annoying English accent. You *vill* speak *vitt* an erotic *French* accent." She snapped her fingers, and Tommy recovered to an alert state.

Tommy's words were silky smooth, his accent sensuously French, so erotic that the sound of his own voice gave him an immediate erection. Tommy felt sorry for those who didn't believe in hypnosis. Tommy believed all this had happened, but he wasn't sure.

Later, Tommy related the event to Sophie who heard him out, no matter how fanciful his story might be. When his tale was finished, Sophie said, "Now, Tommy, we don't use hypnosis here."

"Rance," Tommy said. "I am called Rance."

————))(((())))((————

Rance was a German model who had come to the spa for a facelift. He shared a room with Tommy for three weeks, and, during that time, he regaled Tommy with stories of modeling all around Europe. He told Tommy about adoring groupies thronging around him in Denmark.

"How I love Copenhagen," Rance said.

"Me, too," Tommy agreed.

The closest Tommy had ever been to Copenhagen was a pinch of Pop's bourbon-flavored, long-cut tobacco snuff of the same name.

Rance described how fans swooned when he twitched his hips while modeling a new line of pants in Prague. Tommy listened to every word with rapt attention.

"Like a latter-day Elvis," Tommy whispered.

Tommy plagiarized the stories for his own use during his sessions with Sophie. He told her about modeling cologne in Köln. He made her blush when he recalled a scene on a Cannes beach. Fatigued by modeling sunglasses, he had torn his Speedo from his body with one powerful thrust and marched stark-naked into the sea followed by a band of disrobed, enchanted women in a scene reminiscent of the Pied Piper, *sans vêtements*. Tommy related Rance's exploits as his own, and he refused to emigrate from this realm of his own invention.

"Now, Tommy . . . ."

"I am called Rance."

———— ((|)) ————

Tommy awoke from a stupor, his muscles flaccid. He sensed warmth radiating out of him as if an electric coil had been stuffed into his body. He was a heating pad with appendages. He could see that he was stretched out on Sophie's couch, but he felt as light as air as though he were levitating above his own physical body. Objects glowed with incandescence. Sophie's voice made harmony with itself. What was that humming? It was the Earth sighing. A warm breeze wafted through an open window.

"Who do you love?" Sophie asked him.

"Lori Tolliver. I never knew how much I loved her until I left her behind."

"She is perfect for you?"

"Yes. Perfect. But I ran away. What if she's forgotten about me?"

Tommy fell into a trance. He was Rance. Rance was in a trance. Rance was flying in white suffused clouds like Superman in civilian clothes — no leotards, no cape — weightless. Voices surrounded him as though amplified – tones enriched and the range of frequencies expanded from the highest tinkle of a crystal glass to the deepest bass of Igor's incessant questioning.

"Where is money, Tommy?" Igor roared.

"Blown away," Tommy said feebly. "Gone."

"I *keel* you."

Igor's frightening apparition faded, and Lori appeared to Tommy as iridescent as an angel.

"Come home, Tommy."

"Igor and Puff want their money," Tommy said.

"Get a receipt," Lori whispered, her face almost obscured by a shimmering fog.

"I should have just laid the ball in . . . ."

"Come home to the Bluegrass." Lori's angelic face faded away.

Tommy's mind jerked him into the present. He was weeping like a baby. Sophie's tenderness at such times comforted Tommy. He drifted into his memories of Rance again. He retold Rance's story about a French model in the first person.

"*Ravissement! Extase!* — those were her words," Tommy said, as he blotted his eyes. "And the German woman longs for me still. She was such a temptress."

He told Rance's stories as his own over-and-over. A

kaleidoscopic tumult of jumbled crystals, gleaming pearls, and wisps of incense smoke blurred his vision as if time and light had been fused.

━━━━◦《◉》◦━━━━

The first sound Tommy heard upon waking on Sophie's couch was the chirping of a bird. Sophie was reading her notes. The lace curtains barely stirred in the breeze that whispered off the lake and into the open office windows. The sensation of floating had passed. He felt as cozy as a swaddled baby. Sophie spoke to him tenderly.

"We have worked together for many weeks."

"Weeks?" Tommy asked. Time had become a perplexing dimension for him.

"Tell me who you are."

"I am called Rance . . . everybody knows that. I'm a super-model." He grew uneasy. "Where's my shot."

"No injection today," Sophie said.

Tommy fidgeted and paused awkwardly. "I was fabulously wealthy . . . then, damn me, I jilted you."

"Tommy, we must . . . ."

"I jilted you . . . and . . . to spite me . . . you stole all my money . . . ."

Sophie showed a flash of impatience.

"Trauma has upset your equilibrium. Let us start again. You are Tommy Gunn."

"My name is Rance." Tommy became more agitated. "Call me Rance or . . . I don't have to lie here . . . I can stroll

━ 88 ━

in the garden . . . ."

"Your name is Tommy. Your roommate was called Rance. He is a German model."

"Don't play games, I . . . ."

"You have adopted Rance's persona to cope . . . ."

"Give me a mirror . . . right now."

Tommy's voice was terse. The light in the room turned harsh. The breeze blowing in through the window seemed cold. Tommy shivered. Sophie handed him a mirror. In an instant, Tommy's facial expression morphed from complacency to discovery to despair.

"I'm so plain . . . just like any other guy from . . . from Kentucky. I want to look like Rance again."

"Lots of people want to look like Rance." Sophie's voice was soothing. "How you look is in your mind. Knowing that is wisdom."

"Did you steal my money?" Tommy's French accent was gone.

"I stole nothing. When you came to us, you were carrying counterfeit American dollars. We shielded you from the police. You have spent almost all of your legitimate American dollars for your care in the spa."

Tommy shivered again, and Sophie covered him with a white wool blanket. Tommy's eyes darted around as he tried to extract meaning from Sophie's words.

"You're my agent . . . the only person who knows my password . . . ."

"I'm not an agent, Tommy . . . I'm your therapist."

"I'm . . . I'm a . . . model . . . ."

"No, Tommy, you're a patient. You were in a bad car

accident when you arrived in Switzerland. You were hitch-hiking in a Fiat that rolled down a steep hillside."

Tommy looked defeated. His tears flowed again.

"My name is Rance . . . Rance . . . ."

"Rance was a German model who shared your room with you in hospital."

Tommy curled up beneath the blanket. His eyes darted around without focusing. His breathing accelerated.

"I modeled in Sweden and Hungary . . . ."

"You never left hospital."

"No. No." Tommy placed his hands over his ears.

"You call this imaginary career your second great chance, but this isn't your second great chance, Tommy. That lies in your future. You are healing . . . so you can go home to the life you love. Stop running . . . find Lori Tolliver. With her, you will create your second great chance."

Chapter 20
POLO, TEXAS

CHAMPIONSHIP BANNERS HUNG in profusion from the ceiling of the hoops palace named Polo Arena. Lighting, sound system, and appurtenances were state-of-the-art. Six hundred expensive bidet-inspired toilets called Polo-spas ringed the opulent arena. Imported from Honshu, each top-of-the-line toilet comprised a solar-heated water douche cycle, electro-warm air-drying, and low-frequency vibrator. Any one of those features was marvelous, but all three together was stupendous. Fans lined up to use Polo-spas at every home game. No tour of the campus was complete without a Polo-spa session, and tour buses from places like Minnesota and Georgia delivered tourists eager to experience the thrill of Polo-spa.

All six hundred Polo-spas were upgraded with door-mounted high-definition TVs and Bose speaker systems that enabled Polo-spa users to keep up with Ponies basketball action while enjoying the luxury that was the Polo-spa experience. Polo-spa revenues exceeded the predicted $146,000 a game, so the toilet upgrades were paid for by halftime of the

Polo-versus-Villanova game.

The visionary who had touted the Polo-spa system was promoted to Executive Assistant Athletic Director or Assistance Executive Athletic Director, he couldn't remember which. The Japanese manufacturer of the Polo-spa system endowed a chair at the Polo University School of Engineering Department of Applied Hydraulics.

Lori learned these minutiae during her preparation for her Polo interview. She had memorized scores of details. For example, the arena's twenty-three thousand spectator seats were warmed by twelve-volt seat warmers invented by a Swedish snowmobile company. The seats were upholstered in Polo Blue Nottyhyde, one of many breakthrough substances created in Polo University labs with a grant from NASA. A great blue halo surrounded a one-of-a-kind playing surface made of wood harvested from the exotic Yang Dong tree, a species native to a Northwestern province of China.

Television talk-show host Livid Detterman asked Polo University President Leif Roren, "What is the significance of making the Polo basketball court out of Yang Dong wood?"

"None," President Roren said.

The host and his guests laughed like hell, which confirmed in the minds of viewers at home that Detterman and his guests were as sharp as tacks.

Yes, Lori had done her homework.

In what felt to Lori like a sacred ritual, the Women's Head Basketball Coach escorted Lori to center court. The Head Coach was over forty, but she had the lean body of a thirty-year-old, thanks to a lifetime dedicated to sports. Her hair was bobbed short. Her business suit revealed muscular calves that tapered to fine ankles; she was an auburn-haired version of Lori twenty years hence.

"Joining our staff is the finest opportunity you'll ever have," the Head Coach said. "Bar none."

Some expressions were meaningless to Lori. *Bar none, flammable,* and *inflammable* fell into her linguistic Bermuda Triangle. Looking past that, she was intrigued by the phenomenal Polo Arena acoustics. The Head Coach's voice sounded like the voice of God, if God were a woman, as so many strident female atheists in the Polo University Divinity School insisted. Lori savored the majesty of the place. In contrast, the KBC gym was a hut.

"I know," the Head Coach said, "Stanford, UConn, Tennessee, Texas — they're traditional powers. But Polo's the future in women's basketball." The venerable head coach asked Lori a simple question: "Is there anything keeping you from giving us a hundred per cent?"

Lori's sad tears made her blue eyes glisten. Polo represented the resurrection of hope for her.

"Not a thing . . . I've got nothing."

The Head Coach presented Lori with a chrome Polo-spa toilet token.

"You mustn't leave without trying it," the Head Coach said. A cunning basketball strategist, she was a wily one. She knew that a single Polo-spa encounter would seal the deal. She was right. Lori used the token, and the course of her destiny was charted.

Lori was bound for Polo.

Chapter 21

FINDING POP

POP WONDERED WHETHER a deaf person thought a volume knob was a placebo. *I'll know soon enough*, he thought. His hearing and his eyesight were heading south. He muted his favorite country music radio station to answer the cell phone vibrating in his right front pocket. Not much had gone on down there for the last few years, so he could detect incoming calls every time. Come to think of it, nothing much had gone on down there even before his wife had left him, a possible direct correlation to her departure.

"Lo," he said.

"I'm leaving the Lick," Lori said right away. It's the best she had sounded in weeks. "I got a job coaching junior varsity girls at Polo University down in Texas."

"I'm proud of you, Lori Darlin'. They're mighty lucky to have you."

"I've about given up hope of seeing Tommy again."

"I don't know any more myself, Sweetie. I'm afraid he mighta run away so far he might never get back."

"At least he didn't tell you to forget about him and start a new life like he did me."

"He didn't tell me nothin'," Pop said. "I wake up during the night with a bad dream that something's happened to Tommy, then I spend all day with my feelings hurt because he hasn't bothered to call."

———— ((●)) ————

Tommy was one of three patients dressed in snow white pajamas seated in the hospital library. He scribbled on a memo pad, moved on to a new web page on the desktop computer, then scribbled some more. The last page he came to put a satisfied smile on his face. He printed Pop's name in block capitals, *CLIFFORD "POP" GUNN, 69, Winnemucca, Nevada*. Then Tommy leaned back in his chair and visualized a reunion with Pop and how good it was going to be under the same roof again with his mentor, his guardian, his grandfather.

Chapter 22

CHICAGO

WITH A SINGLE operative eye, a crotchety Immigration Officer examined Tommy's face and passport photo. The man's eye patch intimidated Tommy. So did the hook in the place of his left hand. He looked like a pirate without the parrot or the ship.

"Your photo doesn't match your face."

The eye patch and hook made Tommy stammer. "I was in a c-c-car accident." Tommy knew that stammering people often are perceived to be guilty people.

"We all have accidents," Captain Hook said. "You don't hear me whining about it. What was the purpose of your trip?"

Tommy heard the question as, *Why are you sneaking around outside of the good old U.S.A., you sniveling piece of crap?* A hook and an eye patch conveyed a lot of subtext.

"T – T - Travel. Tourism. Vacation." Tommy was a nervous wreck. He had been as cool as ice whacked out on Oxycodone on the outbound leg with thousands of dollars taped to his torso, but, coming back to America with nothing in his backpack but pajamas, a toothbrush, and a razor, he was shaking like a criminal at a parole hearing.

"Evasive answers will get you nowhere, Mr. Gunn. We'll be watching you."

Tommy vacated the Immigration Officer's lair and headed toward U.S. Customs. A freckled, cheerful Customs Officer examined Tommy's backpack.

"How about them Cubbies?" he asked.

It struck Tommy as a trick question . . . either that or a mighty presumptuous one. Yet, the officer didn't seem bright enough or devious enough to ask trick questions.

"Awesome."

"Anything to declare?"

Tommy shook his head, so the Customs Officer waved him on and switched his suspicions and attentions to a ninety-year-old lady who wouldn't weigh ninety pounds if you filled her pockets with concrete.

As Tommy moved on to the arrivals hall, the Immigration Officer tracked him with his solitary eyeball. He grasped his cell phone with his titanium hook and used his right index finger to peck in a telephone number.

"Tommy Gunn's back in-country. He's got a ticket on the *California Zephyr* leaving out of Union Station."

"Got it," The Smelt barked. "Give my love to Sis."

The Immigration Officer heard a click. "His face has changed," the officer said. "Smelt? Smelt?"

The Smelt had already hung up.

The Smelt's office was a dump in an ugly warehouse on an ugly street in an ugly part of South Chicago. The Smelt was breathing hard from the exertion of pressing an intercom button.

"Get Banjo on the phone."

A nasal voice told The Smelt she couldn't get Banjo on the phone, because Banjo was on vacation out West with Puff and because the mobster contract banned phone calls during vacation periods. The Smelt slammed the phone down on his desk. Then he slammed his palm on the desk. His scar was throbbing red. He shoved a gun into his left underarm holster. He muttered profanities as he shoved another gun into his right underarm holster. He raised his pants legs to shove a pistol into an ankle holster on each calf. He flipped open a switchblade and tested it on a Chicago phone book that it sliced in half easily. He squeezed his fat fingers into gleaming brass knuckles.

"I gotta do everything around here," he muttered.

———— ((◉)) ————

Principal Bradley sat alone in the Rio Feo High School gym, his sanctuary from despondency. His adobe house was cramped and, most recently, infested with spiders. The fumigation had left the house smelling like a DuPont factory. Breathing the residual insecticide vapors had given him a temple-smashing headache. He dreamed of escaping Rio Feo. He dreamed of escaping his wife, a social climber even though there was no society to climb in Rio Feo. And his son,

Chip: how was he going to afford college tuition? Although he dreamed of smashing his wife's head in, he more often thought about suicide. He feared he might be mentally ill. He noticed Anna Lee walking toward him beside the basketball court.

Anna was a stunning brunette beauty, a seventeen-year-old school girl in the body of a Hollywood starlet. Many a townsman, including Principal Bradley, had dreamed about Anna. She intuitively knew she was the object of fantasies. Dreaming of being dreamed of got her through the tedious sermons of her father, the Lutheran minister in Rio Feo. *What a pious dick-head*, the Principal thought, *and his golf handicap is six strokes lower than mine.* The Principal stood up and patted rebellious tufts of hair down on his scalp. He embarked on a mini-fantasy in which he committed suicide, but only after calling Anna to the office for a wild five minutes of carnal education, followed by a self-administered gunshot to the head. It would put Anna into an asylum and split the community in half, but what did he care? He'd be dead. The rogue thought cheered him. Punishing Rio Feo always made Principal Bradley feel better. It would serve the bastards right. Reality: Anna reached him and stood close.

"Please don't cut basketball, Principal Bradley."

"We *weally* don't want to," he assured her. "My son Chip plays . . . so . . . ."

"I'm the head cheerleader this year," Anna said emotionally. "I've dreamed of this my whole life." Anna pressed against the Principal and tapped an index finger against his polyester tie. "I'd be so grateful I wouldn't know how to thank you."

The Principal inadvertently patted Anna on the derriere and blushed. What was he thinking? *Just because you dream about stuff doesn't mean you get to do it in broad daylight.* Anna was amused by the slip-up.

"I'll do all I can," he said, perspiring now.

"You won't be sorry," Anna whispered.

<hr/>

At a bar in Chicago's Union Station, Banjo and Puff looked like beanbags stuffed into suits as they huddled over drinks at a stand-up table, suitcases and briefcases parked at their feet. Passersby couldn't resist staring. Chicago had its share of homely residents, but seven hundred pounds of polyunsaturated ugliness was special. Dressed in classic consignment vacation attire, Banjo's sailboat tie was blue. Puff's palm tree tie was yellow.

Banjo was in the middle of a joke when he spotted The Smelt coming toward them. Banjo's blood froze and his eyes bulged to the size of ping pong balls, which terrified Puff in turn. Banjo pushed Puff down and out of The Smelt's line-of-sight and signaled for Puff to take the money in the briefcases and run. Puff stooped to take both briefcases and escape under The Smelt's radar. Banjo's knees were shaking when The Smelt arrived.

"I want my money," The Smelt snarled.

"I'm on vacation here."

"Gimme your bag."

The Smelt overpowered Banjo and lifted his subordinate's

bag to the table top. The Smelt rummaged through it — gaudy boxers, three bottles of anti-acid lotion, a speedo the size of a fan belt, but no money. The Smelt stormed out of the pub, his scar as bright red as the neon Molson sign over the bar. Banjo had the feeling that he and Puff hadn't ridded themselves of The Smelt for long.

———— ((●)) ————

Lori, dressed in high heels, wearing her best blue suit, and carrying an expensive bag with *Polo University* embossed in gold, searched for a vacant seat. She found one. Its fabric was threadbare from use by thousands of Amtrak passengers. She settled into the chair and noticed on her left a guy with wall-to-wall tattoos and multiple piercings. He appeared to be dying of something at a faster rate than those around him. She didn't recognize plastic-surgery-modified Tommy, who was dozing on her right. Lori's cell phone chimed. She ransacked her purse, finding an airline ticket stamped *ORD-SAT* and then her cell phone, which she answered.

"I should be in Polo by six," Lori said.

Lori collected her bag and slipped out of her seat to exit the Amtrak waiting area for the nearby airline passenger terminal at O'Hare. Tommy started awake from a dream. The gold ring and chain fell out from his shirt.

"Lori?" Tommy said. "Lori?"

Tommy stretched and rubbed his eyes. He noticed a woman in a blue business suit evaporate into the concourse crowd. He sniffed a perfumed, almost familiar aroma in the air, and then he dozed off again.

————)«(●)» ————

Puff waddled into the waiting area carrying two brief-cases. He made his nest on the seat just vacated by Lori. He kicked the tattooed wonder's canvas bag with his left foot and Tommy's black backpack with his right to make more room for his mass. Within seconds, his beady eyes spotted The Smelt lumbering toward him from across the concourse. Panicking, Puff opened Tommy's black backpack. He took all ten stacks of money out of the two briefcases and shoved them into Tommy's backpack. As Puff leaped up to evacuate, Tommy woke up. When Tommy recognized Puff, he was petrified by fear.

The Smelt intercepted Puff's getaway maneuver, grabbed both briefcases, and slammed them onto a trash container to open them. The first one was empty except for a San Francisco tour guide that had fallen out of an envelope ad-dressed to Banjo. The second briefcase was also empty except for a motorcycle magazine and seven condoms. Puff was an optimist. The Smelt grabbed Puff by the right ear and tugged so hard that Puff's ear obscured half of West Virginia. The Smelt's surly lips spat a warning.

"If I don't get my money, you're done."

The threat frightened Puff and Tommy, too, as he fig-ured out his role in the drama. The confrontation confirmed Tommy's suspicion that Puff had kept The Smelt's legitimate money and foisted off the counterfeit to Tommy. Tommy's hands shook. He found some comfort in the anonymity of his surgically-altered face, but not enough comfort to stick around. He grabbed his backpack and strode away toward the train platform.

The Smelt released Puff's ear and stormed away. Puff composed himself and collected his briefcases. He returned to get his bands of money out of the black backpack, but it and its owner were gone. Puff blanched. If The Smelt didn't kill him, Banjo probably would.

The amplified voice of a bored bureaucrat announced, "*The California Zephyr*, service from Chicago's Union Station to San Francisco, departing Track Seven."

⟨⟨◉⟩⟩

Out on Track Seven, Tommy boarded the *Zephyr* and surrendered his ticket to a conductor.

"Forty hours to Winny," the conductor said in hip conductoreeze.

"Big country," Tommy said.

Chapter 23

THE TRAIN

PUFF AND BANJO CONVENED a two-man confer-
ence in the rear of the penultimate coach. Finding a man in
a black jacket with a black backpack so they could reclaim
their *hundo K* should have been easy. It wasn't. The coach was
loaded with guys in black jackets.

Had Tommy opened his backpack, he would have discovered that his net worth since returning to the U.S. had
increased by a *hundo K*. Had he ditched the black jacket and
the black backpack and kept the money, he would have foiled
the gangsters' search. Instead, he slept.

The two wide-bodied thugs squeezed down the aisle
from rear to front. Puff inspected each candidate. Those who
were awake thought, *Please don't let this amorphous flabby hulk
sit beside me.*

Puff's *Gordian Knot* was to prove soluble because of the
diversity of these men in black. The first candidate was an
Asian man; the next, a black man; and the next, a senior
Native American. Then a white guy with red hair, followed
by a white man with black hair, and then an old white fart

with no hair. The next candidate was a black man with yellow hair. Next, a white man with an Afro. Then an elderly black man with straight, oily hair like Little Richard. Near the middle of the coach was the most distinctive of all candidates – a Rastafarian – a black man with long braided locks stuffed into a *Rastacap*. Finally, Puff recognized the owner of the black backpack wearing noise-canceling earphones and sleeping. The backpack rested in the seat beside him.

"It's him," Puff whispered. Puff still couldn't identify the man as Tommy.

Banjo zipped open Tommy's backpack and spotted the stacks of banded money. His wicked smile revealed his lone rotting front tooth. He lifted the backpack off the seat. The front door of the coach opened. To their horror, Puff and Banjo spotted The Smelt. His face was red with rage, and he was coming straight toward them fast. Puff grabbed the backpack and offered it to The Smelt.

"We found your . . . ."

Banjo ripped the backpack out of Puff's hands and made a dash for the rear of the coach. Puff pushed Banjo from behind, propelling him to move faster as The Smelt was gaining on them. The three obese, eccentrically-dressed Mafiosi trundled toward the back of the train like three runaway beach balls.

"I knew you were holding out on me!" The Smelt shouted.

Too fat to pass Puff in the aisle, The Smelt pushed Puff ahead of him in an attempt to catch Banjo. As Banjo tripped out the rear door, a backpack strap hung up on the door handle. On the outside of the coach, Banjo pulled on the strap to keep the door closed while The Smelt on the inside pulled on the strap in an attempt to pull the door open. Puff was a befuddled spectator stuck to the side.

"Don't let money ruin a beautiful friendship," The Smelt pleaded.

"We found the money for ya," Banjo said, "but what do ya do, ya assume the worst."

The Smelt turned cordial. "I'm not an assuming person," he said. "I'm assuming nothing. Ya found my money, and I'm going to give ya a cut."

"I know you're assuming Puff and me stole the money," Banjo said, pouting. "It's hurtful."

The Smelt glanced at Puff, whose blood pressure was spiking.

"Your feelings hurt, too?"

Banjo's head was bobbing up-and-down like a bobble-head doll as he tried to coach Puff through the pane of glass that separated them. Puff appeased The Smelt.

"Feelings?" Puff said. "I got no feelings."

The Smelt pulled a pistol from his left shoulder holster.

"Let go the bag or I'll blow . . . ."

Banjo released the strap, the door flew open, The Smelt fell to the floor, and his pistol slid out of his reach down the aisle. Puff lunged for the door to get away from The Smelt. Banjo grabbed hold of the backpack and scurried up the service stairs with Puff in trail. Banjo and Puff barely could fit through the opening that led to the roof of the coach. For The Smelt, passage would be impossible. The Smelt struggled to his feet and scurried to reclaim his pistol. He passed through the door and thrust the pistol up the service stairway over his head like a periscope. He aimed blindly. With luck, he might give Puff a lead colonoscopy or shoot off his testicles, but, as so often happens in big-game hunting, the opportunity for a clean shot was fleeting. Banjo and Puff were both on the roof and out of The Smelt's line-of-sight before he fired the first bullet.

Banjo and Puff struggled to keep their footing as they braced for balance in the wind on the roof. Their suit jackets blossomed like drogue chutes, filled with wind that pressed them backwards. Banjo sought cover behind Puff, calculating that bullets might go into Puff's body but not likely out. Puff was perfectly suited to be a human shield. Five shots zinged by harmlessly. Two hit Puff's suit jacket.

"I got lucky," Puff shouted into the wind. He jostled to get ahead of Banjo so Banjo could take his turn at being the target of The Smelt's next magazine of bullets. Banjo and Puff were getting the hang of balancing on the top of the coach as the train whizzed onto a long bridge that bisected a reservoir.

"Beautiful!" Puff shouted. "We should get out of town more often!" He grabbed one of the arm straps of the backpack. He had a right to assert ownership as half of the money was his. Banjo resisted, and the two avaricious thugs competed in a full-fledged tug-of-war with no thought for how they were going to get off the coach roof. In the middle of their intensifying battle, a meaty tattooed arm whipped a leather belt up through a skylight opening and looped the belt around the backpack. The tattoo read

The Smelt

The Smelt's second hand appeared through the opening bearing a sharp, shiny, lethal-looking switchblade. When

The Smelt slashed the arm straps with a single swipe of the blade, Banjo and Puff fell off opposite sides of the coach eighty feet into the reservoir.

The Smelt pulled the backpack into the coach where he was standing on a footlocker with his pants splayed around his ankles revealing mismatched socks and two pistols in ankle holsters, one on each leg. He opened the backpack, saw the banded stacks of money, and smiled, although no one in the coach interpreted it as a smile because of his horrific scar.

"Excuse the interruption," The Smelt thundered as he wrestled up his pants and slid down from the footlocker. He was in as good a mood as he had been in a long while.

The commotion had awakened Tommy. He spotted his backpack in the tattooed arms of The Smelt, but Tommy wasn't about to object. For his own safety, Tommy had to accept that his chattels, including his bribe money, were gone. Tommy was learning that wealth was easier to acquire than to retain.

Chapter 24

WINNEMUCCA, NEVADA

TOMMY KNOCKED ON POP'S trailer door using his signature pattern – three knocks followed by three more knocks as in *Jingle bells, jingle bells*. The theft of Tommy's backpack left him with forty-three legal U.S. dollars. He was traveling about as light as you can travel. Pop cracked open the front door, but Tommy's appearance didn't strike a chord of recognition for Pop.

"Who're you?"

"It's me, Pop . . . it's Tommy."

"Don't fiddle with me, you scalawag. I ain't some senile old codger who can't see through the likes of you." Pop pulled the door more toward closed in case the stranger entertained any ideas of a home invasion.

"No, really, it's me," Tommy said. "I was in a crash, so I look different."

Pop looked confused. He opened the door wider. The stranger had nailed Tommy's voice.

"Ask me any question that Tommy should know and I'll answer it."

It was a chore for Pop to remember what *he* knew and hard labor to remember what *Tommy* knew.

"How many fingers Catfish Parker got on his left hand?"

"Two."

Pop calculated that, counting a thumb as a finger and *zero* as a possible answer, the stranger had a sixteen per cent chance of guessing the right answer, and, he had to admit, it *was* Tommy's voice.

"At's right, Tommy . . . get in here, boy."

Tommy wanted to hug Pop, but hugging wasn't Pop's way. Given his long absence, his new face, and his unannounced arrival, Tommy felt it best to act as though nothing had ever happened. Fatigued by the heat outside and inside the trailer, Tommy slumped in an upholstered chair. He tipped his chin toward a window air-conditioner.

"That's the quietest contraption I've ever come across," Tommy said.

"I don't plug it in, 'cause it makes a whole lot of noise and doesn't cool much, just *kindly* stirs up the air."

"I'll fix it up for you."

"Right now, you just rest up and drink a beer." Pop opened a can of beer for each of them. "I'll be honest with you, Tommy, I was flat worried about you."

"I had a rough time, Pop. I . . . ."

"Well, we're back together now, and I'm damn glad to see you again safe and sound."

That was all the emotion Tommy was likely to see in Pop, whose eyes had gone misty. They sat quietly for a while and drained their beers. Pop opened another round.

"It'll take time to adjust to your new look. Is that the best the doctors could do?" He meant no insult.

"They didn't have much to work with." It was a modest quip for a chap who had strutted around in his delusional fog as a world-class model not so long ago. "Doctors over in Switzerland know what they're doing."

"Never been to Switzerland," Pop said. "Knew a gunnery sergeant name a Muff who married a Swiss girl one time . . . out in Oceanside. The girl's parents were real rich. Gunny Muff got a bunch of us new Marines to cross swords for him and his bride to walk under after they was hitched. They didn't want a bunch of drunk Marines around for the reception, so Gunny Muff – we called him *Diver* behind his back – gave us two hundred dollars and *tolt* us to get scarce. We got under the influence down in Encinitas and called the country club where the reception was going on. A kid from Iowa . . . forget his name . . . didn't make it back from Chu Lai . . . pretended to be Colonel Manley. He *tolt* 'em he was commander of a top secret outfit that had just gone to Level Nine, and one of their special agents was gonna have to be picked up by helicopter right away. Agent Muff. Colonel Manley *tolt* 'em to clear the parking lot for the helicopter that was inbound and he *tolt* 'em that under no circumstances was Agent Muff to consume alcohol . . . the success of the mission depended on Agent Muff being stone sober. Colonel Manley also recommended setting off the fire alarm as a method to clear the parking lot for the helo. Dicked the reception up real good. Gunny Muff never got his hands on us before we shipped out to Chu Lai." Pop chuckled. "Colonel Manley, my ass. Don't you ever do nothing like that, Tommy. It's unacceptable, and the only reason

I mention it is to warn you off that kinda' behavior." Pop wiped tears from his eyes. "I guess Gunny Muff was right about not wanting a bunch of Marines at his shindig. Nope, I've never been to Switzerland."

As Pop and Tommy pounded beers to beat the heat, the fears that had driven them from Toxic Lick seemed to diminish. When Tommy told Pop how much he had missed Lori, Pop didn't volunteer information about his weekly calls with Lori. That could wait. Tommy skipped the details of his season of hallucinations, dreams, and pretenses to protect his granddad from upset and to diminish the magnitude of his own stupidity.

"I ain't used to the desert, yet," Pop said. "I still miss the hollers and the creeks."

Pop opened a fifth beer for each of them. Tommy's pump was primed. He quaffed half a can in one swallow.

"I've heard you gotta stay hydrated out here in the desert," Tommy said.

"You're doing a fine job, far as I can tell."

Tommy didn't want Pop to regard him as a permanent parasite, so he said positive things. The beer elevated his mood to *hopeful*.

"I blew my opportunity of a lifetime, Pop, but I've come to believe in second chances. First thing I'll do is get me a job. I'm gonna be a world-class coach some day."

"That's a powerful enterprise," Pop said. "Think I'll take me a nap."

A month later, Tommy and Pop were lounging in Pop's tiny living room. Tommy's resume of harvesting tobacco leaves and bucking hay bales did not make him the most sought-after laborer in Winnemucca. Pop's Social Security check was being stretched to the limits of economic elasticity, but he never complained about the added expense of boarding Tommy. Because he'd already read every book and magazine in the trailer, Pop was reading Tommy's new basketball magazine.

"Here's a sad deal," Pop said. "A high school basketball coach up in Maine got eat up by a shark while he was surfing. It was the coach who was surfing, not the shark. I always say, 'Pick one sport and stick to it.'"

"How old?"

"Twenty-two . . . same as you."

Tommy took the magazine to read for himself.

"His name was Bobby Joe Bates . . . a graduate of the University of Oklahoma. His mother says he died the way he wanted to, but about fifty years too soon."

"You want to coach basketball . . . well, there's your opening."

"We don't have to go to Maine, Pop. There's a summer league coaching job here in Winnemucca. 'Course, I'm about six weeks short of a college degree."

"I reckon you better stop fartin' around in this trailer and go get that degree."

Tommy gazed at the ceiling. He was visualizing.

"There could be a faster way," he said.

———⟫⟨⦿⟩⟪———

Tommy and Pop had been waiting for forty-five minutes, long enough that Pop couldn't hold his tongue any longer.

"I ain't convinced it's right. It ain't natural."

Tommy had steeled himself to Pop's reservations. The gap between their generations showed.

"Messing with nature can bring you to grief," Pop said. "You read about men becoming women and women the other way around."

Tommy left his chair to stretch his legs and improve the flow of oxygen to his brain, so vital for clear thinking.

"I'm changing my name, not my sex."

"What's the difference?"

"Big difference."

"Same thing. You'll be something afterwards that you wasn't before."

Tommy exercised the full extent of his logic.

"If you don't know the difference between cutting off your dick and getting a new business card, I'm glad you're not the guy who fixed my finger. Times are changing." Tommy pointed to his father's analog watch. "There's more computing power in this watch than there used to be in a whole room full of computers."

Pop was underwhelmed by the argument, but his rebuttal remained unspoken.

"Pop, I gotta tell you something. I'm ashamed to say it, but some bad characters are after me . . . over some financial dealin's."

"Oh . . . Tommy, no."

"Some of the money I took wasn't real, but they're just as pissed off as if it was. They don't want me or any other witnesses testifying about their dealings, either. On top of it all, what little money I had left was in a backpack that got stolen. So, I got nothing to show for all my fancy footwork. These guys'd just as soon kill me as look at me."

"Well . . . I'm just saying that lying and deceiving charges a hefty price."

———⟨⊙⟩———

Anna ran across Rio Feo's main street to wrap her arms around Principal Bradley. Despite the pleasing sensation, Principal Bradley knew that violating the three-second rule on public embraces could stimulate the rumor mill. He squirmed free of Anna's clutch.

"We're so excited," Anna said. "We heard that you're advertising for a basketball coach."

"We're committed to having a basketball team, even if it's our only sport," he said.

Anna gripped his forearm and blinked coyly.

"You're a great leader," she said. "Now I'm going home to think of some way to thank you."

Principal Bradley basked in the glow of the compliment. He could think of half a dozen ways for Anna to thank him, but every single one was illegal in the State of New Mexico.

Pop and Tommy loitered at the bottom of the stone steps in front of the Humboldt County Courthouse.

"I never knew a name change could go so smooth," Pop said. "More like changing a spark plug than a transmission."

"It's a great country for fresh starts. The judge has spoken . . . my name is Bobby Joe Bates. Just call me B.J. Say it over and over in your head."

"B.J. . . . B.J. . . . I think I got it."

"The late Bobby Joe Bates isn't using his Social Security number or his diploma, so I believe I'll borrow 'em both for my comeback."

"At'sa problem with not being yourself . . . one thing leads to another, Tommy."

"B.J."

"B.J.," Pop parroted.

Chapter 25
Summer League

GOWRY HIGH SCHOOL was Winnemucca's only secondary school. The school's mascot reflected the historical importance of sheepherding brought to the area by Basque immigrants. The boys' teams were called the *Gowry Gonads*. The girls' teams were called the *Gowry Lady Gonads*. The original Basque settlers could have played it safe with Bears, Tigers, or Wildcats, but they were adventurous people who hung it all out there.

The mascot took the form of two orbs – pink and fuzzy — made of sheep's wool. They looked a lot like the Ohio State University Buckeye mascot *Brutus* minus the dumbfounded facial expression. Nominations to be *Gonads* were traditionally limited to twins, which resulted in slim pickings during some years. The job description included qualities not found in every set of twins: "Must be able to tolerate temperature fluctuations, strenuous activity, and occasional pain."

In 1955, the only set of twins enrolled at Gowry was selected to be *Gonads* by universal acclaim. At six-feet-five-inches, the Ibarra brothers were taller than every member of the Gowry basketball team. The team recorded not a single victory that year, but the *Gonads* delighted crowds all season long by cartwheeling onto the court like a pair of runaway casino dice, only rounder and pinker. Some men reported mild testicular discomfort watching the spectacle for the first time.

A few years after the *Gonads'* only all-loss season, dissention descended on Winnemucca. About the time that civil unrest rocked Selma, Alabama, controversy that had simmered in Winnemucca for years came to a head. While on a senior trip to Washington, D.C., the *Gonads* mascots were filmed at the base of the Washington Monument. The Associated Press ran a picture nation-wide, and it went viral before people knew what *going viral* meant.

The wife of the pastor of the Third Baptist Church called the picture *pornographic* and the mascot an *abomination*, extreme positions in the minds of most residents of the town. Hallowed tradition won out in the end, and the school board reached a compromise among ranchers, veterans, and church-going parents by settling on the *Gowry Fighting Gonads*. (The *Gowry Lady Gonads* never incorporated the "Fighting" descriptor.) It was considered a harmless, long-standing joke to most Winnemuccans, and they accepted with good humor the traditional greeting by every Valedictorian for over fifty years: "Greetings, my *Fellow Fighting Gonads*."

The Gowry High School principal, Mr. Silas Hew, thought of himself as a friend of the student, a mentor to teachers, and the school's athletic director. Principal Hew also directed the Winnemucca Summer Basketball League. He hosted a half-day conference of summer league coaches to keep them on the same page, strengthen the bonds of collegiality, and shoot the breeze. He quoted the inspiring words of Mark Twain, Søren Kierkegaard, Benjamin Franklin, Winston Churchill, and himself.

"Let me introduce our new summer league junior basketball coach, B.J. Bates," Principal Hew said. Tommy, who was getting the hang of being B.J., nodded modestly. "B.J.'s an Oklahoma grad who's been coaching basketball up in Maine. He's agreed to take on the job of coaching the *Junior Fighting Gonads* this summer."

The *senior* summer league coach, who was keen to replace Principal Hew as soon as destiny permitted, jumped in with his raspy voice.

"You jumped from the meat locker to the oven, Coach Bates. Welcome to Winnemucca."

The senior girls' basketball coach could be counted on to throw in her bid for recognition, too. "Did you know Sandy Jones at O.U.?"

"Great guy," Tommy said cordially as though he were a close friend of every athlete and coach ever to pass through Norman, Oklahoma, a city Tommy Gunn had never, in reality, visited.

"Sandy's a woman."

"Gal . . . really great," Tommy corrected.

The girls' coach glared at Tommy with transparent suspicion. Tommy perceived the intent of the glare loud and clear. He remembered Pop's observation that the problem with lying is that *a lie breeds like a rabbit*, and *keeping up with offspring is a full-time job*.

"Who knows what *AMI* stands for?" Principal Hew asked.

Hands were raised, the hands of all the coaches except Tommy, the new guy on campus. Principal Hew adored group participation.

"Let's say it together," Principal Hew prompted.

They all recited together, "Accountability, morality, and integrity."

Principal Hew winked at Tommy. The newbie had the secret code.

"That's our motto here at Gowry," the principal said. "The children in our care might be dumb as stumps, but, if they're accountable, maintain high morals, and are chock full of integrity, they'll make good citizens. Let's take it backwards. *IMA*. B.J., what is integrity?"

Tommy was perspiring. Pretending to be someone else, faking confidence, and answering trick questions was demanding work.

"Telling the truth." The words were hard for Tommy to speak with conviction, seeing as how he recently had told so many whoppers.

"That's right. Not just on Sunday, but seven days a week . . . twenty-four-and-seven. We've gotta ooze integrity, even in our sleep."

The girls' coach corralled Tommy when the meeting was over. She invited him to join her for lunch so they could swap stories. Because he had no stories to swap, Tommy declined the invitation by saying he had to get home to his grandfather for lunch. The girls' coach was used to full-court pressing, so she invited *Mr. Bates*, too.

"Everybody just calls him *Pop*," Tommy said. "He's doing poorly, so thanks anyway." The object of the lady coach's glowering stare, Tommy wished B.J. Bates had graduated from the University of Maine instead of the University of Oklahoma where Sandy Jones was a woman.

⸻ ((◉)) ⸻

Tommy was supervising a junior summer league game on an outdoor court when Principle Hew approached him from behind during halftime and swatted him on the buttocks with a clipboard. Tommy almost leaped out of his skin with surprise. The butt-swat suggested that Principal Hew was a macho athlete himself back in the day. The swat suggested comradeship, respect, trust.

"You giving them a spoonful of *AMI* every day?"

"Yes, sir . . . right after we pray."

"You're not praying for victory, now, B.J.?"

Tommy assured the principal that his team prayers consisted of requests for strength, safety, wisdom, and humility, but never victory.

"Good, good. It's not fair to pray for victory. If we did, God's favorites would win all the time. The Israelites would dominate the Olympics every four years and the Arabs would raise holy hell. No, sir. We gotta treat those Muslim boys right or they'll run off and get radicalized." Principal Hew came up for breath. "Now, I understand that maybe in an overtime game you might have to bend the rule . . . ." Principal Hew located his *to do list* among the sheets clamped to his clipboard. "Hey, the office needs your Oklahoma transcript. Also, drop in to clear up some problem with the IRS.

Something about your W-4."

Tommy swallowed hard.

"I won't tolerate even a whiff of impropriety, B.J. This isn't Maine. That corruption and evil-doing back East doesn't cut it here in the Heartland."

"I'll take care of it, Principal Hew."

The principal gave him a reassuring clipboard swat in parting. Tommy could hear Pop's voice in his head, *Lies breed like rabbits.*

———— ◉ ————

As quiet as a cat, the red-faced, dumpy girls' coach approached Tommy from behind. When she spoke, Tommy almost popped a gasket. He turned around to face her just as she started hissing at him.

"Bobby Joe Bates, you bastard!" She pressed her mammary magnificence against him, and he retreated under the pressure as if pushed by matching sofa cushions. I know what you did, you son-of-a-bitch. And I know why you went to Maine, you sorry-ass . . . ."

Tommy was at a huge disadvantage. His only defense was to reveal that he was an imposter. That was out of the question, so he had to stand his ground and take the abuse.

"Can you be more specific?"

"They told me you'd play stupid," she said. "Jerks like you . . . always think you're smarter than everybody else." Her finger, roughly the shape of the chisel point of a jackhammer, started pounding his sternum. "I'll be watching you.

You make one wrong move . . . and I will give you a molten lava enema." Her threat was impractical, but effective. "You're a disgrace to the University of Oklahoma!"

The rotund, but proud, alumna stalked away, leaving Tommy to question the quality of Bobby Joe Bates's character. Tommy had enough trouble answering for his own failings. Now he was answering for Bobby Joe Bates's flaws, too. Perhaps shortcuts weren't all they were cracked up to be.

Chapter 26
THE RIVER BANK

TOMMY AND POP were back in high clover, as Pop put it, with the deposit of B.J. Bates's bi-weekly pay checks. Their needs were few. They could eat on twenty dollars a day. Pop's rented trailer cost one-hundred-eighty-dollars a month. Tommy bought a clunker for eight hundred dollars. Rust was a stranger in Nevada's low humidity, and a car could last a long time. Beer for a month was about two hundred dollars. Pop bought a fishing rod and reel for twelve dollars. High clover, indeed. Pop and Tommy were sipping suds down on the banks of the Humboldt River on a Sunday afternoon. A red-and-white fishing bobber drifted downstream at the end of Tommy's line.

"Life's a funny thing, Pop."

"Yes, sir . . . it sure is. I was just thinking about an ol' buddy of mine name a' Tibby. He was older than the rest of us . . . he was a Coon-ass from Bayou Cane, Louisiana . . . don't know how I can remember that . . . back in Sixty-eight . . . and I can't find my cell phone that I used an hour ago. But Thibodaux . . . we called him Tibby . . . rented a car to drive down to Tijuana the week before we left for Chu Lai. We was partial to this one bar . . . *kindly* low class . . . but we liked it 'cause it had a urinal built in to the bottom of the bar . . . it was convenient. We took a likin' to this girl sittin' with the rest of 'em in a ring around the bar. We had a five-minute romance with her. Tibby said she was great, but, to me, it was like mountin' a sack of grain. We ran out of money and had to vamoose *kindly* quick . . . dragging the oil pan on a curb in the process and trailing oil all the way back to San Diego. Tibby told the car rental girl that it was a miracle we were able to take the car back from the bandits who'd *stolt* it. Tibby's daddy ended up wiring money for the deductible. Tibby and I had to get some shots because of the girl and I swore I'd never go to Tijuana with Tibby again . . . which I didn't, because he was in a body bag six months later . . . got *kilt* in Phú Bài . . . I sure liked ol' Tibby. The way we acted was unacceptable, though, and the only reason I mention it is so you know not to conduct yourself that way. Now, Son, let that be a warning."

Tommy gave Pop time to blot the tears that always accompanied Pop's recollections.

"I guess you were lucky to get back to the Lick with your dick in one piece," Tommy said.

"Guess I was."

"You think about Toxic Lick and Kegg County much?"

"I sure do. Hard to explain to someone who ain't from Kentucky, but . . . you know." Pop pointed at Tommy's bobber, which was making ripples on the surface of the water. "I don't mean to meddle, but why ain't you called Lori?"

"She's probably got a new guy by now . . . maybe married . . . ."

Tommy's bobber went under the surface, but he failed to hook the fish.

"I doubt that," Pop said. "She called a while back."

"You ever think about telling me?"

"I wasn't sure . . . after you changed . . . I just didn't know . . . ."

"You're not a psychiatrist, Pop. You gotta keep me informed."

"I guess that's the kinda' misunderstanding that happens when you're not who you are."

Tommy sighed and pulled his worm out of the water for inspection. The worm still had some kick left in it, so he cast the worm and the bobber back up-river.

"I'll give that crawler a second chance," Tommy said. "Is Lori still in the Lick?"

"No . . . she's down in Texas to coach freshman basketball at Polo."

Tommy's eyebrows shot up. He was happy for Lori, but, by contrast, her lofty position diminished what he was doing in the summer league.

"That's a big-time move," he said.

"That Lori Tolliver's a big-time girl."

Chapter 27
POLO UNIVERSITY

THE POLO UNIVERSITY Athletic Director dressed impeccably to set a high standard for all the coaches who served Polo at his pleasure. He didn't ask anything of his coaches that he didn't ask of himself. He jogged five miles a day. He refrained from using profanity. He drank modestly at all times, unless he was on vacation in Mexico or Hawaii, at which time he set his hair ablaze like normal people. He was a stately sight to behold in his Perugini suit and coifed hair standing on-stage in front of all of Polo's coaches – every sport, men's and women's.

"Across the board . . . all sports . . . it's gotta be the same . . . discipline. We take these kids . . . a lot of 'em dumber than a slab of concrete . . . and we feed 'em the best food, put 'em in the best housing, tutor 'em so they can scrape by in academics, and tell 'em they're the greatest thing since sliced . . . whatever."

Lori was seated in the second row of the spectacular new auditorium not knowing where the AD's thoughts might ramble, but glad to be along for the ride. She was wearing khaki shorts and a navy blue Polo University knit shirt like every other coach in the crowd. It was the uniform of the day.

"Discipline's a real bugaboo for some of these kids. We got to impose the rules — else they'll go haywire. We got to hold 'em accountable . . . except . . . maybe, if a guy's really good – like, maybe, a running back or somethin' . . . shucks, we don't want to lose a game. You gotta use judgment." He pointed to his head, suggesting that his cranium was the seat of good judgment.

Lori sneaked a peek at the faces of her colleagues in the lecture hall. Oddly, they appeared to be following the AD's drift without tripping on irony. The AD clicked a remote control and the house lights dimmed. A video played on a huge screen in the background.

"Now — look at this clown."

A Polo running back scored a touchdown and celebrated with an elaborate end zone dance.

"You'd think the dumb son of a . . . you'd think he just invented penicillin for Christ's sake. All he did was carry a football through a hole the size of Montana . . . this knucklehead's little sissy dance cost us fifteen yards."

A second video showed a basketball player dunking a ball and then grimacing, showing his teeth, and shouting.

"Here's another prize-winner in the Discipline Hall of Shame. He's seven-foot-two, so he sure as . . . he oughta be able to dunk a basketball. So, while he's doing his chimp thing, Arkansas runs the length of the floor to score. We lose. Why? Lack of *discipline*."

A third video clip appeared on the screen. The action

froze as Tommy Gunn was high in the air tipping an inbound pass. Lori recalled the final seconds of the NCAA
basketball tournament championship game.

"Lack of discipline leads to disaster. Here's the March
Madness final between Brut and Kentucky Barber College.
The chances of KBC ever being in the finals again are about
a zillion-to-one, but they coulda won that game. All this kid
-- Tommy Gunn -- had to do was lay the ball in. But, no-o-o.
This moron had no *discipline*. Too busy shining his ass."

The video started up again. Tommy did his 360-de-
gree spin and missed the dunk. The video froze still just as
Tommy's finger was pared by his ring on the rim weld in
a shower of blood. A close-up of the flayed digit evoked a
communal gasp from the audience.

"This silly-ass-buffoon threw away the chance of a lifetime. Now, for the rest of his days, he'll be the guy who gave
away the national championship. The Cutters lost the trophy
because of a lack of *discipline*."

The AD looked out over the assembly. He straightened
his tie and squinted to see past the stage lights and into the
eyes of his coaches. He asked for Lori Tolliver by name. He
asked her to raise her hand. Lori reluctantly raised her hand,
but the Athletic Director couldn't see it.

"You went to school with this bozo, Lori. What was he
thinking?"

Lori moved her mouth, but no sound came out. The
Athletic Director asked Lori to stand up. When she did, a
facilitator thrust a microphone in front of her face.

"There she is. You know this guy, Lori. What was he
thinking?"

"I think . . . he was . . . ."

"Speak up, Lori . . . ."

Tears sprang in Lori's eyes. She felt humiliated. Her comfortable sense of belonging among a throng dressed in khaki and Polo blue evaporated. She felt alone and insecure. Why had the AD singled her out for ridicule? She wanted to run and hide. Her heart ached for Tommy Gunn. The wound was reopened.

"I don't know," she stammered. "I don't know what he's thinking."

Chapter 28
EPIPHANY

POP HELD THESE TRUTHS to be self-evident: *never miss a chance to eat or sleep.* Pop learned this axiom during his Southeast Asia tour in Sixty-eight.

"With twenty-two days and a wake-up 'fore I rotated back to the States, I got wounded twice in about a second. Some ass hole with an AK-47 shot me here," he pointed to the front of his left thigh, "and here," he pointed to his right buttock. "Spun me around. Rounds went in small, but they came out big, here and here," he pointed to the back of his left thigh and to his left buttock. "I got a Purple Heart for the first one but no oak leaf cluster for the second, because it occurred in what they call *the same instance*. Point is, if you're aimin' to get medals, try to get shot on different days." It was a specialized axiom.

Adhering to his faith in eating and sleeping at every opportunity, Pop ate *huevos rancheros* for breakfast and he was deep into the rapid-eye-movement phase of a morning nap in his rocker when Tommy let rip with an exclamation.

"Would you lookey here!"

Pop was not pleased to have his dream aborted.

"What's got you in a lather?"

"Mr. John High of Seminole, Texas has been named the town manager of Rio Feo, New Mexico."

Pop was not a man to rush to conclusions normally, but he made an exception in this case.

"Don't think I'd a' woke up my granddad for that particular tidbit."

"John High's got a kid . . . name a' Rocky High . . . they call him *Rocky Mountain High* in the *Basketball News*. Guess how tall he is?"

Pop indulged in post-nap stretching and yawning.

"No idea."

"Take a guess."

"Six foot six."

"Eight feet."

"Can't be. Nobody's eight feet tall . . . although Goliath in the Scriptures might a' been pressing eight feet."

"Well, Rocky Mountain High is. This could be my ticket back to March Madness and a championship."

"You planning a kidnapping?"

Tommy visualized the action steps falling into place like pavers in a path back to glory, part of a plan that seemed rational, but not without hurdles.

"No. I'll go to *him*. Rio Feo High School has a coaching vacancy. If I can get the job, I could ride Rocky Mountain High to a big basketball college and right back to the Big Dance." Tommy jumped up from his computer and thrust his arms Heavenward. "Thank you, Lord!"

"The Lord moves in mysterious ways," Pop said, "and I guess we're movin', too."

Chapter 29

RECKONING

THE SMELT HAD KEPT Puff and Banjo waiting just for the hell of it. At last, The Smelt ordered them to enter his office. They both had suffered skeletal, muscular, and psychic injuries in the fall from the train coach roof into the reservoir. The two gangsters owed their lives to a bass fisherman. He had been unable to pull them into his boat, but he had lashed them to his gunwales and dragged them with his trolling motor like a tugboat pulling barges.

Puff's left arm was still in a cast. His head dressing covered part of his West Virginia birthmark, so the exposed portion looked like a map of Cyprus. Banjo was wearing a neck brace. The stitches in his flat face were healing, so he resembled Frankenstein less each day. Both front teeth were missing, and his appearance benefitted from the loss. The Smelt poured three whiskeys. He pointed at his henchmen and laughed.

"Ouch," he boomed, "who knew water could be so hard on the surface."

Puff and Banjo laughed obsequiously at their own

expense, a measure of how glad they were to be alive.

"No hard feelings," Banjo said.

"Hey, I got my money back." The Smelt smiled.

"It'll never happen again," Banjo said.

The Smelt's smile turned into a hateful scowl. He pulled a gun from his shoulder harness and aimed it at Banjo. Banjo froze. Puff dove to the floor.

"One thing that pisses me off about people is they think fat guys are jolly," The Smelt said. Banjo scarcely breathed and his eyes were welded to the pistol in his face. "Do I look jolly to you?"

Banjo shook his head in jerky spasms.

"It'll never happen again," Banjo sputtered.

"That's right," The Smelt said.

The Smelt pulled the trigger. The explosion was deafening. The smell of cordite filled the room. Banjo's head had snapped backwards with the bullet impact. His eyes were squinted closed as though he had a headache. Banjo's neck brace held his head erect. Blood dripped from his forehead to the tip of his nose. On the floor, Puff was squinting, too, waiting for a bullet to explode from The Smelt's gun. The second shot didn't come. The Smelt said a few words in memory of Banjo.

"Banjo pissed me off from the minute he started working for me . . . always bitchin' about a dental plan. What am I – IBM? A dental plan?"

Puff peered up at The Smelt with terrified eyes. The Smelt motioned with the barrel of his gun for Puff to reclaim his seat.

"I got a problem with my pants," Puff said.

"Then have a seat while they're still warm," The Smelt said. "When we're through, ya can change into Banjo's pants. He won't be needin' 'em no more."

Puff trembled as he clambered into his seat. Slack-jawed, he was well into the fifth phase of shock where his hands shook like tuning forks and his scrotum shriveled.

"I . . . I . . . I . . . ."

"Ya don't have to talk right now. I'm promoting ya into Banjo's job. There's a pay cut in it for ya. Any problems with that?"

Puff shook his head and noticed that his nose had started to bleed from elevated blood pressure brought on by exertion and fear.

"Your nose is bleedin'," The Smelt said. "Why's it doing that?"

"The anxiety . . . ."

"What anxiety? I was shooting at Banjo, not you."

"My nose didn't know that."

The Smelt dismissed Puff's explanation with a wave of his colossal hand.

"That kid, Tommy Gunn, ain't Tommy Gunn no more. He's going by the name *B.J. Bates*, and he's living in Winnemucca, Nevada. I want ya to go waste this kid."

Puff nodded, agreeable as a person can get.

"When somebody stiffs ya, it's mandatory that ya whack 'em or your reputation gets damaged. I been too nice about this for too long."

"You bet, Boss."

"Not to mention the FBI looking for witnesses to testify against us."

"You bet, Boss."

"And, Puff, don't ever mess with me again. I let Banjo off easy for old time's sake."

Puff regarded his pal Banjo, who was sitting still, his head resting on his neck brace like a golf ball on a tee.

"He was a vegetarian," Puff said.

"A three-hundred-thirty-pound vegetarian?"

"Ate a lot of vegetables. He was proud of his low cholesterol."

"I didn't know that. That's one thing I like about this job," The Smelt said as he cleaned the barrel of his gun. "Every day ya learn something new."

"Old Banjo loved his broccoli," Puff said.

The Smelt was momentarily overcome by emotion as he holstered his gun.

"He'll be missed," The Smelt said.

Puff gasped for air and nodded his head.

The Smelt said, "At the tournament this year, ya only pay guys to take a flop. Ya don't pay nobody to win, got it?"

Puff nodded his bandaged head. He had no intention of contradicting The Smelt, ever.

"No up-front crap. I don't mind if ya threaten the families . . . threaten the players. That's just good business sense. But ya gotta cut down on the cash outflow this year. Can ya do that?"

"You bet, Boss."

Chapter 30
LICENSE TO KILL

IN THE BACK OF a run-down Chicago bar, dead-eyed Igor was listening on his cell phone, grim-faced as always. He had been drowning his liver in vodka for hours, but he sounded about the same as when he was sober.

"I give you second chance." Igor heard his master's voice.

"Second chance for what?"

"To *keel* that *zjilik* who steal my *vziatka*."

"Where is?"

"Winnemucca. Small town at Nevada. You go there and get my *vziatka* back. Then *keel theese mudak*. I don't want him talking to FBI."

The chance to whack Tommy Gunn aroused Igor. Igor had sabotaged Tommy's IV valves, poisoned his IV solution, shot a poison dart at him, and shot him in the temple all to no avail. This time, Igor intended to go with a tried-and-true method; he planned to pump a clip of nine millimeter slugs into the *sooksin*.

"He is change name," the Russian boss said. "Bates."

"I don't care what is name …. I *keel theese zhopa*," Igor said.

Chapter 31
Rio Feo

SIGNS OF RIO FEO'S DECLINE were as plentiful as the tumbleweeds that stacked up in unsightly scrums against the walls of closed stores bordering the two-block stretch called *Downtown*. Tommy and Pop passed shop windows, unwashed, lifeless, and vacant like the closed mines on whose potash the town had survived for six decades.

"Nary a tree in sight," Pop said.

"Think positive. Look." Tommy pointed down a side street toward two bushes depending for survival on condensation dripping from a window air-conditioner.

"Them are called mesquites."

"I haven't seen a mosquito since I got here," Tommy said.

"Mesquites and mosquitos is two different things," Pop said, proving his axiom that *ninety per cent of conversation was pointless ninety per cent of the time.*

"Let's stop at the pharmacy and I'll pick up the keys to our ranch house."

"Ranch house?" Pop asked.

"That's what the ad said."

Tommy parked his clunker in front of two rustic adobe houses situated on the edge of Rio Feo surrounded by miles of desert and distant mountains. A sign in front of the house on the right read, *ROOMS TO RENT.* The house on the left was Pop's new residence according to the half-page rental agreement bearing his signature.

"A tad outside the metro area," Pop observed.

Tommy ignored Pop's sarcastic throw-away lines during times of upheaval. He knew that seniors were more resistant to change than young folk.

"So where's this ranch house you've been ravin' on about?" Pop asked.

"I believe the ad was referring to the architectural style of the house."

"No architect ever had any dealings with that thing," Pop groused, nodding at the structure which was shaped like a Kleenex box.

That pushed Tommy's button.

"I sure do apologize for not finding a replacement home as splendid as what you just moved out of — that aluminum pizza oven sitting on dry-rotted wheels by the side of the Humboldt River."

Tommy's annoyance fit surprised them both. They held their tongues for a while as they explored the desert that ran right up to the four walls of the house. A roadrunner whizzed by them as they reached the rear of the dwelling. Tumbleweeds bounced along after it, propelled by a warm, dry wind. Tommy wondered where the weeds ended up when they stopped tumbling.

"Might get me a metal-detector and hunt for artifacts

and heirlooms out there," Pop said in an effort to cultivate a more favorable atmosphere.

"The Conquistadors trucked most of it back to Spain," Tommy said. There was no use in letting Pop inflate his hopes too high too fast.

Pop and Tommy were startled by a shot-gun-toting woman who appeared from around the corner nearest the adjacent house.

"You *pajaros* steal my sheets?" she asked.

"I'm sorry for your loss, Ma'am," Tommy said. "But . . . ."

"We ain't crooks," Pop said. "We don't steal sheets."

"Or anything else," Tommy said.

"Not recently," Pop said.

"We're your new neighbors," Tommy said.

"Nobody told me." She lowered the barrel of her shotgun and allowed her more pleasant qualities to shine through. She was about forty, of medium height, and no stranger to the dinner table. "Maria Hernandez," she said.

Pop extended his hand. "I'm Pop. This is To . . . ."

"B.J.," Tommy said.

"Welcome to Rio." She said it with a big smile. They were getting along famously.

Pop swept his arm across the horizon of desert sand and foothills. "Mighty dry," he said.

"Three bars in Rio." Maria had second thoughts about Pop's meaning. "If you mean the weather, we get four inches of rain every year whether we need it or not."

A sheet hanging from the clothes line was billowing in the wind and dragging on the desert. Maria pointed at it with the barrel of the gun held in her right hand.

"Keep your laundry off the sand. Scorpions'll get on the sheets and get into the house."

Pop liked the look of Maria – her chocolate-stained apron, caramel skin, and brilliant white smile. He had been partial to women from an early age.

"Any other critters we should know about?"

"Tarantulas . . . rattlesnakes . . . coyotes . . . that's about it unless you throw in the ass holes who stole my sheets." The wind blew a strand of thick, black hair across Maria's forehead, partly obscuring one eye. A toss of her head put it back in place.

Pop picked up on small signs like Maria's apron, for example, and he steered his conversation by those signs as though they were navigational buoys. On the off-chance that Maria's kitchen and Pop's stomach could establish a relationship, Pop kept chatting, with the goal of getting off on the right foot with her.

"Where's the property line?"

"It doesn't matter. You can hike for miles in any direction. No one cares."

Maria gave Tommy a good look-over. He was blond, muscular, and not hard on the eyes.

"Are you the new basketball coach by any chance?" she asked.

"You heard already?"

"No secrets in Rio. *Buena suerte.*"

Tommy was convinced that coaching Rocky High was his best path to redemption. Rocky was sure to be a top recruit. Tommy might go as a coach along with Rocky to a top college as part of Rocky's recruitment package. Then, Tommy would be back on the fast track, climbing up the coaching ladder on his way back to March Madness. Neither his hopes nor his nerves permitted a delay in meeting the High family. He didn't dare wait until the start of basketball season assuming that Rocky would just waltz into the gym with his sneakers laced up.

Tommy arrived in the town manager's reception area early enough to do some light reading. *Western Homeopathy* took his fancy. An article titled *Seven Things You Don't Know About Your Hemorrhoids* was promising until he got to the photographs. Their gruesome detail induced him to jump to page fifty-two to read the *Eight Benefits Of Breast Feeding*. The text was forgettable, but the photos were spectacular. The town manager's door popped open and there he was, all six-foot-six of him – John High. When John waved Tommy into his office, Tommy noticed John's huge Texas Tech class ring.

"Come on in here, young man."

Tommy discarded his magazine and stretched his posture to lessen the quantum difference between their statures. Standing next to a sky-scraper like John made Tommy feel at a disadvantage. He transmitted a brief prayer for the gifts of a sharp mind and a glib tongue . . . just for a few minutes; he would be content to return to mediocrity after the meeting was concluded.

"I appreciate your time, Mr. High. I'm Coach B.J. Bates."

"Call me John, Coach. I heard you're a Sooner."

Tommy had nearly perfected the art of lying. "Yes, sir. I'm a proud son of the University of Oklahoma."

"I won't hold that against you . . . ."

Tommy pointed toward John's class ring.

"Yep," John said, "I'm a Texas Tech Red Raider."

"I reckon there's room in Rio . . . ."

"That's right. I'm satisfied as long as we kick y'all's ass in October."

Tommy faked a convivial laugh. He was aware that this was what they called yakkin'-and-scratchin', preliminary sniffing, phatic communication.

"I'm looking forward to coaching Rocky."

Instantly, conversational clouds obscured the conversational sun.

"Guess you haven't heard . . . Rocky's going to New Mexico Military Institute."

The news was a shocking setback. Tommy had traveled a long way for this second chance, a second chance that was suddenly floundering on stormy seas.

"I hope he's not dead set on Roswell. I've got big plans for Rio this year. I'm packing the schedule with marquee names like Las Cruces, Lubbock Monterey, El Paso Bowie, Hobbs . . . ." By *I'm packing the schedule*, he meant *I hope to get one or two of these schools to play Rio*. He was pulling out all the stops.

"The discipline at the Institute'll do Rocky good."

"I'm widely-known for my discipline," Tommy interjected too quickly. His delivery was starting to sound like a sales pitch. "I teach my boys life lessons like accountability . . .

morality . . . and integrity."

John knew how to keep his schedule on-track and how to keep visitors moving, and he escorted Tommy to the door. Time, apparently, was up.

"Those are mighty important lessons. I wish we had more coaches like you. Half the coaches I've run into care more about diddling cheerleaders than teaching ethics. Good luck, Coach."

The meeting was over so quickly that Tommy scarcely could recount what had happened. It was like going to a dental appointment for a root canal and ending up with just a cleaning: it was a relief to get out of the dentist chair quickly, but you were stuck with the toothache. His time with John High couldn't be called a negotiation, because a negotiation was where you gave and you got. True, all Tommy had given was bullshit, but he had gotten zero in return. Seeking repose in his old sedan, Tommy found, instead, a baker's oven on wheels heated to over one hundred, thirty degrees Fahrenheit, hardly an incubator for creativity. Nevertheless, an idea germinated in his clunker-turned-hothouse, and he called Pop on his cell phone right away, before the virtual kiln baked the scheme right out of his head.

"Pop," Tommy said, "I need a fortune teller."

Pop took a seat at the counter in the Rio Café where Rocky High worked part time. Rocky was so tall he made the cafe feel like a dollhouse. Pop couldn't take his eyes off the big man, by far taller than any living primate or mammal of any kind he had ever seen first-hand. Pop gawked as he ordered a BLT and a Coke.

"Yes, Sir," Rocky said, "regular, diet, Zero, caffeine-free, classic, black cherry vanilla, cherry Zero?"

"Naw, I ain't partial to any of them sissy kinds. Just a plain ol' Coke."

Rocky wrote down his order with a pencil the relative size of a toothpick in his gigantic hand. Rocky's shoulders were wide, too. Pop reckoned Rocky's pituitary gland must be the size of a cantaloupe.

"You're a tall 'un . . . ."

"They call me Rocky Mountain High."

"How'd you come by them dents?" Pop was pointing at Rocky's head.

"Banging up against basketball rims. I make the defensive basket a *no-fly zone*. They wrote that in the *Sentinel* back in Seminole."

Rocky delivered Pop's Coke, and Pop took a draw on the straw.

"You'll make big news at Rio. The new basketball coach is extremely gifted."

"Dad's got me going to Roswell, not Rio."

"The Institute? Military training can be mighty tough. My nephew went there . . . almost went over the edge with the hazing and the pressure." Pop lied so seldom that he felt entitled now.

Absorbing this fiction made Rocky uncomfortable. He polished the chrome on the counter with a hand towel, his brow furrowed with concern.

"It took a while for the shrinks to bring that boy back," Pop said.

"That's a worry," Rocky said, "because pressure doesn't set well with me."

"You'd be a spectacular target on a battlefield. A man of your proportions might be better suited for the civilian sector."

Rocky served up Pop's BLT.

"I can't be a pilot. My legs ud get tore off if I ever ejected. There's drawbacks to being eight feet . . . ."

"I reckon life in a submarine doesn't much appeal to you, neither."

"I can't swim, so I haven't even thought about the Navy."

"Well, it takes a special person to see the future."

"Sure 'nuff."

Pop's pause was dramatic. He swallowed his bite of BLT, followed it up with a slug of Coke, and, then he said, "I know this lady . . . ."

Rocky looked huge perched on a wooden chair across a card table from Maria Hernandez, a fortune teller with a vital mission — to synchronize everybody's *karma* toward the goal of recruiting Rocky to play for Rio Feo. Tommy was hiding behind a closed door trying not to sneeze. Pop sat to one side mentally complimenting himself on getting Rocky to the *séance*. Maria's low-cut white cotton blouse, paisley skirt, bandana headband, and hoop earrings put her solidly into Gypsy Territory.

Any mystery about the origin of the crystal ball was dispelled for Pop when he noticed Alfonso the fish swimming laps in a water pitcher by the sink. Alfonso looked naked out of his normal environment, a plastic anchor and an aluminum pipe-cleaner simulation of coral. Perhaps Alfonso had new insight into how Pop felt about moving from Kentucky to Rio Feo.

"Stare into the crystal ball," Maria urged Rocky, "and think of . . . nothing." Maria was winging it.

Rocky's eyes sparkled in the candlelight as he stared at the fish bowl as commanded. Pop took heart. This might work.

"I see you in a straight-jacket . . . no . . . a tight suit. Your shirt is stiff. It's rubbing your neck like . . . sandpaper. You're boiling hot." Maria's voice was soothing, mystical, the tone of voice that seduced you into believing gobbledygook. Rocky's aspect trended toward serious. His powers of visualization appeared to be intact. "I see more clearly," Maria continued, "you're in a uniform. Heavy. Hot. Officers are shouting at you . . . ridiculing you. You're so lonely. No friends. Torment."

Rocky was agitated, perspiring.

When Maria's head snapped backwards, her eyelids fluttering and exposing the whites of her eyes, even Pop got a start. Her pseudo-convulsion jolted Rocky.

"No, no!" Maria wailed. "Don't hurt him . . . oh . . . what can this mean?"

Rocky stood up abruptly, bumping his head on the ceiling fan and dwarfing the fortune-teller.

"I know what it means," Rocky said. "Don't say another word."

Chapter 32

ASSEMBLY

STUDENTS AGED FIFTEEN through eighteen filed into the old-fashioned Rio Feo High School gym. Assemblies were popular, because every hour spent in an assembly was an hour *not* spent in a ball-buster like calculus or physics. Principal Charles Bradley eagerly mastered the ceremonies. Of all the duties shouldered by a principal, talking into a microphone was his favorite. An earnest and affable man, he often labored to project a severe countenance, but his loose grip on his *R*s, where "red" became "*wed*" and "rough" became "*wuff*" and so on, made him a target of ridicule by scruffier elements of the student body. He often heard the cruel jokes, but he never let it bother him. His secret was *not caring*. With fewer than twenty years remaining until retirement, he could look past the aggravation and pretend to befriend the adolescent *pwicks*.

"Good afternoon, Weevils. *Pwincipal Bwadley* here. Before I deliver my *inspiwational* message, let me *intwoduce* two new teachers. First, teaching *Algebwa* and *Geometwy*, a *wecent gwaduate* of Texas Tech University, Miss Sandi

Wamirez." The Principal looked behind him to where the faculty sat teetering on metal folding chairs at half court. A curvaceous and foxy Sandi Ramirez stood amid mimicking whispers and an inappropriate cat-call.

"I need help with my square *woot!*" shouted a notorious miscreant in the back row.

"Be *wespectful,* students," the Principal chided, "a few words, Miss *Wamirez?*"

Sandi tilted the microphone down to her height.

"I just want y'all to know I'll put everything I've got into this year, and I hope y'all will do the same."

"I'll give you all I got!" shouted another savant.

Sandi sat down to thunderous applause. She was a hit. The Principal readjusted the mike, producing amplified phonic squeals powerful enough to cauterize nerve endings.

"Now, let me *intwoduce* our new basketball coach, the *pwide* of Sooner Nation, Coach B.J. Bates."

Tommy strode to the mike with an object in his hand about the size of a hand grenade. He tilted the mike up to his height while garnering token applause.

"Principal Bradley, Fellow Academics, Janitorial Staff, and students, I come to you with a hopeful heart even as our student body keeps shrinking."

Tommy was distracted by a stunning beauty in the first row. Seventeen-year-old Anna Lee didn't belong here. Her flashing brown eyes, her coifed mahogany hair, the confidence of her posture was out-of-place. She was a princess among peasants.

Some students were growing restless. Their finely-tuned attention spans – molded by hours of flashing images on

MTV – were stretched to the limit. So much mediocrity in one place put a damper on wise-ass cat-calls. Jaws were slack. Minds were numb.

"This year, we're going to put a winning team on this court, this Sacred Hardwood Shrine, this Cathedral of Hoops, to bring glory back to our belov-ed Rio."

"Joker!" It was the wise-ass in the back row again.

Tommy ignored the heckler. Tommy was on a roll. He couldn't resist once again checking out the goddess with the long, incredible legs. Did she wink at him?

"*AMI* will be our foundation. *A . . . Accountability.* What does it mean? You, chewing gum and mouthing off in the back row."

"*Accountability?*" the heckler responded, pleased to have the attention. "It means, you know, like adding up columns . . . numbers."

BRRAUGGHH!

A fog horn blasted a sharp, painful audio wave that filled every corner of the gym. Tommy's hand-held air horn frightened the students and the faculty out of their respective daydreams and wits.

"Wrong," Tommy said as though nothing had happened. "*Accountability* means taking responsibility for what you do. *M* is for *morality* — doing the right thing. And *I* is for *integrity* — telling the truth."

A great deal of auditory damage had been done by the air horn, but, hearing-impaired or not, the students were motionless — stunned and attentive. Pop had told Tommy long ago to *believe in what you say, because, if you don't, who will?* Therefore, Tommy spoke with the self-assurance of a teacher who had actually graduated from college, a man who answered to his birth name, a man who actually lived by the principles of *AMI.*

"We're going to be a powerhouse in New Mexico basketball this year. We'll be *accountable* and *moral,* and we'll do it with *integrity.* That's all I got."

Tommy gazed for an extra second into the seductive face of Anna Lee before returning to his seat. This was edgy stuff, scaring the piss out of young punks with a fog horn and telling them a fable about excelling in basketball with a team that didn't even exist yet. But minds – the kinds of minds steeped in a tradition of Darth Vader slicing adversaries in half with a flashlight beam and movie heroes slaughtering dozens of villains without ever reloading their guns — those kinds of minds believed anything. Six hundred hands came together in celebration of Tommy's preposterous promises.

The Principal chuckled as he returned to the mike he loved so much. "After stemming the *wiver* of blood gushing from my *eardwums,* we'll move along." How he loved to talk. "As I look out upon you," Principal Bradley declared, "I see future leaders, landlords, *lauweates,* lawyers, *lectuwers,* lieutenants, linguists, locksmiths, logicians, and lumberjacks." He beamed a radiant smile in the manner of a cat digesting a canary. Nobody laughed. Stupefaction reigned.

Funny thing, Tommy thought, he was surveying the same mass of humanity, and all he saw were lard-asses, lead-bellies, lechers, leeches, lesbians, loafers, loners, looters, losers, louts, and lunatics. And Anna Lee.

"Ask yourself the fundamental question," Principal Bradley said, "why am I here?"

The kid in the back row had a lot of lip left: "Cause the jail's filled up."

———— ❖ ————

Teachers milled around the faculty lounge, some drinking coffee from a pot that looked like a relic from the Oregon Trail. Others drank punch made of indeterminable ingredients from a cheap glass punch bowl ladled into cheap glass cups. The plates and napkins were recycled products of China. An assessment of the quality of educators in the room might cause a skeptic to despair for the future of the nation's youth.

"I almost soiled my diaper when you tooted your horn, Coach," the history teacher said.

"Pure passion," the literature teacher chimed in.

"Pure something," said the chemistry teacher, a dour, alcoholic, over-weight, paroled sex-offender. "You do know this town's dying with the mines shut down?"

"It's infectious," the history teacher said. "The Mundo Circus came to town last weekend and went bankrupt this morning."

Their interest piqued, the teachers clustered closer.

"Just what Rio Feo needs," the chemistry teacher complained, "a bunch of out-of-work circus clowns."

"Success is the triumph of courage over consensus." It was just one of a dozen stirring quotations Tommy had memorized for occasions like this. Tommy's plagiarized philosophy was a real show-stopper. Nothing could kill a conversation like an obscure Polish proverb.

"Good luck, B.J. I'm glad I'm teaching geography, not trying to build a basketball team in a land of dwarfs."

Tommy took the geography teacher aside. "Who was the brunette woman in front?"

"That's not a woman, that's a girl." The wistful look in the teacher's eyes implied that he understood what Tommy was thinking. "Anna Lee's the daughter of the Lutheran minister here in town."

"She's a student?"

"Yep. Anna lives in a different century than the rest of us. She's seventeen and a hundred-and-fifty at the same time. We had an English literature teacher here last year named Victor Pedrosa. He fell under Anna's spell and went from being a raging Catholic to being a Protestant. He attended the Lutheran church so he could get an extra dose of Anna every week. It was pathetic. Back in the props room behind the stage is where he shot himself. What a mess. Rumor says the Sheriff destroyed the suicide note to preserve tranquility in the town. Anna showed up at the funeral looking like Jackie Kennedy. You never saw so many guys in black suits with hard-ons in your life. I hope you don't think I'm a gossip."

Chapter 33
REALITY CHECK

FOUR STUDENTS REPORTED for the first afternoon basketball shoot-around – Chip, Felipe, Rondo, and River (yes, River). The tallest player was Chip Bradley, the Principal's son, at five-feet-eight-inches. Tommy took a deep breath to hide his disappointment. He reminded himself that Hadrian's Wall was built one stone at a time.

Felipe, a pudgy kid squinting through thick glasses, was wearing his jock strap on the outside of his bright yellow gym shorts. Tommy called him to the side for fashion counseling.

"What's your goal here, Felipe?"

"I want to be a priest." He seemed sincere.

"Well, regardless of your aspirations in the clergy, the jock goes *inside* your shorts, Son."

"I'm rubber intolerant, Coach."

"Then you'll have to wear cotton underwear under your gym shorts."

"I can't . . . my . . . ."

Felipe stretched out his waist band to give Tommy a clear view of his genitalia. Tommy recoiled from the sight with a mixture of awe and respect. Tommy slapped Felipe on the shoulder.

"Congratulations, Felipe. We'll special-order something for you."

At that moment, a skinny, zit-afflicted kid trotted by wearing elbow pads, knee braces, wrist bands, and a head band. Tommy motioned to him. Teacher and pupil met at mid-court.

"What's your name, Son?"

"Rondo," the kid said, flattered to get special attention.

"Rambo or Rondo?"

"Rondo."

"Lose the roller derby outfit, Rondo."

"But, Coach, my mom says . . . ."

"Has your mom ever coached basketball?"

"No."

"Didn't think so. Your mom is being irrationally exuberant about the amount of playing time you're going to get. Take off the gladiator stuff. You won't get hurt."

A native-American kid glided by on tip-toes. He had two studs in his nose and a metal piercing of some kind on his tongue. Dangle earrings swayed below his silver tragus rings. Tommy crooked his finger at the boy, who seemed delighted to be singled out. He swished toward Tommy at a canter like an uncoordinated colt.

"Name?" Tommy asked.

"River."

"Really?"

"Do you want to know my last name?"

"No," Tommy said, "It'll be a miracle if I remember your

first name." Tommy rested his hand on the boy's skinny shoulder to hint at sincerity. "See, River, the Boy George thing won't work with basketball. Dennis Rodman is an anomaly. It's a physical game. Lose the ball bearings and the wind chimes."

"Okay, Coach."

River cheerfully skipped away as if he were chasing butterflies without a net. Later, when River returned with holes in his face where jewelry used to be, Tommy called the hopefuls together. He told the diminutive crew to show him their two-handed chest passes. Tommy discovered about what he had expected – incompetence. A gleaming exception was Chip, whose crisp pass put River on his back howling as though he had been permanently disabled. Tommy reset River's dislocated finger, which wasn't as skinny as it had been moments before.

"Now we know where we stand on passing," Tommy said. "Let's dribble one-at-a-time to the basket and lay the ball in the hoop."

What followed was even worse than the passing. Chip stood out from the crowd once again. He dribbled between his legs, spun the ball around his back, and flipped it into the hoop. Tommy lined his youngsters up for the last drill. One-by-one, they jogged to the top of the key and fired off a ballistic prayer at the basket. Disaster. All the hopefuls mangled their shots except for Chip who jumped high and swished nothing but net from twenty-two feet. Tommy called in the want-to-be hoopsters and they formed a ragged cluster. Tommy invited nominations for team captain.

"I nominate me." It was Chip Bradley.

"Any others?" Tommy asked. He allowed no more than a millisecond for them to think about it. "No? Okay, let's vote. All those in favor of Chip, raise your hands."

"It's s'posed to be a secret ballot," Rondo said.

"These are not normal times," Tommy replied.

All four kids raised their hands to vote for Chip, and so did Tommy. Chip pumped his fist in the air, a silent celebration of cream rising to the top.

"Democracy is a precious thing," Tommy said, moving on without a transition to, "think about that while you give me ten laps."

While the boys jogged, Sandi appeared by Tommy's side. When the boys caught sight of her, they lengthened their pitiful strides and expanded their chests, which is to say from thirty inches to thirty-one inches.

"Which one's Michael Jordan?" she asked.

Tommy shrugged.

"You have an admirer," she said, gesturing toward a window in a gym door framing Anna's face. "Anna's my head cheerleader. She's quite a dish for a preacher's daughter. Have you heard the ballad of Victor Pedrosa?"

"Yep."

"Nobody ever shot himself over me," Sandi said.

"Be patient . . . you're still young. How about dinner at my *casa* tonight?"

———

Pop, Maria, Tommy, and Sandi were wrapped in fleece

blankets and sitting in a circle around a fire pit on Maria's rear patio. For two hours after sunset, they had been drinking wine and dipping *sopaipillas* into honey. Enveloped by stars above and moonlit desert below, the foursome's banter and laughter made Pop more light-hearted than he had been for a long time. The subject was favorite actors of all time. Maria said Gregory Peck was her choice. Sandi raved about Robert Redford.

"I've always been partial to Porky Pig," Pop said. He was serious. "He had that funny little chatter . . . ."

"That's a stutter," Tommy said. "Chattering is what you're doing."

"Stutter," Pop corrected himself. "I don't like my actors too perfect. Throw in a stutter and you got yourself a character with humanity."

Pop's perspective on life was such a hit with the ladies that he kept on talking, one story after another. Ignoring Tommy's subtle signals to abort the revelation, Pop told about the time he got caught in another man's bed.

"Wouldn't have been so bad," Pop said, "but between the mattress and me was this feller's wife . . . and she was hollerin' and twitchin' . . . I could see why he was so fond of her. Anyway, I lit out of there like a scalded-ass orangutan . . . hit the window buck naked . . . almost de-nutted myself on the window sill . . . and hopped into the ol' Studebaker and laid tracks. The husband was a jealous kinda' guy and he fired so much buckshot in my direction that my trunk looked like a pepper shaker. Only reason I mention this embarrassing episode is to warn y'all off minglin' with the spouses of jealous folk. Might save you a heap of embarrassment."

"Where was this?" Maria asked.

"Pulaski County, Ke . . . ."

"Oklahoma," Tommy said, cutting Pop off before damage was done. Tommy steered the conversation back to present-day concerns, chief among which was the sad reality that his predictions of basketball supremacy looked like the rantings of a lunatic in light of the afternoon's practice. He realized what a fool he had made of himself at the assembly. It was time to admit his pending failure to these friends before the rest of Rio found out.

"If I don't get this Rocky Mountain High kid on the team, the Weevils are going to make the *Titanic* look like a minor capsize."

"Rocky's committed to the Institute," Sandi said.

Tommy winked at Maria Hernandez. "Yeah. I was hoping a week of neckties and harassment might send him back to Rio in full retreat."

Sandi's eyes sparkled as though she knew more than she was saying. "I know his dad from Texas Tech. Let me work on that for you."

"Even if he comes to Rio," Tommy sighed, "I still don't have enough players for a team. All I've got besides Chip Bradley is a budding porn star, a hypochondriac, and a pansy."

"Young'uns still want letters on their letter jackets, don't they?" Four glasses of wine had got Pop thinking. "Football and wrestling have folded, so get some of them jocks to play hoops." Maria and Sandi praised Pop's idea. Easily beguiled by female flattery, Pop said, "I ain't known as an intellectual, but once in a blue moon . . . ." Pop rose up stiffly. "I didn't get this good-looking by carousing all night. I'm turning in."

He shed his blanket and draped it on Sandi's shoulders, giving her two layers of fleece to ward off the chill. He kissed his fingertips and touched Sandi's cheek.

"Desert turns right cold of an evening," Pop said.

Maria followed Pop's lead, wrapping her blanket around Tommy. "B.J., these range cattle out here are wild. They don't come to the rancher. He's got to go after them. It's the same with these Rio kids." Maria kissed Pop on the cheek, and he trundled off to his house. "Saddle up and go round them up." Maria bent down to kiss Tommy and then Sandi. She baby-stepped out of the circle of firelight to steer toward home by her porch light.

The reflection of flickering flames played on Tommy's and Sandi's faces.

"This whole town's given up," Tommy said.

"Well, don't you go giving up, too, B.J. You're a nice guy."

Tommy wasn't accustomed to getting compliments from anyone but Lori, so he didn't respond.

"I wish I'd never shot off my mouth about a basketball powerhouse. I was counting on having Rocky."

For the first time, Sandi detected a thin suture line that ran below his eyes and across the bridge of his nose.

"What are you running from, B.J.?"

"Why do you say that?"

"Because nobody comes to Rio unless he's got a good reason to get away from the place he was before. Rio's the end of the line."

"Then, why're you here?"

"I'm running, too. When I know you better, I'll tell you all about it."

Tommy leaned sideways to hold his cheek against Sandi's, but Sandi pulled away.

"Let's don't, B.J."

"Why not?"

"I already told you. You're a nice guy." Sandi shed her blankets and stood up. She leaned down to kiss Tommy's forehead. "Don't ask me why, but I believe you're already spoken for."

Tommy watched Sandi retreat from the circle of light to walk in near-darkness toward her car. He remained huddled beside the dying fire surrounded by miles of sand and cactus laid out beneath stars and entire galaxies that shimmered in the cool night sky. He felt very much alone.

Chapter 34

RECRUITING

IN THE SOBER LIGHT of dawn, Tommy's changes of venue and name seemed like schemes of a crackpot. Tommy had made promises he couldn't keep, and he was feeling low. Over breakfast, Tommy moaned the *Rio Feo Blues*, and Pop didn't hesitate to suggest a remedy: *help someone less fortunate than yourself.*

"Even if the poor bastard's beyond help, you'll feel better knowing you ain't the sorriest son-of-a-bitch on Earth, if you'll excuse my rustic *vernakler.*"

Pop hadn't always followed his own advice. Back before Pop's wife had deserted him, back when he got fired from the tobacco exchange, the best plan Pop could come up with was to binge on Jim Beam for two weeks. With an aching liver and a smashed pickup truck to show for his depression, Pop said, "I realized I *was* the sorriest son-of-a-bitch on Earth."

Tommy was in the same boat. Death threats, bodily injury, disorientation, loss of Lori, and his shattered dream of building a super team — who could have bigger problems than that? His answer came at the funeral of Rio Feo High

School's long-time janitor, Miguel Otero.

Grizzled old Miguel had ascended into Heaven on Thursday at the age of ninety-five. *Stress-related illness* was cited as the cause of death, but it was widely viewed as an unlikely cause, given the janitor's motto — *mañana*. Wrinkle-free Miguel had lived all of his days impervious to worry. The woman who owned the Rio Café whispered that *stress* was a cover-up and that it was AIDS that had taken Miguel to his reward. The café owner also believed that President John Kennedy had been an undercover agent for the Pope, that movies of America's first lunar landing had been filmed near Rio Feo, and that the government used televisions to read viewers' minds.

The AIDS theory was debunked by the town barber, who based his common sense argument on the central question: *how could anyone get AIDS in Rio Feo?*

"Ain't no perverted activities goin' on in this town," the Barber said. "Fact is, ain't a whole lot of activities of *any* description goin' on in this town, neither perverted nor *un*perverted."

It was Pop's opinion that stress, indeed, was the culprit that struck Miguel down. "Stress is silent and cumulative," he said authoritatively. "It'll sneak up on you like a thief in the night." Pop purloined Biblical metaphors to add a gloss of gravitas to his speculations.

Maria said she didn't care about causes *post mortem*. She was concerned about causes *pre mortem*, while she could still do something about them. Maria wore more black to the funeral than Mrs. Ortega. When it came to mourning, Maria knew what she was about.

Sitting in the tenth row of the crowded church, Tommy searched for the town's most unfortunate person. If Heaven was as cosmic as advertised, it sure wasn't Miguel. The deceased was, presumably, no longer less fortunate than anyone this side of the veil. Despite the declining fortunes of Rio Feo, Tommy considered no one in town worse off than he was, not even Miguel's bereaved wife who was having the time of her life wailing and sobbing in the front row. The answer came to him during the third verse of *Amazing Grace*. The bankrupt Mundo Circus! Surely the Mundo Circus would be a breeding ground for hard-luck stories, an epicenter of misery.

———— ‹‹()›› ————

Tommy strolled through the park where the Mundo Circus wagons and trailers were parked. He meandered among the carnival rides stacked on flatbed trailers until he met a man of about forty years named Tony Lopez, a short, trim man wearing the sequined outfit of a circus performer. Tony said the bankruptcy wasn't a total surprise, because Mundo had run off to visit his sick aunt in Santa Fe again, a red flag meaning he couldn't make payroll. Two drunks stumbled by, one wearing floppy clown shoes, the other a red ball for a nose and smeared pancake makeup. Under present circumstances, they were the Anti-Laughter.

"The clowns are shit-faced," Tony explained. "We had a mutiny last night after the Sheriff left. The clowns broke into the liquor vault. Mundo loads up on Mexican booze every time we play south of the border. Customs guys stay clear of the tiger cage."

Tony greeted a dwarf named Bryan who ambled by leading a scraggly camel.

"Cairo doesn't stop eating just because Mundo's broke," Bryan said.

"How old is he?" Tommy asked.

"Bryan or Cairo?"

"Cairo."

"They're both about forty, come to think of it. It's a toss-up which one will pass on first. Bryan's in decline on account of booze and drugs."

An obese woman waddled by with a leg of lamb in hand. Even the dimple in her chin was fat.

"It's straightforward for the Fat Lady," Tony said. "Just keep eating. But the animals have to be cared for. The acts have to keep practicing."

"What's your act?"

"The Leaping Lopezes, jugglers and acrobats."

Tony led Tommy past a derelict performer nursing a Tequila bottle. He took a swig and exhaled a huge flame. *Employment on the outside was probably elusive for a specialist like the fire-eater,* Tommy supposed.

"Rafael's a one-trick pony," Tony said.

Tommy and Tony entered a tent where three identical-looking young men with rubber tendons and the balance of cats were warming up with flips. Next, they juggled bowling pins.

"My boys – Alberto, Carlos, and Ernesto."

"Isn't Mrs. Lopez in the act?"

"She ran away with a Navajo guy up in Gallup. The crazy bastard came to every show and hung around like a love-sick teenager. That silly crap works for some people." The triplets performed stunts that seemed to defy gravity. "She left a long note, but her writing's so bad, I still don't know why. Anyway, the boys and I had to redo the show."

"What was her name?"

"Can't say. The boys and me took an oath never to speak her name again." Tony spat in the dry dust. "God, I miss her *tortillas*."

A roustabout led a mangy panther into the tent.

"Do y'all do anything with balls?"

"Our balls are a big part of the show." Tony opened a locker and threw several balls to his sons. "You've got a one-man crowd, boys."

The triplets spun the balls on their fingers, on their heads, and on their noses. They juggled smaller balls while kicking larger balls to one another. Unadulterated talent.

"They're awesome," Tommy said. "Do they do anything with basketballs?"

Tony rummaged in the locker again. He tossed several basketballs to the boys and they amazed Tommy with their dribbling, passing, and tumbling.

"I could sure use your boys on the high school basketball team," Tommy said.

"I need to get a job first."

"I wish you'd stay in town for a while."

Tony gave the proposition some thought.

"You'd have to watch Ernesto," Tony said. "He has an attitude . . . a resentment . . . about being born last. He plays games rough sometimes."

"Which one's Ernesto?"

"The one who plays rough."

Tommy speed-dialed Maria Hernandez.

———⊷«()»⊶———

Tommy escorted the Lopez family past the *ROOM FOR RENT* sign to Maria's front porch where she was waiting for them in an apron that blew in the breeze like a regimental flag. Maria's eyes sparkled when Tommy introduced Tony, *el caudillo* of the Leaping Lopezes, and his boys as potential boarders. Maria was taller than Tony, and she outweighed him, too, but he was an attractive man, and she took an instant shine to him.

"Encantado," Tony said as he shook Maria's hand.

It was just a hunch, but Tommy felt sure that Tony Lopez could charm the habit off a nun. The triplets shook Maria's hand respectfully.

"Your boys are so polite," Maria said.

"They're good boys." Tony was proud of his litter. "I teach them to be accountable and to live morally and to act with integrity."

Tony had charmed even Tommy, what with the *AMI* and all. Tommy recognized in Tony a kindred spirit. Tony offered Maria two hundred dollars a month to park his small trailer in the desert behind her house. He said he could rig an outdoor shower so the Lopez Family would need to enter her home only to use the toilet.

"I'm accepting your offer faster than Seward accepted Alaska from the Rooskies," Maria said. "I'm reading James Michener," she explained.

"For seven-point-two-million dollars in eighteen-sixty-seven," Ernesto Lopez piped up without missing a beat. For that single, shining moment, Ernesto separated himself from his siblings and showed himself to be a juggling, ball-spinning, history buff.

"Polite *and* smart," Maria cooed.

Tommy said the Lopez boys could ride with him to school. By the time Pop arrived on the scene, everyone was in agreement and Maria had opened a celebratory bottle of wine.

"Pop, the Lopez boys are going to be working on our house after school."

"Doing what?"

"Raking the sand and trimming the bush," Tommy said. "Fifty dollars a month."

As usual, sheets on Maria's clothesline were blowing in the wind like torn spinnakers.

"We can do laundry and iron, too," Alberto said.

"Wash dishes, vacuum, wash windows," Carlos added.

"You can live like a king, *Señor* Pop," Ernesto said.

Pop was elated. Maria smiled radiantly, the way women smile when the male-to-female ratio is six-to-one.

"I feel like Snow White," Pop said. "Where you boys been all my life?"

Tommy opened the back door of the gym, turned on the court lights, and tossed some basketballs out to the Lopez boys to find out whether they could shoot a basketball. He placed a call.

"Sandi, I found three kids who're magicians with a basketball."

Sandi had good news, too. While they talked, the triplets dribbled two basketballs each and whirled around the court like dervishes. Tommy was aflame with hope. He gestured for them to shoot at the basket.

"Don't make me beg," Tommy said, "tell me."

"About Rocky Mountain High . . . ."

"Yeah . . . tell me . . . ."

"He's transferring to Rio."

Tommy was so overcome by emotion he couldn't speak. *What a mystery life is*, he thought. *Life can seem so stacked against you one minute and then it'll turn around and roll you in blessings like a catfish filet in batter.* His eyes were afloat in tears of joy.

"B.J.?"

"How'd you do it?"

"I went to dinner with John High . . . ."

"Mrs. High, too?"

"She's long gone, B.J. John and I had some wine, and our conversation drifted here and there and, boom, he just up and decided to pull Rocky out of the Institute. Anyway, Super Coach, you've got your eight-footer."

With renewed energy and soaring hopes, Tommy led the triplets to the free throw line.

"Okay, Studs, let's see you burn up the nets."

Maria blind-folded could have shot free throws better than the Lopez boys. Their shots rarely hit the rim or the backboard. Tommy still had tears in his eyes.

———— ‹‹◉›› ————

Tommy had suffered through many a lonely night in Winnemucca and Rio Feo, but, until the present hour of midnight, Tommy had resisted calling Lori on account of his new face and his name change. He had dialed her number before, but, until this night, he had hung up before the first ring. He speed-dialed Lori's number. Eight rings: no answer, no voicemail. He put his cell phone away. Tommy's days were packed with minutiae that blocked memories of Lori. But during nights such as this, when cool air descended from the high canyons, filled the arroyos, and crept into his bedroom window, absorbing heat from sunbaked adobe walls, that's when Lori's memory came to call. In the still of night when he heard the whine of eighteen-wheelers on the road to Texas and when he shuddered with melancholy at the sound of a coyote's yowl from the rim of the mesa, that's the time that Lori dwelled in his thoughts. Tommy reasoned that God surely would not have let him know the bliss of touching Lori's skin or kissing Lori's lips if he was to be denied such joy for the rest of his life. An *indifferent* god might do that. A *mean* god might do that. *But*, Tommy assured himself, *an omniscient, loving God would not*. Tommy resolved to set aside his guilt and regret, and dare to call Lori again during some other lonely night.

Chapter 35

Ignorance And Confidence

AN AGED TANDEM ROLLER was compacting a rectangle of fresh asphalt laid in the desert behind Pop's house when Tommy got home from basketball practice. A bartender who moonlighted as a building contractor and a horse-trainer had installed a backboard, a rim, and a new net on the northern edge of the rectangular surface. Pop joined Tommy to inspect the work — a couple of asphalt experts toting cold beers.

"You plan on pavin' New Mexico?"

"It's an investment," Tommy said.

"You don't need me to go along with everything you do, you got a shadow for that," Pop said. "Long as you don't think money grows on trees."

Tommy allowed Pop the last word. The Lopez boys showed up eager to start shooting baskets, but Tommy told them to keep their powder dry until the asphalt had cured.

"Better a patient man than a warrior," Pop said. Then,

because no one could take his meaning, he added, "that's from Proverbs."

"Is Pop a priest?" Alberto asked Tommy when Pop was a ways off. "He talks about the Bible all the time."

"If he's a priest, he's got some explaining to do," Tommy said. "Pop talks about a lot of things."

————)((•)) ————

The Rio basketball team, composed of a diminutive point guard, three acrobats, and a post man with dents in his head, rejuvenated Tommy's enthusiasm. He promoted Chip Bradley to graduate assistant status by asking him to teach everyone but Rocky how to shoot a jump shot. Tommy took Rocky aside for a shot-blocking evaluation. Five muscled Mexican-American boys in old wrestling uniforms dawdled in the bleachers, scowling at the proceedings. At the far end of the court, John High set up a camera on a tripod to film the practice.

"Rocky," Tommy said, "I'm going to shoot a jump shot and I want you to block it. First, I'll take a sample shot so you can see the arc I put on the ball."

Chip, his teammates, the five wrestlers, and Rocky looked on curiously as Tommy dribbled expertly before leaping incredibly high in the air to launch a perfect shot that swished through the net.

"Dude's got hops," a wrestler named Raul Santos said. Raul, a second-year senior, sported a mustache worthy of a thirty-year-old man with eye brows to match. The quintet of wrestlers murmured in amazement.

"Okay, Rocky, take up a position in the key and try to block my shot before it reaches its apex. Do you know what *apex* means?"

"I'm tall, Coach, not stupid."

For a second time, Tommy jumped really high. The ring on his neck chain escaped from his shirt and floated in the air as he shot. Rocky pounded the ball right back into Tommy's face. Tommy crumpled to the floor.

"Damn, Rocky killed the Coach," Chip said.

John High continued filming as the team hustled to encircle their coach, slapped down in the prime of his life. The blocked ball rolled to the feet of the dumb-struck wrestlers. Tommy staggered to his feet. His right eye was engorged with blood and his face was starting to swell. He had a big smile on his face. Tommy motioned for Chip and his teammates to return to their jump-shooting seminar as he jogged off the court to the equipment cage.

He returned wearing a catcher's mask. He set Rocky up to repeat the exercise. Everyone watched Tommy as he elevated for a second jump shot. Rocky leaped up and swatted the ball violently with a loud slap. It careened toward John High's tripod. Once again, Tommy jogged off-court. He returned from the equipment cage with a tennis ball auto-serve machine. He aimed the launcher at the rim. He told Rocky to work on his touch while the machine fired tennis balls at the rim relentlessly. Rocky worked up a sweat learning to block more softly. Tommy's swollen face looked like a magenta cauliflower as he approached the wrestlers.

"Boys, I 'spect you're disappointed that football and

wrestling have been canceled."

"Yeah . . . bummer," Raul said.

"You can still earn a letter."

"No way." They were skeptical.

"You can spend practice sessions in the weight room. Suit up and just sit on the bench during games. You'll get out of class every Friday to travel to away games. Plus I'll pay you fifty dollars a month to sweep the locker room and wash towels and basketballs." Tommy detected hints of smiles on their faces. "You're my intimidators. Rub Vaseline on your muscles before game time. Scare the crap out of everybody."

Raul and his *hermanos* liked the concept. They exchanged secret homemade gang handshakes.

Tommy was spending money faster than he was making it, hoping for a breakthrough in time to meet obligations before his scheme came crashing down. He whistled for the team to gather at mid-court where the sets and subsets of boys eyeballed one another suspiciously. Rondo was worried about losing his status on the team, however low that status might be. The acrobats were worried about losing their point guard jobs to the wrestlers. Rocky wasn't worried about anything.

"I have a vision," Tommy said. "We're going to dominate New Mexico basketball. Your names will be immortalized. Years from now, people will still be talking about the greatest Rio Feo team in history."

The triplets were excited because, excluding the circus, they had never been on a team before. The wrestlers were excited because they thought they were getting something for nothing. Felipe, Rondo, and River, destined to be ball-boys, were excited, because they had been outsiders all their lives and would believe anything to be insiders. Rocky thought the Coach was off his rocker. Tommy urged them to keep the vision and the details of their preparations a secret.

"Like the Manhattan Project?" Ernesto asked.

"Exactly like that. We want the element of surprise at our opener at Clovis. When that game's over, shock waves will rock the basketball world."

Tommy's hyperbole inspired even himself. He passed out ten dollar bills as payment for deep-cleaning the locker room after practice. He ordered the boys to get haircuts like his by the following day's practice. The boys took the ten dollar bills greedily.

"Does this end our amateur status?" Felipe asked.

"Does *what* end your amateur status?"

"The ten dollars."

"*What* ten dollars?"

"You said integrity was our big thing."

"It is. If you've got integrity, you'll keep all this secret including the ten dollars."

Everybody finally understood how integrity works.

Across the court, Sandi was doing calisthenics with her cheerleader squad. Lithe bodies in Spandex were stretching in unison. Anna's dark all-seeing eyes focused on Tommy. When Tommy noticed her intense stare, he imagined the back of Victor Pedrosa's head splattering against the props room wall.

That evening after sunset, Tommy and Pop were drain-ing beer cans sitting in lawn chairs in the middle of the new asphalt court in their back yard. The moon was rising over the eastern hills and gilding every shape in the desert with a layer of silver.

"Can't beat the smell of new asphalt at day's end," Pop said. He pulled the tab on a new beer. "You got shot in your sleep last night by a guy name a' *Smelt*."

Tommy wiggled in his seat uncomfortably.

"You was yellin' and thrashin' around like you was wres-tling a gator in there. You still got worries?"

"I shoulda told you a long time ago, Pop. I took a bribe to lose the Brut game by more than three points from a tough guy name a' Igor."

"Igor?"

"He's Russian — ugly as the back end of a pole cat."

"That's a Rooskie for you."

"I also took some money to *win* the game from a dude name a' Puff ."

"A dude name a' Puff?"

"Yeah. Big Italian dude . . . works for The Smelt. I was s'posed to give the money back if KBC lost to Brut. Well, I didn't just lose the game, I didn't give the money back, either. Didn't give the money back to the Italians or the Russians."

Pop removed his John Deere hat and rubbed his fore-head. He didn't care for what he was hearing.

"If I got this right, you lost by a point, so you didn't please either one a' them *yayhoos*," Pop said. "Tarnation."

"The FBI's interviewing players to try to nail the bookies making the bribes. The Russians and the Italians take a special disliking to being ratted on. I figure they want me dead more than they want their money back." Tommy moaned. "It was greed that got me into this fix."

Pop put his John Deere cap back on. "I reckon you thought you was smarter'n everybody else."

"For a while there, I did. I'm ashamed Lori saw that side of my nature."

"I ain't givin' you no speeches. I did somethin' about as dumb forty years ago with a guy's moonshine. Had to hide out in Tennessee for purt' near a year."

Tommy was relieved to have a fellow *desperado* in the family to take some of the weight off his shoulders. It appeared that the men in the Gunn Family had a proclivity to engage in dodgy deals.

"The thing I learned," Pop said, "is that my real enemy was *me* – my own fear. I finally went back to the Bluegrass to face up to it and I worked it all out."

"You got any more details?"

Pop drank a gulp of beer. "That'll do for now."

"Well, I'm too far down the road now. It's too big a risk to come clean right now. I gotta make this plan work, get me a good coaching job, and then I'll work it out. I got aspirations, Pop."

Pop became philosophical by seeing the lighter side of things. "You got all you need for success – *ignorance* and *confidence*." Pop chuckled and glanced over toward Maria's porch where she and Tony were drinking wine and chatting intimately. The happy couple waved. "Where you been and where you're going ain't nothin' compared with what's lying inside you," Pop said.

Tommy recognized inspiration when he heard it. He speed-dialed Sandi's telephone number.

"I gotta keep banging away 'til I get 'er done," Tommy said.

———————⟫((◉))⟪———————

On the other side of Rio Feo, brilliant moon beams invaded the darkness of Sandi's bedroom. Her cell phone was vibrating on her bed-side table. She and John High were naked in bed wrapped up in each other's arms and swaying rhythmically in the act. Sandi ignored the cell phone.

Chapter 36
MAKING WINNERS

ONLY A FEW DAYS remained before the first game at Clovis. Principal Bradley was fully invested in the team. He paid extra for vanity auto license plates: *WEEVIL*. He insisted that Tommy cancel scheduled games with Kermit, Monahans, and Lovington to *upgrade* to games at Carlsbad, Artesia, and Alamogordo. Principal Bradley got so worked up over the team's potential that he submitted Rio's name to the annual competition for State Turnaround School of the Year. Such an honor would strap a booster rocket to his career. Never before had he been in a position to nominate Rio Feo without getting laughed out of the state educators' convention. He told Tommy about it.

"We'll be merciless," Tommy assured him. "It'll be *Blitzkrieg* . . . Sherman marching through Georgia."

"It's uplifting to have a coach with a *gwasp* of *histowy*," the Principal said.

"The fire-bombing of Dresden. Little Big Horn."

"I get the idea."

"College scouts from major colleges will be coming in

droves," Tommy exaggerated.

"We could win the *Turnawound* Award."

"Pro scouts will be poking around."

"Maybe even National *Turnawound* Sch . . . ."

"Maybe," Tommy agreed. "I want to buy new uniforms for the kids."

"Go for it. You've got the football and *westling* budgets to tap into."

"And shoes."

The Principal brooded over this one.

"I have a vision of National Turnaround School," Tommy said, his hand panning an imaginary banner.

"Get 'em shoes."

———— ((()) ————

Each Fighting Weevil prepared for the season opener in his own way. Raul and his posse of wrestlers lifted massive weights four days a week. They consumed gallons of Gatorade. Raul had more electrolytes in his body than a truck battery. Alas, all five of the strapping former grapplers contracted the same malady. On day one, they thought it was measles. By day three, Raul was guessing leprosy. As the coarse red splotches in their crotches spread, they asked River for his opinion.

A view from any angle of Raul's heavily-forested *crotchal* area was no bargain in the best of times, but, by the time River took a look, the view was nothing short of revolting. River dashed off to vomit in a toilet, leaving in his wake his latest dream of a career in medicine. Tommy was made of sterner stuff. He delivered his diagnosis: raging cases of jock itch. He addressed the problem right away. He quarantined the wrestlers to the weight room and to the lockers in the south end of the locker room. He ordered fifty tubes of *Nitrolim*. The entire team scrubbed their hands several times a day as a precaution. Felipe, who insisted on wearing a surplus gas mask, rubbed down the entire weight room with a chlorine solution. By midweek, the Weevils had bacteria of all kinds on the run.

The starting five hoopsters practiced relentlessly. The triplets choreographed a series of amazing weaves and slights of hand to break a full-court press. Rocky High dominated the paint. Chip Bradley screened off the triplets and fired off thirty-foot jump shots that swished the nets almost half the time. When he missed, Rocky was there to gather in the rebound and smash in a dunk. The Weevils were a scoring machine. Tommy blew his whistle. He sent River to fetch the boys from the quarantined weight room. After the wrestlers joined their teammates, Tommy lined up his ragged squad and inspected their haircuts as he had every school day for two weeks. The ball boys – Felipe, Rondo, and River – were in the inspection line, too.

"We're all in this together," Tommy said.

He growled encouraging comments the way platoon leaders do before sending their men into battle.

"Nice pecs, Raul," Tommy said.

"Thank you." Unaccustomed to compliments from his dysfunctional parents, Raul relished the praise.

"Thank you, who?" Tommy corrected him.

"Thank you, *sir.*"

Rondo wheeled in a trolley loaded with cardboard boxes. Tommy pointed to shoe boxes with names scrawled on them and told Rondo to pass them out. The boys tore into the shoe boxes like crazed children at Yule Tide.

"Put 'em on, My Champions, My Viking Kings, My *Conquistadores.*"

The boys were flushed with excitement, even if they didn't take Tommy's meaning. Pandemonium broke out when the neophyte hoopsters found the main attraction — boxes containing navy blue jock straps and dark blue uniforms with white lettering — *RIO FEO* — on the front and their surnames on the back. They stripped right on the spot, performing male ritualistic acts of horseplay such as *smack-the-noodle* using their jockstraps as slingshots and *giddy-up* using their new jerseys as pony whips.

Anna watched the revelry from a tunnel leading past bleachers out to the court. She ignored Felipe's majestic phallus. She took no heed of Rocky's immense nude body. Her brilliant, sparkling eyes were focused only on Tommy.

Even Felipe, Rondo, and River received warm-up suits, which delighted River no end. Tommy happened to glance at the doors leading to the gym and he saw Sandi ogling the orgy of box-opening. Tommy called her cell phone as the Weevils continued their childish celebration.

"Ooh-la-la," Sandi said.

"Hard to find good free entertainment," he said.

"I want to see the coach put on his new suit, too." Sandi's face disappeared from the door window. Her petite squeal ended when her cell phone went dead.

A second later, John High entered through the same doors and began recording a video of the Weevils in their new livery. When the boys were dressed in their new uniforms and new shoes, they modeled and posed for John's camera. The triplets turned their backs to the lens, revealing three *LOPEZ* names over the numbers *1*, *2*, and *3*. Rocky spun around to show off his *HIGH* and *55* on the back of his jersey.

"From now on," Tommy said, "we practice in our game uniforms. Scrimmage like we play. Last thing today, we're going to practice cutting down the nets. We're going to think like champions. Now, clean up this mess."

————))(((————

"Are your conditioning methods permitted by the Geneva Convention?" Principal Bradley asked.

"What?" Tommy had just strolled into Principal Bradley's office.

"I saw Chip and the *west* of the team jogging in the desert *dwagging* cinder blocks."

"Builds up the legs and the lungs."

"And my snitch informs me that you make them leg-*pwess* enormous weights."

"I've done that for years myself. I can do twenty reps of six hundred pounds. I'll have your son dunking before we're done."

"He's five, eight. He can't dunk."

"You wanna bet on it?"

The Principal measured Tommy for a long time.

"No, I don't think I do," the Principal said. "You do have a flair, . . . Coach Bates."

The Principal flipped his hand, *get on with it*.

"Almost all of our games are away. We have to travel to get teams to play us. I want the boys to look good, to represent Rio the right way."

"I'm amazed that you got them to cut their hair."

"I want travel blazers and slacks for the kids."

"Do it."

"And good leather shoes."

"Do it."

"And iPods and headphones."

"You're insane."

Tommy stared at the Principal without blinking.

"Do it," the Principal said.

"And I want to paint a school bus metallic blue."

"Do it."

"With chrome wheel covers."

"You're exhausting me. Get outta here."

Tommy winked at the Principal's secretary as he left the office. He told her, "I just had a conversation with the Principal of the Year." He said it loudly enough to be overheard by the man with the swollen ego – Principal Bradley.

Chapter 37
THE WRONG STUFF

A RED LAMBORGHINI braked to a stop in a driveway fronting a mini-mansion. The driver was a big, muscular, handsome, conceited man named Quentin Tanner. Around Polo, back in Tyler, Texas, and on ESPN, they called the former professional offensive lineman *Q.T.* After blowing out his knees in successive NFL seasons, Q.T. had accepted an assistant coaching job working for the Polo University Offensive Line Coordinator. Five seasons later, Q.T. *was* the Offensive Line Coordinator.

The three gardeners manicuring the lawn showed deference to the big man for two reasons – Q.T. was their employer and Q.T. could crush the life out of any of them. Q.T. flipped the car keys to the young Hispanic man who had opened Lori Tolliver's door for her. The young man drove the car into the garage as Q.T. escorted Lori through the majestic front doorway of the extravagant home. The young man was already dusting every centimeter of the Lamborghini with a pink feather duster. Every move orchestrated by Q.T. was intended to impress Lori.

The stage for Q.T.'s next act was an outdoor bar adjacent to Q.T.'s sparkling swimming pool. Q.T.'s muscles rippled as he blended Martinis in a stainless steel cocktail shaker. His dark blue Triple-X golf shirt stretched to cover his massive biceps. His pale yellow shorts revealed muscled calves the size of Lori's thighs. Q.T. poured cocktails into two pretentious Martini glasses. All the while, Lori's ears were getting a workout.

"One used to knock down the brewskies like a maniac, but at one's (chuckle) advanced age, one must corral one's waistline or one will become a fat-ass." He pulled up his shirt tail to reveal abdominal muscles worthy of a statue. He slapped his abs adoringly. "Martinis'll pickle one's brain, but they're easy on the abs."

Q.T. made a show of serving a Martini to Lori who radiated apathy.

"Polo's dedicated to excellence," he said. "Polo's committed to winning. You'll make a bundle here and fix your resume up for life. Drink up."

Lori took a tiny sip, really tiny.

"I got a lush on my hands. Ha. You're a good-looking woman. You're not a . . . you know . . . a . . . ."

"A *what*?"

"You know, playing for the other team, like a . . . ."

Q.T. had a great tan, big muscles, and a fancy house, but some acquaintances, including Lori, concluded that he was missing a brain. Q.T. kept on yakking.

"No, one didn't think so. One had to ask. One doesn't care to drive too far down the wrong boulevard . . . know what I mean? It's counterproductive."

"I appreciate lunch, Coach, but I ought to be going."

Lori couldn't take any more of Q.T. Her barely-disguised rejection was a severe rebuff to a man not accustomed to brush-offs.

"Whoa, Pony . . . whoa, whoa, whoa. One went out of one's way to make you feel welcome, and one doesn't get any thanks?"

"I just thanked you."

Q.T. moved in close, too close. Lori edged away from him until she felt his massive arm squeeze her toward him.

"I mean . . . thanks of a more . . . intimate nature. You want me on your sideline, Girl. You don't want me on the other side of the field. I'm the big dog in this pound."

"I wish the big dog would take me home."

"That ain't the way the game goes."

Lori wiggled free and stepped away from the pissed off, muscle-bound Offensive Line Coordinator.

"I'm just a country girl from Kentucky, and the things that matter to you don't matter to me, so . . . ."

"Damn right you're country. You can drag your ungrateful red-neck-country-ass right outta my house and foot it back to campus. The walk'll do you good."

Lori didn't fight it. She turned away and moved past the pool toward the big house. Q.T. downed his entire Martini in one swallow and reached for Lori's glass.

"You ain't going very far and you ain't lasting very long here at Polo, Miss Tolliver. You got the wrong stuff!"

During her walk back to campus, Lori wondered how she had found the courage to stand up to Q.T., whom she loathed and feared, when she had failed to stand up to Tommy, whom she loved. Why hadn't she steered Tommy away from greed? She had let Tommy's appetite for wealth and fame trespass on their happiness. The extended communications blackout between Tommy and Lori troubled her. Pop hadn't called in several weeks, either. She worried that Tommy might have found someone else. Terrifying dreams of gangster reprisals against Tommy made her sleepless and restless in her bed, but patience sustained her hope. She could hear her mother's voice reading from Psalms, "I waited patiently for the Lord, and he heard my cry." She would wait for Tommy because she couldn't bear to think of living without him in a world populated by nincompoops like Q.T.

Chapter 38
HOBBS

WHEN TOMMY WAS nervous, he subconsciously scratched his battle-damaged pinky. Principal Bradley had once asked about the habit, and Tommy had explained that an accident had damaged his finger's nerves and that he was plagued by phantom itch, a strong urge to scratch an itch that wouldn't go away. Tommy was scratching away as he waited outside the Principal's office. Finally, the secretary gave Tommy the green light, and Tommy hurried into the Principal's office.

"What's got you all *fwothed* up?"

"Who's won sixteen state championships? Who's produced fifteen NBA players?"

"I'm not Alex *Twebek*."

"The Hobbs Eagles, that's who . . . and I've got 'em coming here."

"You got Hobbs? To come here?" The Principal was impressed.

"Last game of the season. I told 'em there'd be fifty college scouts in the bleachers. It was like baiting a mouse trap with a block of cheese."

Tommy and Principal Bradley shared a high five. The Principal eased Tommy over to his office window and the two of them looked out on the parched lawn stretching to the flag pole and the curb bordering the road to Texas.

"B.J., for the first game at Clovis, make *woom* for *weporters* and *camewas fwom* Albuquerque and El Paso TV stations. The council and the town manager, too."

Tommy looked worried. Was the Principal hyping this thing too much because Tommy himself had hyped it too much? What if the Weevils – the Fighting Weevils – were all frosting and no cake?

"We don't have enough room."

For the first time in Tommy's experience, the Principal revealed his dark side. He stroked the tufts of hair sticking up from his semi-bald dome, grabbed Tommy by the upper arm, and leaned in close.

"This has to happen, Coach . . . Bates. Find a way."

———◗◖———

At first, Felipe, Rondo, and River were flattered to be summoned to a meeting in Tommy's office. Perhaps the ball boys were about to harvest overdue gratitude. That hypothesis was shattered within seconds.

"Boys, we've run out of seats on the bus to Clovis."

The boys moaned and groaned as though Tommy had shot their dogs and burned their girlie magazines. River pouted, his chin slumped against his chest. Rondo's face flushed. Felipe's jaw dropped.

"So, us losers don't get to go," Rondo said.

"We're second class citizens," Felipe whined.

"I didn't say that."

"I ain't going in no mini-van," Rondo said.

Tommy produced a picture on his lap top computer.

"What's second-class about this?"

The picture showed a long, black limousine beside a manicured lawn and a slender palm tree. Such a lawn or palm tree didn't exist within a hundred miles of Rio Feo, but the youngsters' lively imaginations filled in the blanks. They celebrated with high fives, low fives, and in-between fives. Being from Rio Feo, it didn't take much to excite them. There was nothing that money couldn't buy. Clever exploitation of the purchase order procedure had solved Tommy's transportation problems.

As soon as the ball-boys had clambered out of the office, Tommy speed-dialed Sandi's phone. A second later, Anna appeared. Her lips were soft and parted and her eyes were languid. The nubile maiden laid a hand on Tommy's arm.

"Coach, I wish you all the luck in the world."

While his cell phone dial tone rang, an insane notion crossed Tommy's mind: he could whisk the ravishing beauty into his office, satisfy his basest desires, and . . . spend the rest of his life in jail. Anna just had that look that induced temporary imbecility in men. A flash image of a wall splattered with Victor Pedrosa's blood got Tommy back on track.

"Thank you, uh . . . ."

"Anna . . . Anna Lee," she purred.

"Thank you, Anna."

Sandi answered his call. Tommy held up an index finger. Disappointed, Anna fixed her intense gaze on Tommy until the door was closed. Tommy asked Sandi to come over to Pop's house for a beer that night, but she declined. She had too many papers to grade. The rejection chilled Tommy's optimism about the success of the Weevils. Was he betting on a lame horse? Everything depended on Rocky and his eclectic supporting cast. A shiver ran down Tommy's spine. What if the Weevils were headed for humiliation at Clovis?

Tommy had commissioned the painting of a new Weevil mascot icon at mid-court. The old Weevil's face had projected a benign laissez-faire image, a cross between the likenesses of Daffy Duck and Winnie the Pooh. The new Weevil face was a frightening countenance – a splotch of Genghis Kahn with a spatter of Jack the Ripper. The new Fighting Weevil was a mascot to be taken seriously. Tommy stood beside the Weevil and admired it for several seconds before blowing his whistle. The giant, the point guard, the jugglers, and the wrestlers ran over to huddle around Tommy.

"You boys ready to make history?"

He was answered with jostling and throaty growls.

"I'm not calling you *boys* anymore." That stilled the huddle. "I'm calling you *men*. You *men* have trusted the system and you've worked hard. That's what *men* do. They don't run from adversity, they face up to it. I'm proud of you. Now, give me ten laps and call it a day. Give me everything you got!"

Sandi was on top of John High naked in her bed. The heavy breathing of the two lovers and the rhythmic cadence of the mattress beneath them beat like a pulse past a stack of ungraded papers and out through Sandi's open window into the cool desert air that settled on Rio Feo after every glorious sunset.

On the other side of town, Tommy, Pop, Maria, and Tony sat in a circle on Maria's porch, warmed by fleece blankets and hot apple cider spiked with rum.

"Here it is," Pop said, "the night before the big game. It used to feel this way in Vietnam just before a firefight." (Who knew if he was just making this stuff up?) "Your nerves *kindly* tingled and made you shiver when it wasn't cold."

"You're making *me* shiver," Maria said.

"Not knowing how it's going to turn out," Pop said, "adds pepper to life, don't it?"

Had an Angel of the Lord offered a guaranteed two-point victory over Clovis, Tommy would have taken it without a second thought.

Chapter 39
PEARL HARBOR

TELEVISION CAMERAMEN CAROMED around in the crowd outside the Rio Feo High School gym. The Weevil Pep Band screeched and squawked through a Sousa march. Fans waved blue-and-white flags. The throng was a hybrid — political convention, lynch mob, and county fair. John High and Sandi Ramirez, dead ringers for Tom Brady and Giselle Bündchen, were among the first dignitaries to board the shiny, metallic blue team bus. Pop followed wearing pressed jeans, a crisp white starched shirt, a bolo tie, and cowboy boots polished to a high luster. Maria, the next person to board, was dressed for a coronation in a tiara resurrected from ancient times when she had been crowned Weevil Queen. Pressing through the crowd, Anna boarded with her squad of cheerleaders showing off their lovely, tight derrieres – derrieres that, within ten years, most likely would turn to whale fat.

Principal Bradley and his long-suffering wife were next. Inexplicably, the Principal wore a tuxedo. His wife had plastered his hair sprigs down with a viscous substance that darkened the strands of hair and stuck them to his head like black fishing line to a watermelon. Huge speakers boomed an amplified deep base – thunder under a clear sky. A man with a voice as deep as a tractor exhaust announced the arrival of the Fighting Weevils.

"And now . . . ."

Music pounded a sonic wave onto the crowd. Partisans winced, part pleasure, part pain. A rented fog machine worked overtime. Never before had Rio Feo witnessed this style of exciting-multi-media delirium.

". . . your Rio Feo Fighting Weevils!"

Rock music rent the air. The Weevils — dressed in polished black shoes, gray flannel slacks, navy blue blazers and blue-and-white regimental ties — strutted through the crowd. Tommy wore the same travel uniform and a style of wrap-around sunglasses worn by the finest golfers. Women cried and men cheered for the magnificently groomed Weevils as they navigated through the fog toward the bus. Mimicking what they had seen on television, each player wore earphones and was listening to God-knows-what. The players hadn't scored a single point yet, but they waved to the crowd like astronauts returning from space.

The three ball-boys, any one of whom gladly would have accepted any seat in the limo the previous week, now squabbled over seats like blue jays over sunflower seeds. As a result of secret negotiations with Tommy, Felipe had lost three pounds of blubber and Rondo had gained two pounds that he alleged was muscle. Tommy had bought Felipe a properly-sized pair of pants that didn't look as though he had a Kielbasa stuffed down the front. Rondo had sworn off

Cokes and other sugar-laden beverages and had begun lifting weights with righteous zeal. He was down to a single zit on the end of his nose. His biceps, which he self-consciously referred to as his *guns*, were almost eight inches in circumference – a start.

River, the Weevils' native-American salute to sexual ambivalence, had jettisoned facial ornaments. He no longer wore ruffled shirts. He seldom reverted to flapping his hands like the flippers of a penguin suffering a seizure.

The eclectic convoy of Fighting Weevils pulled out of the parking lot — the limo, the blue bus, and a column of dusty pickup trucks. For an instant, Rio Feo's dreary aura of peeled paint, cracked barrel roofing tiles, and chipped stucco was obscured by the magic fairy dust of optimism.

⸺ ◉ ⸺

The Clovis High School gymnasium was packed to capacity. Rumors about Rocky Mountain High attracted spectators from Portales, Fort Sumner, and as far away as Tucumcari. Curious fans remarked on the Weevils' unusual pregame warmup. Rocky was the headliner. Standing near a backboard, he made the rim look too low as if the custodian had got his measurements wrong. Rocky paused during his stretching exercises to sign autographs. Seeing the triplets shoot free throws was as entertaining as watching zoo pandas — they were just so damn cute. Ernesto smiled stupidly when he missed a shot to make it look as if he was just clowning around, as though he had a higher purpose in

SALVATION AT RIO FEO

life and was dabbling in basketball as an ephemeral distraction. Chip drilled jump shots from freakishly long distances. Raul and his fellow menacing wrestlers stood with their massive arms folded over their massive chests hawking the Clovis shoot-around. On a signal from Tommy, the Fighting Weevils gathered in a circle beside the visitors' bench.

"Men, courage is the greatest quality of the mind next to honor." Tommy quoted the line from Aristotle, a line he had memorized the night before. The quote had stirred him no end in the glow of eight glasses of rum and cider, but, in this setting, with this audience, it fell flat. Aristotle had lost something between Athens and Clovis. Tommy shifted gears.

"Men, we didn't come here to be nice or to make new friends. We came here to kiss ass!"

"*Kick* ass," Raul said.

"What did I say?"

"You said, *kiss* ass."

"I meant, *kick* ass."

The buzzer sounded and the huddle broke before Tommy could conclude his pep monologue with an inspiring quote from Winston Churchill. The teams squared off at center court. The Clovis center craned to look up at Rocky in wonder. The six-foot-four-inch Clovis center protected his dignity by keeping his feet planted on the floor when the referee tossed the ball into the air to start the game. Flat-footed, Rocky tipped the ball to Carlos Lopez. He and his siblings performed amazing weaves and dribbling maneuvers, unfortunately headed for the wrong basket. Tommy was screaming "the other way" at the top of his voice, but his warning was drowned in a sea of delirious cheering. Alberto Lopez missed an easy layup on the wrong goal. A Clovis player tipped the rebound into the basket. The Clovis crowd went nuts. Confused, Alberto threw the ball in-bounds, but the same Clovis player intercepted the ball and scored again. Clovis fans roared.

CLOVIS 4 – VISITORS 0. The scoreboard dazed Tommy as though his brain hadn't yet processed the first ten seconds of action. He had day-dreamed about this moment dozens of times, and, in those dreams, the present scenario had never once occurred. Tommy's face showed pain, surprise, fear, and disbelief. His right pinky was itching terribly, and Tommy scratched it vigorously. He called for a time out, and his Weevils gathered around him, Tommy remained calm. He was, of course, faking it. He could see Principal Bradley, a blanched face teetering on top of a tuxedo collar in the fourth row. Tommy also could see Sandi cradled by John High's right arm. Pop looked daft in his skewed Weevil antennas as he asked Maria what the hell was going on. Rio Feo cheerleaders were stunned into motionlessness, their pompoms sagging. The Clovis pep band played their hearts out.

"Men," Tommy began, "perhaps I'm remiss for failing to mention that we're shooting at that basket down there. Got that?"

Felipe shouted, "Seven-hundred-and-sixty-eight to nothing."

"What?" Tommy yelled in reply amidst the din.

"That's the final score if . . . ."

Tommy's malevolent stare silenced the pudgy mathematician.

"That's not going to happen. Men, this is just like practice, except we're on a different court . . . with an insane crowd . . . with the future of civilization in the balance. Now, *Rio* on three. One — two — three."

"Rio!" the boys shouted in unison. They had mastered that part of the game.

The Lopez triplets amazed the crowd with their inventive, synchronized gymnastic moves as they brought the ball down the court. Chip used a Lopez screen to launch a twenty-six-foot jump shot that missed. Rocky's giant paws extended high above everyone else's, and he slammed the rebound into the basket. The Principal got his color back. Sandi stopped hiding her face against John's chest. Pop straightened his Weevil antennas.

Rocky blocked a Clovis field goal attempt. Carlos Lopez dribbled the ball down court. The Weevils ran the same play as before. This time, Chip's long jump shot hit nothing but net. *Swish* – Tommy's favorite sound. Rocky blocked another Clovis field goal attempt. Ernesto flipped over Alberto's back and Carlos passed the ball between Alberto's legs so Ernesto could receive the ball as he landed like a cat on his feet. This was entertaining stuff.

When the game was over, the scoreboard read, *HOME 32 - VISITORS 80.*

———◦———

Principal Bradley's arm rested on Tommy's shoulder almost affectionately as both men gazed out the Principal's window. A skinny coyote with a mangy coat sniffed at a garbage can, unaware of being observed by the very humans who might have had first crack at some of the can's edible contents.

"The phone's been *winging* off the hook," the Principal said. "We got five-minute segments in Albuquerque and El Paso." Principal Bradley could not have been any more pleased if he had won the Masters.

"We won't surprise anybody anymore," Tommy said. "That was our Pearl Harbor."

"How'd you like to fix up another bus? We'll charge ten bucks apiece for fans to *twavel* to away games."

"Where's the money coming from?"

"We cut the baseball *pwogwam* last night. What was the point? We don't have nine guys in this town who could hit a beach ball if you tossed it to them underhand. Basketball is *Wio's* future."

Chapter 40

FAME

THE RIO FEO FIGHTING WEEVILS pushed their winning streak to six games. News of the small school's victories spread, so the element of surprise was a thing of the past. Nevertheless, the Weevils overpowered Carlsbad, Artesia, Alamogordo, Socorro, and Roswell.

Rio Feo community spirit got a boost from the successes. The curmudgeon who owned the hardware store replaced his dry-rotted sign. A few homeowners painted the stucco exterior walls of their houses. Marigolds appeared in flower boxes in town hall windows.

The mayor removed twenty broken-down parking meters on main street. The chemistry teacher bought them for a pittance and repaired them in his spare time. He doubled his investment by selling the refurbished meters to Principal Bradley. The Principal was intoxicated by their potential as a new revenue stream. He tripled his money by selling the parking meters at the full price of new meters to the school district. He had them installed outside the high school gym. *Cha-ching*. Capitalism. Progress.

———— ((O)) ————

Principal Bradley styled himself as the Big Kahuna behind the Weevils' winning streak. At cocktail parties, he often said, "My first order of business was to *suwwound* myself with top-quality staff." Invariably, the statement earned him a slap on the back from the person with whom he was speaking, a person who hoped he was included in the *top-quality* circle. The Principal's notoriety inspired him to make positive personal changes. He goosed his network by sending out two hundred *celebration* cards extolling the Fighting Weevils' undefeated season. He hired a yoga instructor to help manage the stress brought on by his high school's sudden regional prominence. The yoga instructor knew about as much about yoga as Principal Bradley knew about nuclear physics, but she was one-fourth Asian, so her vaguely Asian appearance gave her instant street credibility in Rio Feo.

———— ((O)) ————

Not content with improvements in his professional standing and in his spiritual life, Principal Bradley tuned up his physical well-being as well. He shunned carbohydrates. He hired as a personal trainer a former prison guard from Bosnia named Zdravko. Acquaintances called him Z. A humorless, single-minded man, Z whipped the Principal into shape, sort of. The Principal lost twenty pounds and shaved his head. No more tufts of wispy hair for smart-alecks to ridicule behind his back.

Mrs. Bradley wasn't about to let her husband leave her behind in the race for a hard body, so she spent two hours with Z every weekday. Two hours a day with anyone could lead to familiarity, maybe intimacy. It was just a matter of time before Z and Mrs. Bradley gave in to passion on a workout mat in the garage. At a particularly intense moment, Mrs. Bradley's manicured fingernails scraped eight bloody furrows in Z's back, four on either side of his swastika tattoo. The secrecy of their rendezvous was compromised by Mrs. Bradley's screams of ecstasy and Z's Bosnian whoops, inspired by either climax or laceration, or both. The chemistry teacher was delivering reconditioned parking meters to the Principal's garage at the time of the spontaneous coupling. Who could have turned his eyes away from such a sight? Not the chemistry teacher, for whom gossiping was a sacred duty.

In fairness to Mrs. Bradley, it was the first time she had ever broken her matrimonial vows. On the other hand, no one had ever put moves on Mrs. Bradley before, so talk of sainthood would have been premature. Fortunately for everyone, Principal Bradley refused to believe that anyone with the gift of sight would seduce or attempt to seduce his wife, so Z got a free pass. Mrs. Bradley's course of antibiotics was completed and the scandal was forgotten within a month. For his part, Z promised Mrs. Bradley never to give in to her charms again. Z's wounds healed quickly, leaving pink chevron scars that he bore proudly. When asked about the scars, Z insisted that they were remnants of torture from his time in a Serbian prison.

Pleased with his strides in the area of self-improvement,

Principal Bradley ambled in to Tommy's office with his sleeves rolled up to expose rippling muscles in his forearms, muscles unseen for years. He plopped in a chair at Tommy's desk and started chatting away while admiring himself in a wall mirror.

"You're not going to burn out, are you, Coach?"

"There's a time to jog and a time to sprint. Now, it's sprinting time."

"Man, I'm glad I hired you."

Chip, the Principal's son, stuck his head in the doorway, waved to his dad, and assured Tommy that his athletic realm was cleaned and secured.

"Thanks, Captain Bradley," Tommy said. Tommy believed that titles enhanced accountability in youngsters (accountability being the *A* in *AMI*).

Chip closed the door behind him. Tommy took two Cokes out of his mini-fridge and poured each into a plastic glass. Then he poured in a few fingers of Jim Beam each and passed one of the glasses to the Principal.

"You've got yourself a wonderful son, there."

"I'm blessed," Principal Bradley said. He tried not to brag about Chip, the star of his universe. "*Twuly* blessed. I got a question for you, B.J. How come you don't want your picture on the web site or in the yearbook?"

"I'm kinda' shy when you get right down to it."

"I've known a few shy guys in my time. None of them ever blasted the wax out of my ears with a fog horn at an assembly full of delinquents." The Principal downed a slug of Beam-and-Coke and focused on Tommy for a long time. "Modesty's *ware* in sports. Are you sure you don't want your picture on the Net?"

"No, sir. I'd prefer to keep a low profile and concentrate on the team."

"Between Maine and here, you spent part of a year in Winnemucca, *wight*?"

Tommy looked worried before remembering that a cool demeanor was vital to keeping a secret.

"How'd you get along in Nevada?"

"Good. I liked everybody fine."

"I never did call *Gowwy* for a *wefwence*. You were our only applicant. If they'd a told me you *waped* sheep for a hobby, we wouldn't have a basketball coach *wight* now. The *wule* is, don't ask if you can't stand the answer."

Tommy smiled to conceal his apprehension.

"How about Maine?"

"Never had any trouble up in Maine."

"During a *wecords weview,* I noticed your birth date on your Social *Secuwity* card is *diffwent* from your Nevada *Dwivers* License. I imagine only one of those can be *wight*? Maybe you ought to fix that."

That got Tommy wondering about how many other loose strings were out there waiting to trip him up.

"I'll sure look into it."

Tommy accompanied the Principal to the door. The Principal laid his hand on Tommy's shoulder.

"I'm your *fwiend*, B.J. I want to get out of *Wio* at least as bad as you do. If you can beat Hobbs and go undefeated, we'll both be out of here like a couple of SCUD missiles." He paused for a second to decide whether to continue. "I'm a *capwicious* son-of-a-bitch, though. If you *scwew* up, our *fwiendship'll* be . . . *stwained.* I've *weceived* a disturbing phone call *fwom* Winnemucca that, if *twue*, doesn't shed a positive light on your time at Oklahoma."

Tommy froze. The chunky girls' coach was back to haunt him with allegations against Bobby Joe Bates. Was he a rapist? A sex-offender? An extortionist?

"Anyway, B.J., if you ever want to spill your guts, come on by." The Principal left the office.

The gods of drama weren't through with Tommy, yet. Anna appeared in the doorway and struck a pose that was guaranteed to make nine out of ten sets of knees buckle. Anna was smug in the knowledge that she was a knockout. Tommy wondered if she practiced her moves in front of a mirror.

"Coach, we're all pulling for you."

Tommy moved toward the door to preclude being in the office alone with the young seductress.

"We love you to death, Coach, that's why . . . ."

"I'm just leaving, Anna. Actually, I'm late."

Tommy grabbed his keys and gestured for Anna to make way for him to close the door. Anna batted her eyes flirtatiously and reluctantly stepped backwards. It seemed that the more Tommy resisted her charms, the stronger her desire for him grew.

"You just tell me if you ever need . . . anything," Anna said, "anything at all."

That evening after dinner, Tommy and Pop sipped their beers and admired the flaming western sky above the mountains as they had done many times before.

"Pop, you ever given in to pleasures of the flesh?"

"I have done so on a number of occasions," Pop admitted. "What do you have in mind?"

"I've been feeling lonely for a while, and there's this little girl . . . ."

"How little?"

"About five-foot, six- . . . ."

Pop raised an eyebrow and glared at his grandson as if to say *you know what I mean.*

"About seventeen . . . ."

"You'd be better off slammin' the door on your pecker ten times," Pop said. "It'd be less painful in the long run."

Tommy sighed. He could picture Anna. He also could picture the back of Pedrosa's head splattered against the wall like a buck-shot-blasted pumpkin.

"Your Dummy Bucket's already full, so stay away from temptation. If you got a choice 'tween pleasure now or pleasure in the future, pick the future ever' time. If I was you, I'd concentrate on getting my life straightened out for Lori. You oughtta call that girl. Don't wait 'till you're world famous. She could be long gone."

"Not yet. Not until I'm in the Big Time with the Russians and the Italians off my back. Not until I got my name back. I have no idea what she'll think of my face."

"If you think Lori's going to care about your face, you don't know her very well. Hell, your face didn't matter none to me."

— 207 —

"You're an old tobacco field hand, not a beautiful young woman. Young women are all about shapely bodies and beautiful faces."

"You just described yourself, not Lori."

————))((((————

In the game against Albuquerque Sandia, Ernesto got his fourth foul just fifteen seconds before the halftime intermission. One more foul, and Number Three would be out of the game. With Ernesto out of the game, Tommy could say goodbye to his perfect season. In the locker room, Tommy pointed to Carlos and told him to trade jerseys with Ernesto. Tommy took Ernesto aside for a one-on-one intervention.

"How many times do I have to . . . ."

Ernesto was doing his James Dean stare, soaking up attention. Tommy was tired of Ernesto's stubbornness.

"Look at me," Tommy said.

Ernesto tucked in his brother's Number Two jersey and stared directly into Tommy's eyes.

"You're choppin' wood out there when you're supposed to be playing defense . . . every game, Ernesto. If you foul out, we're gonna lose. Do you understand that?

"I got anger issues, Coach. I'm the youngest . . . ."

Tommy lost his temper and he threw a towel.

"You were born two minutes after Carlos. Get over it. Stop thinking about yourself. Think about the team."

"You're racial profiling . . . ."

B.J. popped Ernesto on the head with a clip board.

"How do you like that, *La Raza*? You silly shit, get out there and play defense."

It wasn't the first time Tommy had cheated to keep his starting five players on the floor in defense of his undefeated season. Even if the officials didn't know it, the Fighting Weevils did. Up in the stands, Pop knew, too.

———•(()•———

When Tommy walked in from work, Pop was perched on a kitchen stool watching the triplets shoot baskets behind his house.

"I used to play golf when I was a youngun'. I'd take Mulligans left and right, off the tee, out of traps, do-overs on the greens. I never took penalties on a lost ball. I was shooting in the seventies." Pop kept looking out the window as he talked. "One day, a good ol' boy asked me what my handicap was. I said, *about a six*, and he said, *not likely*. He *tolt* me if I didn't play by the rules, I'd never know what I really could shoot."

"What's your point?" Tommy was bone-tired. He wasn't in the mood for a lengthy parable to illustrate one of Pop's theories.

"I know you're switching jerseys with the triplets to keep Ernesto from fouling out. It's cuttin' corners. I have to speak up even though I was a fast-dealer myself. I can't let my own failin's be an excuse for saying nothin'."

"You done?" Tommy asked curtly.

"You listenin'?"

Tommy didn't respond.

"Reckon I am," Pop said.

———◄((●))►———

The following evening, Tony and Maria were spectators as Tommy shot baskets with the triplets on the asphalt court in Pop's back yard. In addition to the Lopez boys' extraordinary ball-handling skills, they now were able to hit the backboard with their shots more often than not. Maria appeared with a can of beer for Tommy.

"This'll cool you down, Coach."

Tommy took a big swig. "Mmm."

"You should be glad Tony came along. I used to look over here and see you catching rays and my mind imagined things . . . sexy things."

"It's a good thing you didn't tell me . . . I couldn't have resisted the temptation."

"Liar."

Tony rambled over with a beer in hand.

"Hey, Coach."

"Tony."

"I was just telling Coach that I used to fantasize about seducing him."

"I guess I got to Rio just in time, Coach. Maria is quite a woman."

"Pop wishes she was twenty years older."

"And you wish I was twenty years younger," Maria said to Tommy.

Alberto hit a shot, and the triplets went into spasm.

"You've worked miracles with these kids," Tony said. "They love basketball more than the circus."

"You beat Monzano by fifteen points," Maria said.

"And Sandia. That's eight in a row. You should'a seen their faces when we rolled into the Duke City in blue buses with speakers blaring. It watered their eyes."

"Who's next?"

"Santa Fe, Los Alamos, Las Pretendas, Taos."

"Rocky keeps swatting shots like flies," Maria said.

The sun dropped below the horizon. The triplets retired to their trailer. A sliver of a moon was perched overhead like a dim street lamp.

"Pop mentioned Kentucky a few times the other day," Maria said. "I thought y'all were Oklahoma people."

Pop wasn't there to defend himself. Maria's comment raised caution flags for Tommy. Pop was known to flap his gums way too much once he got wound up.

"Pop gets confused sometimes."

"How did you enjoy coaching up in Maine?" Tony asked.

"I've liked every place I've ever lived, Tony. Listen, I appreciate the beer, but I gotta go."

The pressure was mounting on Tommy. The television news said that the FBI was deposing college players for testimony to use against Russian Mob suspects and the syndicate under the control of Francis "The Smelt" Frantupo. Anna was paying too much attention to Tommy. Sandi wasn't paying enough. Lori was only five hundred miles away in Polo, Texas, but she felt as inaccessible to Tommy as when he was in Switzerland. The girls' coach in Winnemucca was on the warpath, Principal Bradley was acting weird, and Pop was giving free lectures on morality. Even Maria and Tony were poking around. Tommy poured a stiff Jim Beam and went to bed, locking his bedroom door for the first time since he and Pop had moved to Rio Feo.

————)((●)) ————

Lori lay awake in her bed in her apartment down in Polo. Her junior varsity girls' team had lost only two games so far, a home game against Texas and an away game at Texas A&M. The girls on the team were gifted, more than a little spoiled, but generally hard-working. Coaching collegiate junior varsity girls was like running a strip club in Saudi Arabia: you could have the best talent in the world, but almost no one came through the doors to watch. Lori would have traded her one hundred die-hard fans for one call from Tommy. Pop didn't call any more, either. She was certain that something was wrong, but she was just as certain that it would be a mistake for her to initiate contact. Chasing Tommy down would be a mistake. He had to come to her.

Chapter 41
ROAD TRIP

A PROCESSION OF tricked-out cars was attracted by the Weevil buses parked beside a Los Alamos fast-food joint. Low-riders, routine. Chrome twenty-inch wheels, standard. Stereos producing harmonic distortion at decibel levels a notch below the threshold of pain, mandatory. Sub-woofers that vibrated the filaments of light bulbs and windows in their panes, indispensable. Drivers of the cars couldn't conjugate a verb, but they could explain the logarithmic variation of sound volume to acoustical output power. A Dodge representing the driver's entire net worth rumbled by. Only his forehead could be seen above the window sill like a partial eclipse of the face.

The Weevils gorged on burgers and fries with the cheerleaders inside the fast-food restaurant. Sandi and Tommy lunched in front row seats on the team bus prior to the trip from Los Alamos to Las Pretendas. Tommy offered his French fries to Sandi. She shook her head, but then she took the biggest one as an afterthought.

"John High couldn't make the trip?" Tommy asked.

"He's at meetings down in Corpus."

"Y'all have got close."

"John and I were close before we got here. He was a big jock at Texas Tech in his day, and he still goes back to Lubbock for games a lot. We met one night after the Texas game and we clicked."

"How much older is he than . . . ?"

"Twenty years. I prefer 'em mature. I was dating Tech guys when I was a junior in high school."

Sandi licked the salt off the second longest French fry in Tommy's meal before devouring it. For a lady sworn off fried foods, she was granting a lot of exemptions.

"John sponsored me as an intern in his office. Mrs. High found out we were involved, and the town fired him."

"How'd you feel about that?" Tommy was copying Sophie's counseling technique.

"Being a home-breaker's nobody's first choice. Rocky didn't go live with his mom because she turned sour on men after that."

"That explains why you haven't been stalking me."

"You're sweet, B.J. John even says so."

"John says I'm sweet?"

"He says you show what's in your heart by the way you treat kids who can't give you anything in return . . . like the ball boys. He says you're a saint."

"Being celibate doesn't make you a saint."

<hr>

The Las Pretendas fans were going berserk. In the middle of an astounding acrobatic move, Alberto was fouled hard, sending his body to the bench. The location of his mind was yet to be determined.

"How many?" River asked as he waved three fingers in front of Alberto's glassy eyes.

"The Father, Son, and Holy Ghost," Alberto replied. Alberto was sitting this one out for a while.

"That was flagrant!" Tommy shouted at a referee.

Rocky tried to get revenge, but Chip held him back. Tommy called a time out.

"Stay cool, Rocky," Tommy said, "we can't afford to lose you." If he couldn't keep his starting five on the floor, his perfect season was in grave jeopardy. Without a perfect season, his scheme was dead-on-arrival. He asked a referee, "What does it take to get a technical? That guy could have killed my guy." When the ref ignored him, Tommy made four substitutions. He barely controlled his fury as he spoke to his squad. "Okay. These pricks wanna rumble. I'm putting the wrestlers on the court with Rocky." The wrestlers grinned with malice. "I told you guys you didn't have to play, but if teams figure out they can mess with us, we'll get drilled the rest of the season."

"Coach, we can't dribble and stuff," Raul said.

"You know how to deck somebody, right?"

Raul nodded. Of that there was no doubt.

"Look," Tommy said, "we're up by over twenty. You saw how Number Twenty-One fouled Alberto? Pay back. Double. Try to get the ball to Rocky."

The buzzer sounded and the teams returned to the court.

Raul went to the free throw line to shoot for Alberto who was still addled. Raul missed both free throws, but Rocky got the second shot rebound and scored a dunk. The wrestlers pursued the Pretendas players like cats chasing mice. Raul swiped at the ball and knocked a Pretendas player down like a sack of mulch.

"Foul!" the referee shouted.

The Pretendas player couldn't get up, so his coach sent in a substitute. On the in-bounds play, three wrestlers decked Pretendas players simultaneously as Raul swiped wildly at the ball and pounded the throw-in man again.

"Foul!" the referee said. "That's Rio's last foul to give. The next foul will put Las Pretendas in the bonus."

The Las Pretendas coach was bobbing up-and-down on the sidelines like a rooster on a hot asphalt driveway.

"Flagrant foul!" He yelled. "Flagrant foul!"

He replaced the injured player who needed help back to the bench. The muscular wrestlers had intimidated the Pretendas players. The substitute player got forearmed like his predecessors and he flopped on the court, almost eager to go down.

"Foul. Third foul on Number Ten."

The referees were earning their pay. The gym noise was deafening. The local fans were outraged at the carnage. The Las Pretendas coach signaled for a time out.

"These fouls are flagrant," he wailed at a referee, who called the two coaches to the scorers' table. Another referee had to restrain the Las Pretendas coach.

The lead official said, "Gentlemen, get your teams under control or we'll suspend this thing."

"This is basketball, not karate," the Las Pretendas coach bellowed.

"You want basketball?" Tommy shouted. "We'll play basketball. But, if you hatchet any of my guys again, you'll need a MASH unit . . . nine-one-one, Baby!"

"Gentlemen, are we playing basketball?" The official's question wasn't hypothetical.

The coaches nodded. Tommy put his regular team back in and the wrestlers returned to the bench looking self-satisfied.

———— ((◉)) ————

Hecklers shouted insults at the Weevils when they passed through a cordon of police to board the team bus.

"Thugs! Criminals!"

"Seventy-nine to fifty-two," Tommy said.

"Animals!"

"Seventy-nine to fifty-two."

As the Weevil buses pulled out of the parking lot escorted by police cars, Tommy texted Pop.

Won. BTW, dont talk KY w the naybrs member?

———— ((◉)) ————

The following night, after Rio's victory over the Taos Tigers, Sandi sat beside Tommy in the front of the players' bus. The Weevils were listening to their iPods as the bus droned through the night southward toward Rio Feo. The cheerleaders were hooked up to their earphones, too, except for the mouthy one and her bosom buddy. The two prattling maidens hadn't stopped talking for four days. Tommy could imagine them in the future driving their husbands to divorce, insanity, suicide, or murder.

"You've got some gangster in you," Sandi said. "Girls are partial to tough guys."

Sandi squeezed the immense muscles of Tommy's left thigh, a gesture more than collegial but less than sexual.

Tommy's mind had been replaying continuous loop stock footage of Lori. When he wasn't thinking about basketball, he was thinking about Lori. He could conjure up a picture of her at will – her soft face and trusting gaze.

"What's bothering you," Sandi asked.

"Are the Lopez boys flunking geometry?"

"Probably."

"We can't win without them. Can you tutor them?"

"B.J., if I tutored every kid who . . . ."

". . . this is special. They're good kids."

"You don't care whether they know geometry . . . you just want them eligible." Then, Sandi nodded.

Tommy squeezed Sandi's right thigh – more than collegial, a tad sexual, but mostly grateful. Tommy glanced back at the bus window and noticed Anna's image reflected over his right shoulder. Anna was watching him with her big owl-like eyes. Tommy closed his eyes and imagined Lori.

If he was so tough, why were tears streaming down his cheeks?

Chapter 42

SHORTCUTS

THE GREENS ON RIO FEO'S municipal golf course were brown. The fairways were even browner, thanks to a strict water-conservation policy. Principal Bradley brought Z along as a caddy. Tommy had never had a pardoned war criminal for a caddie before. Z might have known a lot about prison administration back in Bosnia and he might even have known a lot about personal training, but he didn't know his ass from a boxcar on a golf course.

Dressed in desert camouflage and a Tilley hat, Z looked more like an Outback trail guide than a caddy. His piercing eyes would have made even cool-as-ice Phil Mickelson uneasy during his backswing. Principal Bradley teed off first. He raised his hand toward the fairway in a manner replicating Babe Ruth pointing to the stands before a home run. It wasn't clear to Tommy for whose benefit this bit of theater was intended – him, Z, a vulture settled on a broken golf cart nearby, or an armadillo burrowing under the eighteenth green.

"Chip told me about what happened up north," the Principal said to Tommy.

"Had to do it."

"I know. Glad you're on my side."

"If I let a team bully us, they rest of the teams will be on us like vultures on a dead armadillo."

Principal Bradley drove his ball 240 yards down the hard, bumpy, parched fairway. Z grunted in Bosnian or Bozniak or something.

"You don't have to explain it to me. It's all about survival. About Darwin. I get it. *Wecwuiters* are calling for tickets *evwy* day . . . even for the *Wuidoso* game."

"No one called me," Tommy said as he teed up a yellow low-compression ball he had found under a tumbleweed beside a portable toilet at the practice tees.

Although Z molested golf etiquette by chatting on his cell phone during Tommy's backswing, Tommy's drive landed near the Principal's ball.

"You don't need the *distwaction* of *wecwuiters*, do you?" the Principal asked. "You're modest . . . shy."

"Who's calling?"

"*Nebwaska, Missouwi*, TCU."

Tommy drove the beat-up golf cart down the fairway with Z jogging in trail. Z made a big deal out of not breathing hard even though Rio was almost a mile above sea level and oxygen molecules were scarce.

"By the way, B.J., I still need a copy of your Oklahoma *twanscwipt* for the *wecords*."

"I'll get right on it."

Z picked up the Principal's ball from the scorched fairway, laid down a sixteen-inch-square section of green outdoor carpet, and laid the ball on the square. Z didn't even know he was trashing the rules; he was just doing the Principal's bidding. Z then amused himself by playing with his biceps, oblivious to the alleged golf that was going on a few feet in front of him.

"*Semper pawatus*, Coach . . . Bates."

The Principal thrashed at the ball with a four iron and it sliced off to the right like a defective frisbee. It ricocheted off a golf cart on the eighteenth fairway and an outraged player swore a blue streak in Spanish.

"Heads up!" the Principal shouted. Better late than never.

"Fore!" Z shouted at last.

"What'll you do if the *twiplets* flunk *geometwy*?"

"Slit my throat."

"If you don't take care of the *pwoblem*, the fans will slit it for you."

The Principal pointed to the square patch of green carpet at his feet and Z placed a new unblemished golf ball right in the middle of it.

"I'm taking a Mulligan," Principal Bradley said.

His second approach shot landed in a bunker fronting the putting surface. Tommy knew from past experience that getting out of Rio's sand traps was like pounding concrete. The Principal should have no trouble getting up and down in five, maybe six.

Tommy's instincts told him it was going to be a long round of golf.

My Old Kentucky Home was Pop's tune of choice for the evening. Norman Rockwell would have drooled over the sight of Pop whittling in his rocking chair and Tommy moving *Xs* and *Os* around on a whiteboard secured to the refrigerator by carpenter's clamps.

"Maria said you've been yakking about Kentucky," Tommy said.

"I got your text. I'm a little forgetful . . . ."

Tommy pointed to Pop's trousers fly.

"You forgot to zip up your pants."

Pop tugged his fly up.

"At least I still remember to zip 'em down."

"I'm at a critical point, Pop. I can't have my cover blown before Rocky gets his scholarship. Keep the spotlight on Rocky and off of us." Tommy could tell that Pop's feelings were hurt ever so slightly. "This has to work. It's got to all come together."

<hr />

Black-and-orange was the theme on Halloween night in the Perez High School gym. The Fighting Weevils had gotten into the spirit of All Saints Day. The five wrestlers looked like Mexican drug lords in their black skull caps and fake mustaches. Felipe was dressed like Zorro. Rondo was a Pilgrim and River was Peter Pan. Tommy was dressed like Coach Bates.

A Perez player charged into Chip, but the official called a blocking foul on Chip.

"That's four, Chip," Tommy said. "I'm leaving you in until halftime, so play soft."

In the locker room moments later, Tommy told Chip and Raul to exchange jerseys. River barely could pull Chip's medium Number Five jersey over Raul's massive chest. Raul's XXL jersey Number Ten fit on Chip's lean frame like a condom on a pencil. Raul stuck a costume mustache – a bulkier, bushier version of his own — above Chip's lips and pulled a skull cap over Chip's blond hair.

"Chip," Tommy said, "you are now Raul Santos, got it?"

Chip nodded. The real Raul Santos was squeezed into Chip's jersey Number Five like a hippo into a corset.

"Who are you?" Tommy asked him.

Raul wrestled with the question.

"Justin Bieber?"

Tommy looked exasperated.

"Chip Bradley?" Raul said.

"You're the ugliest Anglo I ever saw," one of Raul's posse said.

When the jeering subsided, Chip and the wrestlers were sporting mustaches, warmup suits, and skull caps. The impromptu name changes flipped Anglo-Hispanic stereotypes on their heads. Tommy had taken the Weevils even deeper into the dark world of rules infractions.

At the start of the second half, Chip, wearing oversized jersey Number Ten, a skull cap, and a fake mustache, checked into the game.

"Santos for Bradley," Chip said.

A few seconds later, Chip Number Ten scored on a jump shot and fell to the court beneath a pile of players. Chip found his mustache lying on the hardwood, and he stuck it back above his lips. By the time Chip toed the free throw line, Tommy realized that Chip's mustache was inverted, Picasso style. Tommy called a time out. In the huddle, Carlos flipped Chip's mustache. The switch got by the officials and the Perez faithful without notice.

Later, on the bus ride back toward Rio Feo, Chip shouted to be heard over the drone of the bus engine.

"What did we learn tonight?"

Ernesto said, "If you're not cheating, you're not trying!"

Tommy scowled at the most jaded of the triplets.

"Who taught you that?"

The boys prodded and poked one another as they hooted and hollered like a band of renegades celebrating their lawlessness. The undefeated Fighting Weevils from Rio Feo High began to chant.

"AMI! AMI! AMI!"

Tommy imagined he could hear defiance in their voices, perhaps traces of vengeance. The boys from a sad, broken down junction of roads in the desert were thrashing the big boys from towns with shiny store front windows and houses with green lawns. The impudence in their chant made Tommy uneasy, unworthy, as if he had joked around during the National Anthem or whispered during The Lord's Prayer. Not only was he bending the rules, he was flaunting them, mocking them, and he was dragging these boys along after him.

Pop used to say, *the time you get too big for your britches is about the time you get your ears pinned back.*

Tommy had the troubling sense that he would pay for

what he had done that night. He regretted it, but it was too late to make it right.

———— ❊ ————

The United Spirit Arena in Lubbock was a sea of red seats surrounding Tommy and a recruiter in khakis and a blue Polo University knit shirt.

"Monterrey couldn't stop your big man," the recruiter said, stating the obvious. "Your Rocky Mountain High kid would fit in real good at Polo next year."

"He'd be perfect . . . ."

"If he commits to Polo, it could be a helluva a career move for you."

"I'll get with him," Tommy said. Tommy was metering his words. He didn't want to mess this up.

"Some programs have rarefied air . . . Kentucky, Kansas, North Carolina. The air at Polo is filled with thousand dollar bills just waiting to be snatched."

"I'll do what I can."

"You know what I mean?"

"Sure do."

Their staccato conversation was just about done without too many trespasses on the NCAA regulations. As an afterthought, Tommy asked one last question.

"You know a coach at Polo named Lori Tolliver?"

"Hell, yeah," the recruiter said. "She's the best-looking chick coach on campus. I'd love to check her vitals, and so would every other swinging Ricardo at Polo."

Tommy's face turned bright red. His heart pounded like a piston.

"Gotta get down to the team," he said.

He didn't shake the recruiter's hand. He just walked down the stairs. He hated himself more with each step he took down the aisle to the arena floor. He wished he'd killed the son-of-a-bitch, but he wouldn't have known where to stash the body.

Chapter 43

DISASTER

WEDNESDAY AFTERNOON. TOMMY closed a filing cabinet drawer, turned, and bumped into Anna. Her makeup and sultry eyes insinuated a decidedly inappropriate teacher-student atmosphere. Anna reached out for his hands and pressed close to him.

Anna whispered, "Thy tender touch hath . . . ."

Tommy made a half-hearted attempt to move away, but Anna clasped his hands and stared into his eyes.

"B.J. – may I call you B.J.?"

She pressed his hands against her breasts.

"There is nothing, nothing, nothing I won't do for you," she moaned dramatically. The third *nothing* got Tommy's juices flowing as his mind flashed through a catalog of possibilities. Tommy kept some of his strength in reserve as he made futile attempts to remove his hands from Anna's breasts. Tommy knew that his underwear was shrinking, and, judging by the wanton twinkling of Anna's eyes, so did she.

Unknown to Tommy and Anna, Sandi was observing the encounter from her position at the narrow opening in the doorway to Tommy's office. She stood there quietly, holding two large tumblers of Coke.

"I know what pleases a man," Anna panted. "I'll give you anything you want for as long as you want."

Tommy succeeded in extracting his hands as Anna slid against him, pushing him against the wall.

"You're a lovely girl, Anna . . . ."

"*Woman*, B.J., a woman who won't be satisfied until she has possessed you. Take me."

Tommy slid out from Anna's body press.

"Anna, think . . . ."

"This is a heart thing, not a head thing, my love."

She grabbed Tommy's hands and tried to thrust them under her blouse. Anna and Tommy froze when the door opened.

"Break time," Sandi said as she entered the office.

Anna's and Tommy's hands flashed away from Anna's blouse. Anna spun around and stepped toward the door, walking right past Sandi.

"Good luck in El Paso, Coach," Anna said.

Tommy waved weakly and accepted one of Sandi's tumblers. As soon as Anna was out the door, Tommy poured Jim Beam into their Cokes. He swallowed a manly portion. Sandi smiled mischievously. Tommy took another mighty slug from his glass. And then another. The burn in his throat and sinuses was what he needed.

"You can have all the Beam you want," Sandi said, "but keep your hands off the candy, you naughty boy."

"I wasn't . . . ."

"Be glad it was me at the door. Can you imagine Principal Bradley?" Sandi sat on Tommy's desk. "You want to tell me your problems?"

"I got problems if the Lopez boys don't pass your geometry class. You tell me if I got problems."

"I don't know. I tutored them last weekend."

"Isn't there some quick fix? Without them, we're going down."

"B.J., these kids grew up in a circus wagon. They have a lot to learn. They're trying. Trust them and trust me. There's no shortcut."

"There's always a shortcut."

"Not to anything worthwhile."

The stress was getting to Tommy. He rubbed his palms on his forehead. It got worse.

"B.J., I'm moving to Texas."

Tremors shorted out synapses in Tommy's brain. For a second, he was unable to move, think, or breathe. Tommy chugged his Beam-and-Coke to replace the stuffing that had been knocked out of him.

"John's accepted the Polo city manager job. I guess you know what that means for Rocky?"

Tommy looked as though he had just been hit in the head with a dull ax. Everything he had counted on was toppling off a precipice. Order was jumbled; reason, upended.

"No one told me," he said. He was trying to be brave. Pop had often said you shouldn't give anyone the pleasure of seeing you sweat, or whine, or cry, depending on the situation. He wanted to hold Sandi, to kiss her at the same time he wanted to ring her neck for saying those awful words so full of doom for him.

"Has Rocky committed?"

"They're waiting for John's hiring to be announced so it doesn't look like *quid pro quo*. They'll do a big P.R. thing after you beat Hobbs."

"I was counting on getting a coaching job wherever Rocky went." Tommy's voice tapered off.

"That's what I'm trying to tell you, B.J. Your ship may have already sailed. Find a life preserver."

The same old ache rose in Tommy's chest. It squeezed his heart like a vice. The pain followed the same artery as before – hearing the true story of his parents' death, loss of the national championship, loss of Lori, and now, the loss of his second . . . maybe last chance. It no longer mattered whether Rio could beat Hobbs. Tommy was cut out of the spoils. He had wasted his chance of a lifetime back in Lexington. Now, he had stolen a man's identity all for nothing.

"If you'll excuse me, I have to go," Tommy said.

"I wanted this to . . . ."

"I can't stay here right now."

"I'll go with you," Sandi said. "Where do you want to go?"

"Nowhere. I don't want to be anywhere."

Chapter 44

GLORY

THE LEANER, TANNER PRINCIPAL BRADLEY stood out as the lone stud muffin among the four principals at the head table in the auditorium of an Albuquerque resort. His eyebrows were plucked, his ear hairs clipped, and the cut inside his right nostril had stopped bleeding after thirty minutes of ice pack therapy. Those nasal hairs were stout buggers, and Principal Bradley had learned to expect occasional collateral damage when harvesting them.

Z's disciplined conditioning program had turned the Principal into an AARP cover boy. The Principal declared that he had never felt better in his life. Of course, he had, but it was so long ago, the memory had faded. The other three principals were dog meat compared with Principal Bradley, and they knew it. Principal Bradley's tuxedo was beautifully tailored in contrast to the gunny sacks his competitors wore. As an added accent, Principal Bradley's cummerbund was Fighting Weevil Blue. *Très chic.*

The master-of-ceremonies was a jolly Hispanic guy, who, although an unknown in educational circles, was a close friend of the Governor, who regrettably was unable to attend that evening. Some well-meaning person long ago had told the master-of-ceremonies that he was a comedian, and audiences around Albuquerque had been paying for it ever since. He couldn't decide if he was a Latino Steve Martin, a bald Lee Trevino, or a dead-pan Dom Deluise.

"It's time to announce the winner of the award for New Mexico Turnaround School of the Year." His speech was tinged with sadness from knowing that his time at the microphone was waning. He fumbled with an envelope the size of a kite, hoping to milk one last laugh out of the audience, semi-stoned on Margaritas and wine. "The most improved high school in the Land of Enchantment is . . . Rio Feo High School . . . Principal Charles Bradley!"

Courtesy of an open bar, the applause was wild and sustained. Principal Bradley leaped out of his chair as though propelled by a bottle rocket. He still had a napkin tucked into his collar. The master-of-ceremonies removed the napkin and squeezed out an encore laugh with a pantomime of blotting Principal Bradley's lips. The honoree went along with the gag good-naturedly, because he was, if for only an instant, the center of the universe. For once in his life, as he cradled the turquois trophy, Principal Charles Bradley didn't want to be anyone else.

"Good evening. *Pwincipal Bwadley* here. As many of you know . . . ."

Two full-figured, fairly ferocious female protesters stood abruptly in the audience and screamed for attention.

"More women principals! More women principals! More women principals!"

Their voices were as shrill as hungry seagulls. Some attendees booed. The booing swelled in a second wave of protest to the protest.

"I hear you . . . and I'll defend to the death your *wight* to speak your mind," Principal Bradley said. It was the wine talking. "Now, if *Secuwity* will chuck these chicks out, I'll continue with my auspicious *wemarks*."

Muscular security guards with shaved heads and wires in their ears removed the squealing protesters.

"Can you imagine a night with either one of those *gwowlers*?" the Principal said.

Laughter drowned out a couple of high-pitched boos. He had gotten away with an *ad lib*.

"As you may know, *Wio* Feo is in decline."

In the front row, an elderly man wearing hearing aids leaned toward a bearded colleague and asked, "What did he say? What's a *wio*?"

"Decline," the whiskered colleague responded.

"Decline?" the old man repeated.

"Rio Feo is going down the shitter."

The old man settled back into his chair and adjusted the volume on his hearing aids.

Principal Bradley continued undeterred, "The mines played out and families moved away. Our tax base shrank and we had to make some tough choices."

A skinny, naked man sporting a long, thin scarf and a purple *Mardi Gras* mask leaped on-stage and danced around behind Principal Bradley.

"More gay principals!" he trilled. "More gay principals! More . . . ."

A security guard tackled the skinny man. Something cracked, maybe a bone. The guard whisked the emaciated exhibitionist off stage. Principal Bradley seized the moment for another *ad lib*.

"You know you're in a university town when all the *cwazies* come out." No one laughed. "We had to make some tough choices. It's all about leadership . . . ."

"What's it all about?" the old deaf man asked.

"Leadership," his bristly colleague replied.

". . . although I couldn't have done this alone. I established *thwee* pillars as our foundation – accountability, *mowality*, and *integwity*."

Principal Bradley took a sip of water. He wanted this night to last forever. He lost his place and fumbled his note cards. Desperate to save face, he located his final note card, the one he had written the previous evening after consuming six vodkas in two hours.

"Always *wemember*: the poor may be bloated by hunger, but the *wich* are bloated by *pwide*." The note said *PRIDE*, but he couldn't remember . . . . A punchline was on the loose, but the Principal couldn't lasso it. "Stay humble my *fwiends*."

The tan, fit, slightly-snockered Principal of the Year had baffled the audience with his nonsensical speech, but his fellow lushes clapped enthusiastically so they could get back to the bar at the earliest possible moment.

What a night.

━━◦((◦))◦━━

"God, I wish you could have been there, B.J. It was the *cwowning* moment of my *caweer.*"

The Principal's pose was Churchillian, only thinner. He gazed out his window at the wind-swept desert seeing nothing, which, frankly, was all there was to be seen.

"Congratulations, Mister Principal," Tommy said. "This could open some doors."

"The door's *alweady* opened, B.J., and I've *alweady* sashayed *thwough* it. I want you to be the first to know that I've accepted a *Pwincipal's* position in *Sacwamento,* California!"

"Wow."

"*Wow* is the *expwession* I had in mind. *Twiple* the pay. *Gween gwass* in my lawn instead of a *dwied*-up yucca. In-state tuition for Chip. *Wow!*"

"I'm happy for you . . . very . . . ."

Principal Bradley breathed deeply, adjusted his silk tie, and placed his hand benevolently on Tommy's shoulder. Tommy sensed the singularity of the moment; a powerful man was about to bestow a favor on a peon, a symbolic gifting of largesse.

"I know you're busy getting *weady* for the Hobbs game, but, when the dust settles, *wead* up on the *Sacwamento* school system. We'll do lunch and discuss it."

Tommy was jealous for a milli-second, the milli-second in which he realized that Principal Charles Bradley had become *somebody.*

Igor had embalmed himself on vodka again, and he was listening to his cell phone in the darkest, grungiest booth in any bar in Chicago. The Russian Boss on the other end of the conversation believed in the Ninety-Ten rule: the boss talked ninety per cent of the time and the lackey – in this case, Igor – was allotted ten per cent of the time to squirm, apologize, or concoct excuses.

"This Tommy Gunn kid is name B.J. Bates now," the Boss said. "Is coach at Rio Feo, New Mexico. You get him before FBI does. I know their tricks. They give immunity to make talk. I end up in jail."

Tonto had a better command of English than the Russian Boss did.

"I break his *deek*," Igor slurred. He had used up his ten per cent.

"Time runs out. Stop talking and start shooting this *zjelob*!"

Chapter 45
CLOSING IN

A MAJESTIC STATUE of a pony surrounded by verdant lawns was the centerpiece of the Polo University campus. Lining wide campus pathways were hedges grown from tiny cuttings, gifts from the *Jardin du Luxembourg* in Paris. The Royal Congress of Horticulturalists named Polo the most beautiful university campus in the world. A college in Dubai came in a close second, but it was widely known that no students attended Dubai U.

Compared with Harvard, an older center of learning in the East, Polo's faculty was stuffier, the maintenance employees more strident, and the students better-dressed. Polo University was emblematic of the best of Texas – tradition, taste, opulence, and optimism. Students parked their Porsches and Ferraris in spacious lots constructed of marble pavers from Vermont. Professors parked their Bentleys on unique onyx veneer parking spots. South Asian Indian legend ascribed benefits to onyx such as increased intuition, improved liver health, and boosted intelligence. That was the myth that surrounded the choice of onyx for professor parking. The truth was more utilitarian: a benefactor had inherited an onyx mine in Hawaii and had figured out a way to get a tax exemption of ten times the value of the onyx he donated to Polo. Win-win. It was the Polo way.

Basketball coaching staffs of men's teams and women's teams sat around a long conference table in the Polo Sports Center. The table, a gift from the nation of Egypt, was made of fossilized *spinosaurus aegyptiacus* spines, compressed and polished to a high luster. The Athletic Director believed that a piece of furniture more than one hundred million years old might inspire long-term decision-making by his athletic coaches. In fact, it was all the coaches could do to choose the color-of-the-day for their matching Polo University knit shirts.

"We feel confident about landing this eight-foot kid from New Mexico," the Head Men's Basketball Coach said, "so, we're focusing on recruiting guards now."

He handed out blue sheets of paper to male coaches. Efficiency was so thick in the room you could cut it with a steel machete with a pearl Polo logo on the handle.

"That's all I got," the head man said.

The Women's Head Coach took the floor.

"Our season's over. For the first time in ten years, we didn't make the tournament. Do we quit? Negative!" Her staff knew she was entitled to use snappy military terms such as *negative* because her brother was a Navy Seal. "So we start fresh. All assistant coaches will be on the road this week chasing some backyard talent."

She handed out sheets of pink paper. The color was carefully selected, not as dark as salmon pink, but not so pastel as powder-puff pink, suggestive of excess femininity and susceptibility to sexual exploitation.

"Sheila, you've got San Antonio and Austin. Renee, you're in Dallas-Fort Worth. Tracy's back in Houston. And going out to Carlsbad and El Paso is Lori Tolliver.

The Men's Head Basketball Coach addressed Lori by name, considered a feather in a young coach's cap.

"While you're out there, why don't you join Marcus over in Rio Feo? He'll be scouting the Rio-Hobbs game."

"Should be a barn-burner," Marcus said. "Hobbs has been a basketball powerhouse for fifty years. Rio Feo was a virtual ghost town until this Rocky Mountain High kid showed up."

———— ((●)) ————

Puff waddled through the crowded terminal at Chicago O'Hare. He was talking on his cell phone as he scrambled onto every moving sidewalk going his way. Without his cell phone, Puff was just a fat guy blocking the moving sidewalk. With a cell phone held up to his ear, he was substantial, perhaps important.

"He's using a different name now — B.J. Bates," The Smelt said in his voice of thunder. "He's in Rio Feo, New Mexico. You gotta *off* him this time. The FBI is rounding up the kids we bribed to rat on us."

"I don't care if he changed his name to Dustin Hoffman, he's a dead man," Puff said. Since being promoted to replace Banjo, Puff had turned nasty.

"Dustin Who?" The Smelt wasn't nearly as hip or as erudite as he pretended to be.

Chapter 46

SHOWDOWN

PRINCIPAL BRADLEY'S NERVES were stampeding, and he couldn't hide it. Tommy was nervous, too, but he was so depressed it didn't show. They stood facing one another in the dim corridor leading to Tommy's office, the Principal wanting to talk and Tommy wanting to walk.

"Big night," Principal Bradley said. "They don't get any bigger." His babbling was a device to cram his doubts and fears back down to where they came from. "If you beat Hobbs, you flat-ass beat somebody. You'll be able to name your ticket. You'll have a welcome mat laid out for you in *Sacwamento.*"

Tommy wanted the self-important bag of wind to go away. Principal Bradley searched the hallway to ensure they were alone.

"If you lose to Hobbs, all bets are off. The Big Time doesn't deal out second chances." Principal Bradley had fallen in love with the sense of power that came with his new career opportunity, hence his impersonation of Lucifer. "Another thing . . . I still haven't *weceived* your Oklahoma *twanscwipt.*"

Tommy was embarrassed, disillusioned, and angry. The Principal had repeatedly called him *Coach . . . Bates*. How much did he know? What was he holding back?

"You know I'm going to rot in Rio, don't you?" Tommy asked.

"Don't let jealousy say things you'll *we-gwet*."

Tommy spun away from the Principal to retreat to his office. His carefully orchestrated second chance was unraveling. His college coaching future was as illusionary as a mirage, but he had to stay the course for the boys. He had raised hopes too high to abandon them now.

Tommy's Polo dream may have vanished, but a win over Hobbs for a perfect regular season might launch him into the junior college coaching ranks. Maybe Coffeyville, Fort Scott, or Hutchinson up in Kansas. Maybe Cisco, Kilgore, Odessa, or San Jacinto over in Texas. His shortcut had vaporized, but he still had a chance if he swallowed his pride and did it the hard way. First, he had to beat Hobbs.

Anna, super-sexy in her cheerleader uniform, rushed into Tommy's office and slammed it shut. Taken off guard, Tommy rolled his chair back on its casters, and, before he could stand, Anna straddled him as though she were mounting a Palomino. She wrapped her arms around his neck and brushed her lips against his.

"Sh-sh-sh, Darling," she said. "Don't say a thing."

Tommy's struggle for freedom lacked vigor.

"How I long for your touch. How I rejoice at the very sight of you," she panted. Tommy had never read Shakespeare, but to him her words sounded Shakespearean. Anna peppered Tommy's flushed face with kisses, leaving rose-colored track

marks on his cheeks and forehead.

"I offer myself completely to you. I'm a virgin, B.J., a virgin. Do you know what that means?"

Tommy couldn't confirm what he knew, because Anna was sucking the oxygen out of his lungs with a lusty kiss that made Tommy feel as though he had locked lips with a vacuum cleaner. Tommy had never before encountered anyone with such an abundance of panache or with such an enormous capacity for self-confidence.

"I dream of flying away with you. *Come hither that I might sate your desires,*" Anna gasped between groans of what Tommy presumed was ecstasy. Anna rocked her hips and pressed against Tommy's whatchamacallit. She squeezed his head against her eager breasts.

"Take me now, my love. *Let my dreams be thine.*"

Shelley? Keats? Who knew? Tommy saw his office door swing open enough to show River's shocked face. The door clicked shut. If River had been sexually confused before, he had full-fledged sexual vertigo by now.

Tommy's *AMI* was taking a terrible beating in its struggle with *ACL* — ardor, craving, and lust. Fortunately for Tommy and his legacy, only a few minutes remained before game time. He had a job to do. He leaped to his feet with Anna hanging on to him with her legs wrapped around his hips like a koala bear. He unwrapped Anna's grip on his torso and lowered her legs until she was standing on the floor again.

"Anna, you're a beautiful girl . . . ."

"Woman!"

". . . woman. But your dream . . . ."

"One must dream . . . you told us! *I dream not of silk and lace, I dream alone of your sweet face."*

"Dream your own dream. Don't dream for someone else or you'll make them a prisoner."

Anna slapped Tommy. It hurt.

"You bastard! Don't turn your back on me after all I've given up for you. I could have had anybody in this town, but I waited for you . . . my love." Her frown changed to a smile of boundless compassion, *"yearning for the passing of your shadow, oh, love divine!"*

Tommy relaxed. Anna's slap marks on his face looked like four red sausages stamped on his pink cheek. Bam! She slapped him again.

"What the . . . ."

"You bastard!" She was back with the slap the bastard theme. "I can ruin you! I know you've switched the triplets' jerseys. I know you've switched Chip Bradley's jersey. I know how you got Rocky to transfer here. I know every sordid detail . . . *into the tempest torn at last and singed by the inferno's blast!* Tell me you love me or I'll reveal everything to the world!"

Anna moved to clinch Tommy again, but he fended her off. It was eight minutes before tip-off, and Tommy had his hands full.

Anna was just getting warmed up. "And I know about your tawdry affair with Miss Ramirez. You betrayed me. *Alas, my broken heart doth pine for love so pure it must be thine.* Give me your love or I'll yell *rape!"*

"Let's not say that," Tommy pleaded, his hands moving up-and-down, palms down, as if to slow traffic.

"I'll yell *rape,* so help me!"

It had taken Tommy a while, but he was coming to the conclusion that Anna Lee was a certified nut job, an attractive, well-endowed, high-strung nut job. Tommy pulled a chair between Anna and himself.

"Anna, let me just say one thing . . . you're out of your friggin' mind."

The insult worked. Anna ran to the door, spun around to face Tommy, raised her sweater, and fondled her breasts. "You could have had it all," she said theatrically. She lowered her sweater, opened the door, and dashed off, leaving River standing in the doorway, clapping his hands as though he were playing cymbals without the benefit of cymbals.

"We're all ready, Coach."

Tommy bounded over to the boy and forced his hands to clap in a suitably macho manner.

"Clap like a man, dammit."

River looked hurt. "I just came to wish you luck."

"I want you to be normal, River. Not odd, not a sissy. Rio's got enough whackos already. Be normal."

"Normal . . . like you?"

"Yeah . . . ."

"Okay," River said as he teared up and breathed rapidly. "I'll be normal like you. I'll switch players' jerseys and mess around with cheerleaders and . . . ."

Tommy put an arm on River's shoulders.

"River, I don't want you to suffer . . . ."

"I can't be you, Coach. Never in a million years. But I know one thing — you can be a lot more than you are. You should straighten yourself out before you try to straighten me out."

River tried to dip under Tommy's arm to run from the office, but Tommy held on.

"River, tell me something: what do you want? More than anything else?"

River stopped squirming long enough to contemplate the question.

"I want somebody to like me."

Tommy squeezed the youngster in a manly hug.

"*I* like you, River."

River beamed and clutched Tommy in return.

"Why didn't you say so? I like you, too."

River tore off in a trot. When the boy was gone, Tommy looked at his own image in a wall mirror. On a vitally important night, he looked disheveled, bleary-eyed, and lip-stick-blotched. He took a deep breath and rubbed his face with a towel. He heard a knock at the door. All he could see in the open doorway was a single quivering Weevil antenna on top of Pop's head cocked to peer around the corner.

"Join the crowd," Tommy called. "Grab a two-by-four and come on in and beat on me for a while."

Pop showed his entire puzzled face.

"I just came by to tell you that, no matter how this goes, I'm real proud of you Tommy . . . B.J."

Tommy surprised his grandfather with a bear hug.

"Don't think I likely told you enough," Pop said.

"Go out there and get yourself a good seat, Pop. We got us a game to win."

The tired old Rio gymnasium was filled beyond capacity for the battle of the two highest-ranking high school teams in the state. The Fire Marshall fretted about exceeding the gym's capacity before withdrawing to treat an ulcer flare-up. The pep band played the Rio fight song. They were not the Boston Pops. The Weevil cheerleaders flailed around as though they were on hallucinogens. The Hobbs cheerleaders were more mature and prettier than the Rio girls were, but Hobbs didn't have Anna. Manic Anna weaved and bobbed and glowered in Tommy's direction.

Sandi Ramirez and John High made a beautiful couple behind the scorers' table. Maria, Tony, and Pop were wearing blue-and-white Weevil antennas that swayed crazily on their heads. Attired for Oscar Night, Principal and Mrs. Bradley were flanked by two janitors dressed like undertakers but presumably serving as body guards. High in the bleachers noting Rocky's every move, Marcus and Lori were two of at least twenty college scouts on hand. Across the court, Igor-of-the-dead-eyes was dressed in a khaki hunting jacket and an Australian bush hat. He was kitted out for a safari, Ernest Hemingway transported from Mount Kilimanjaro to Rio Feo.

Tommy caught glimpses of Pop, Maria, and Sandi in the crowd. He saw happy townspeople — women dressed in cotton dresses and men in blue jeans and Western-cut work shirts; they were the parents of the wrestlers and the ballboys and the cheerleaders and the band musicians. They were simple and unpretentious, unlike Principal Bradley, who had been called out of the stands to interview on-camera with an El Paso television reporter. Tommy kept telling himself he had to finish the journey for the kids who were trapped in a dying town with no future and who dared to believe they could win on the back of an eight-foot giant. Tommy's big chance of riding Rocky to a college coaching job was lost, but the kids' big chance was still in play. Ernesto trotted up to Tommy.

"Euclid," Tommy said.

"We passed," Ernesto said. "Miss Ramirez helped us. Hard stuff's easier when someone helps you."

Tommy mussed Ernesto's hair and winked at Sandi. He called the team together two minutes before the tip-off.

"How y'all liking the Big Time so far?"

The Fighting Weevils had their game faces on trying to look as though they belonged on the same floor as the Hobbs Eagles, maybe even in Madison Square Garden.

"Hobbs has championship trophies in a glass case as long as this court," Tommy said, in the belief that hyperbole was no defect in a worthy cause. "Rio's never had a winning season 'til this year." Tommy shouted to be heard over the sound of the pep band slaughtering the purloined Notre Dame Fight Song. "Hobbs has turned out dozens of college stars. Not many guys from Rio have ever gone to college. Almost twenty players from Hobbs have played in the NBA. We can't even see an NBA game in Rio without a satellite dish."

"Coach," Raul said, "aren't you supposed to build our confidence *up*?"

"I'm getting to that part. You boys heard about David and Goliath?"

"They stuck 'em in a lions' den," Carlos said.

"That's a different deal . . . ."

"David whacked Goliath with a rock," Chip said.

"Bingo. All the money was on Goliath. David just took care of business and ran his game plan. Ended up cleaning Goliath's clock."

The wrestlers muttered approval at this outcome. Their muscles bulged when they clapped. Three solid months of intense weightlifting had turned them into fearsome specimens, with or without their skull caps. They were enforcers with an attitude.

"Hobbs is going to full-court press like they've been doing since Christ was a Corporal," Tommy said.

The Lopez triplets made the sign of the Cross.

"Find the open spaces. Don't foul. That means you, Ernesto. We can't lose anyone to fouls. On offense, get the ball close to the rim. Rocky'll do the rest. We didn't come this far to lose."

The game started. Hobbs triple-teamed Chip so effectively that he seldom got the ball during the first five minutes of the game. The Lopez Triplets dazzled the crowd by advancing the ball down the court acrobatically until they could throw it near the rim for a Rocky dunk. On defense, Rio double-teamed the ball handler and Rocky defended the lane alone. Hobbs tried to penetrate, but Rocky blocked a bunch of their shots. When Hobbs triple-teamed Rocky, Chip drilled three-pointers. The game ebbed and flowed, but the Weevils pulled ahead. With three minutes and fifty-five seconds remaining, Rio was ahead of Hobbs by 73 to 64. That's when fate intervened in a cruel way.

After making a spectacular rebound, Rocky landed on an opponent's sneaker and turned his ankle badly. He fell to the ground like a giant Sequoia. The crowd went silent. Rocky regained his feet, but he was in pain and limping badly. Tommy rushed out to him to assess the damage.

"Get Rocky to the bench," Tommy said.

"Coach, I can play flat-footed and still block shots."

"To the bench, Rock."

Tommy motioned for Raul to substitute for Rocky.

Raul's eyes were as wide open as fried eggs. "What do I do, Coach?"

"If your man's going to shoot, foul him, but don't hurt him. This isn't a Las Pretendas situation."

Tommy motioned for Felipe and Rondo to escort Rocky to the locker room. River wore a stethoscope strung around his neck and a thermometer clipped into his pocket.

"I'll go, too," he said, intending to reassure Rocky.

Tommy nodded. In the middle of the confusion, red-faced Principal Bradley crowded close to Tommy.

"Put Rocky back in there! There's only three minutes to go . . . he's got the whole off-season to heal."

"I can't risk hurting him worse," Tommy shouted.

"Without Rocky, you're going to lose."

Tommy looked into the face of the highly-decorated Principal of the Turnaround School of the Year.

"No."

"Say goodbye to *Sacwamento*, Tommy Gunn, you *fwiggin'*

phony." The Principal spat the words hatefully. "For the second time in your life, you're *scwewing* up your big chance. It's no wonder you can't make the tough choices, you can't even decide who the hell you are."

Tommy was Zorro with his mask ripped off.

For the last three minutes of bedlam on the court, Hobbs triple-teamed Chip and stole the ball twice. The Eagles managed to strip the ball from the Lopez Triplets three times. With Rocky out of the game, Hobbs began penetrating the lane and making high-percentage shots close to the rim. The whistle blew with five-point-five seconds remaining in the game. The scoreboard showed *RIO 82 – HOBBS 84.*

"Foul . . . right here . . . Number Forty-Three."

Alberto lined up at the free throw line. In the stands, Tony covered his face, peeping through his fingers.

"Who is it?" Maria asked.

"I don't know," Tony said, "none of them can hit the side of a barn."

The noise of the crowd dissipated as Alberto dribbled the ball to calm his nerves. He had shot over four thousand free throws since Tommy had laid the asphalt in the desert behind Pop's house. Tommy tried to project his eyes and hands into the body of Alberto. Alberto's shot arced smoothly, but it rimmed out. The crowd groaned.

"Lane infraction on Number Fifty-Four," the lead referee declared. "We'll shoot again . . . shooting two."

Alberto repeated his pre-shot dribbles as the crowd once again was hushed. The dribbles on the wooden floor sounded different from the asphalt in the desert. The gym basket looked closer against the rafters than the rim out-doors backed by an infinite sky. Everything was different.

Ernesto prodded his brother, "For God's sake, take the shot."

Alberto shot. The ball arched gracefully into the air and swished through the net. The crowd exploded.

Tommy glanced up at the scoreboard: *RIO 83 – HOBBS 84.*

The gym became as quiet as a graveyard as Alberto drib-bled the ball before taking his second shot. His shot clunked hard against the rim and Chip rebounded near the free throw line. He dribbled to free himself for a jump shot. He leaped high in the air. The ball left his hands. The buzzer sounded. The ball rolled around the rim two full circles and spun out of the basket. The game was over.

Disappointed fans booed and threw paper cups onto the floor. It wasn't hard for Tommy to decipher the mood of the angry, disappointed crowd. Pop's antennas were askew. Maria bawled like baby. Tony consoled her. Sandi sobbed. John put his arm around her, but he was having a hard time, too. Principal Bradley's face was as red as a tomato. A stroke was seconds away. Tommy ran past Anna and the cheerleaders to the scorers' table and grabbed a microphone.

"Attention . . . your attention, please."

The crowd noise diminished.

"My friends," Tommy said, "the great Coach Ralph Tasker made the Hobbs Eagles the best team in this state for almost half a century. He's gone, but Hobbs is still Number One. What's more, they're our guests. They honored us to come here and play."

The crowd was silent and motionless except for the tiny balls on the tips of Weevil antennas bobbing merrily, oblivious to the tragedy that had squeezed joy out of the gym.

"Our town is blowing away in the wind . . . right in front of our eyes. But *we're* not gone, not yet. We fell short tonight, but not because we didn't try. We gave it our best shot. We didn't turn into dust without a whimper. So, let's honor Rio Feo and show our respect for the Hobbs Eagles with a big hand."

At first, only a few fans in the crowd clapped their hands with Tommy, but, then, the applause grew in volume until it filled the gym.

Principal Bradley applauded his fabulous future in California, far removed from this forlorn, dusty town in the middle of nowhere.

John High applauded memories of his own years as a player and he applauded Rocky and the joy that lay ahead for him in the game of basketball.

Sandi applauded Tommy, who had protected Rocky and who had inspired the Weevils to accomplish as a team more than they had ever dreamed of.

Tony applauded Maria for the love she had brought into his life; he applauded his three sons and the sense of belonging they had found in this unlikely place.

Maria applauded Pop and B.J. who had chased loneliness out of her life and brought spontaneity into her simple existence on the edge of the desert.

Pop applauded Tommy for his basic goodness and for the gift of his love that gave meaning to the life of an old man.

Lori Tolliver applauded hopefully because she

recognized the voice – if not the face – of the boy who had been her best friend, for the man who had been her lover. Her brimming heart told her she had heard the voice of Tommy Gunn.

Chapter 47

REUNION

THE THUMP OF CRUTCHES sounded in the hallway outside Tommy's office. Rocky and his father John paused at the threshold peering in at Tommy who was slumped over his desk. They waited silently at first, fearful that the wrong words could do harm.

"The doctor said you were right, Coach," Rocky said. He held a hat in one hand and he leaned on the longest pair of crutches Tommy had ever seen.

"Some coaches would've played Rock," John said.

"I've made enough mistakes for one life." Tommy gazed up at the big kid. "What a star you're going to be."

John asked Rocky to wait in the car, but before Rocky left the room, he reached down to shake Tommy's hand. Rocky's voice didn't work, so he let his grip and the tears in his eyes do the talking.

"Before you go," Tommy said, "did you decide?"

Rocky put on his cap that read, *POLO*.

"You and the Ponies are going to roll."

After Rocky exited, John and Tommy listened to the

thumping of Rocky's crutches receding down the hall.

"Coach, I get vicarious pleasure out of watching Rocky play the game. I videotaped a lot of practices and games this year. You know that." John produced a Manila folder from which he extracted two eight-by-ten-inch photos. "Here's a picture of you shooting a jump shot one afternoon." John laid the photo on Tommy's desk. "Look at those legs. Look at your vertical. Only one other time have I seen a guy go that high." John laid a second picture on the desk. "When Brut and Kentucky Barber played in the tournament final. That's a picture of Tommy Gunn. What's the difference in those two pictures?"

Tommy examined the two photos. The memories made him weep. His voice sounded constricted.

"The jerseys: WEEVILS and CUTTERS."

John said, "Same arm position . . . same legs . . . same elevation . . . same guy. Only the face is different." John seated himself in a chair next to Tommy's desk. "You stood up to the crazies tonight. I wish you'd stood up to 'em back in Kentucky. Don't you think it's time to get back to being Tommy Gunn?"

Tommy rested his head in his hands, elbows on his desk, tear-filled eyes locked on the photos. John extended his hand and Tommy took it.

"Thanks for everything you did for Rocky . . . for all of us," John said.

Raul and the other wrestlers were cruising in Raul's tricked-out Chevrolet Impala. The engine exhaust rumbled through chrome mufflers as the car rolled slowly down Rio Feo's main street. The Hobbs bus had left Rio, taking the undefeated Eagles back to their town near the Texas border. Curious fans from Artesia, Portales, and Eunice had convoyed back home in their ranch trucks. No other cars were on the streets, not even Officer Guerrero. Depression had descended on Rio Feo.

"Coach shouldn't be alone," Raul said.

———————————

Anna's tears had streaked her face and smeared her makeup. She was dressed for her mission in black leotards, black pumps, and a black tee shirt. Her parents' adobe home was still and dark. Anna slipped into her father's study, closed the door behind her, and switched on a desk lamp. White letters on her tee shirt read ASPIRE. She opened a desk drawer and pulled out a thirty-eight caliber pistol. She opened the cylinder and confirmed that each of the six chambers contained a bullet.

———————————

Alone at his desk, Tommy stared at the two pictures of himself for a long time before bending over to tighten the laces of his sneakers. Leaving the photos on his desk, he stood up and took a ball from a basketball rack. His shoes squeaked as he walked on the wooden floor the length of the dim corridor. He tripped the master switch that powered the lights over the court. He dribbled onto the littered court, kicking away a paper cup here and a Weevil antenna there. When he leaped high in the air to launch a thirty-foot jump shot, the gold ring on his chain floated in the air at the apex of his jump. *Swish.*

A shadowy figure descended from the darkened bleachers into the bright lights of the court.

"Only one guy I know of can break the laws of physics like that," Lori Tolliver said.

"Lori? Is that you?"

"Where you been, Tommy?"

Tommy wanted to rush to her, but, because of her tone and her manner, he balked.

"I've been all over."

"I didn't know it was you until I heard your voice on the PA at the end. I'd recognize your voice anywhere . . . and I recognize that gold ring, too."

Tommy cradled the ring with his fingertips.

"What're you doing here, Lori?"

"Scouting . . . and recruiting . . . for Polo."

"I heard. I'm proud of you."

"But not proud enough to come back to the Lick."

"It's complicated. I told you to get on . . . ."

Tears were flooding Lori's eyes. She sniffed, and that gesture put another ache in Tommy's heart.

"You're not God, Tommy. Girls don't have a *Love Switch* that you can turn on and off any time you want to. A girl can't stop loving you just because you disappear . . . oh, I gotta stop crying."

"Crosses were burning. Bombs going off . . . ."

"It wasn't Baghdad. Those knuckleheads tossing dynamite had the attention span of a fence post."

"I wasn't safe anywhere. The Russians and the Italians were all pissed off."

Tommy's nerves were too raw to accept blame for his misdeeds even when he knew he deserved it.

"You could've come back for me the week after you blew the game."

"Blew the game?"

"Yeah, you did. You were show-boating and you missed a dunk. Big deal. Humans make mistakes."

Revelation, hopelessness, and guilt pushed Tommy to confession.

"I shouldna run . . . I shouldna taken that money. I lecture to my boys about integrity all the time, but, when it mattered, I didn't have any."

Lori was close enough for him to embrace her and Tommy wanted to hold her more than anything else in the world, but her body language stopped him.

"I don't know your face, Tommy. I know your voice and how your body moves, but I feel like I'm with a stranger."

"I had an accident. Guess I'm accident-prone." Lori was distressed, but she refused to go to him. "You wouldn't believe what I've been through on the run. I just wish I hadn't tried to be world-famous."

"You about were for a while . . . more like Jesse James than Elvis."

That zinger took more starch out of Tommy.

"Ever since that night, all I've wanted was a second chance."

The distance between them was awkward for both Tommy and Lori. So was their nearness.

"How's Pop?"

"'Bout the same. He's always about the same."

Behind Lori, a hundred feet away, Marcus appeared as a silhouette in a doorway at the edge of the court. Lori gestured for him to wait.

"I gotta be in El Paso by morning," she said, wiping her tears on her sleeve.

"That your squeeze?"

"No, that's another coach at Polo. I haven't had a squeeze since the night you ran off. Girls with broken hearts don't have squeezes."

Tommy reached out for Lori. Her elegant melancholy was suffocating him.

"Lori, I'm truly sorry I let . . . ."

Lori turned away, sobbing to catch her breath.

"You don't know what sorry is," she said.

Lori walked away from Tommy.

Tommy removed the chain from his neck and extended the ring in his hand toward her.

"Wait . . . ."

Lori didn't turn around. She continued walking across the court and out the door.

The ring and chain fell from Tommy's hand. When he stooped to reclaim them, his knees buckled. After a pause on his hands and knees, he collapsed at mid-court. He curled into a ball and clasped the ring against his chest.

A man wearing a khaki safari jacket and a bush hat emerged from the shadows. Tommy rolled out of his fetal position, keeping his eyes fixed on the gun Igor was pointing at his face.

"You think you hide from me?"

"I intend to pay you back when I get the money." Lying had come easier for Tommy recently, but Igor's gun made lying the easiest thing Tommy had ever done. "Can we work out a payment plan?"

Stepping between dark columns of bleachers behind Tommy, Anna stealthily approached, holding her father's pistol as steady as her trembling hands allowed.

"You mess with Russian, you got death wish." Igor didn't appear to be a man interested in issuing a repayment coupon book. "I come to *theese* hole to *keel* you."

"Your timing's good," Tommy said, "because I'm about as low as I've been in a while." Tommy shifted his weight onto his arms braced behind his back. "I don't really give a shit whether you shoot me or not."

Igor looked puzzled, but not deterred.

"I *keel* you slow. I hang genital from that rim." Igor pointed at the south basketball rim with his gun.

Neither Igor nor Tommy spotted the five wrestlers silently approaching Igor from behind. Raul was carrying a folded metal chair like a club in both hands.

"Just do it," Tommy said. "I can't stand listening to your baby talk anymore."

Anna raised her father's pistol to shoulder height with both hands.

Raul lifted the folding chair over his head as he got

within striking distance.

Igor aimed his pistol at Tommy's face.

Raul smashed the folding chair onto Igor's head.

A shot from Igor's pistol blasted into the south backboard and fiberglass shattered onto the floor.

Raul raised the chair to whack Igor again just as a bullet from Anna's gun tore through the metal chair seat.

Anna fired a second round that shattered the north backboard. Fiberglass shards cascaded to the court. Anna spun around and ran out of the gym.

Raul smacked Igor again. As the Russian crumpled to the court, the five wrestlers piled on, pummeling him with their fists. Igor's gun slid away harmlessly, coming to rest on top of the Fighting Weevil logo.

Tommy got to his feet and the boys took a break.

"I want to explain something, boys," Tommy said.

Raul said, "You got nothing to explain, Coach. Everybody's fallen behind on a loan some time or other."

Tommy stopped trying to offer an explanation.

"We're taking this dude for a ride," Raul said.

Tommy shook Raul's hand as Raul's pals dragged Igor toward the front exit. Raul pocketed Igor's gun.

"You'll close down the shooting range?"

Chapter 48

COMING CLEAN

THE SUN WAS A WHITE BALL rising over the eastern hills by the time Tommy drove home to Pop's house. He parked his clunker beside a TV van with *Channel 17 News Live* painted on the side. After he slammed the car door, a woman reporter and a man carrying a TV camera scurried out of the van like ants out of an ant hill to converge on Tommy. They blocked his path, but he side-stepped his way to the front door. He closed the door behind him and tip-toed to the kitchen where Pop was seated at the table.

"Where you been all night?" Early morning after a sleepless night brought out Pop's irritable side.

"Wishing things had turned out different."

"I tried to call your cell phone." Pop was peeved.

"I turned it off. I've been trying to turn a lot of things off."

Pop pointed toward the stove where a frying pan rested beside a messy bowl of pancake batter.

"Slap on a couple. They taste like sawdust, but they'll take the wrinkles out of your guts."

Tommy heated the frying pan.

"It'll take a spell for the hurt to pass," Pop said. "Always does. You did good settling down them peckerwoods after the game."

"I could've done better. I made Rio out to be a cemetery."

"Just about is."

Pop toyed with his Weevil antennas. *Boing. Boing.*

"Last night I was thinking about back when you was little," Pop said. "Your momma and daddy used to spread a blanket by the river and lie there with you all afternoon listening to country music on the 'lectric radio."

"I been thinking about Kentucky, too. Wish I'd never run . . . stood up like a man and admitted I screwed up. Instead, I lit out like a coward, ran off like a crook."

"You can be bullheaded and irritatin', but you ain't a coward or a crook — neither one of them things. Give it time. Us country boys don't end up where we was aiming at very often, but we usually end up where we need to be."

Tommy poured batter into the frying pan. He was stalling, avoiding what really mattered.

"Saw her last night," Tommy said. "We spoke."

"I ain't no mind-reader."

"Lori Tolliver. She was at the game."

"You won't find no better'n her."

"Nope. She shot me in the heart. Made me cry." He was crying now, silent and soft. "Who the hell did I think I was? Takin' that money and leavin' Lori. Acting like a big shot."

He had Pop crying, too, tears long saved up.

"I know that feeling, 'cause I get it every time I think about your daddy . . . how I never *tolt* him . . . and then he was gone . . . ."

"Just when you think the pain in your heart can't get any worse," Tommy said, "it does."

"If I just had your daddy back, hell, I'd tell him."

"I'm not good enough for Lori Tolliver. I'm just a weak-dick pud-knocker who does the wrong thing every time . . . and says the wrong words . . . ."

Pop rose up out of his chair and put an arm around Tommy's shoulders.

"You're a Gunn, Tommy. Us Gunn's always been dicked up royal . . . 'scuse my turn-of-phrase. We keep our peace when we should be talking and we talk when we ought to be . . . . Your daddy believed he was smarter than the rest of us. Run off with your momma to Detroit — got themselves *kilt*. And the closest I ever came to telling him was one time when I was about drunk I *tolt* him, *You know how I feel, Son.* That ain't 'specially powerful. Don't wait no longer to tell Lori you love her. Time's wastin'."

Pop's calloused hand grasped Tommy by the neck and he gazed through cataracts and tears into Tommy's eyes, red with weeping.

"A youngun's afraid of what's under the bed. You and me . . . we're afraid of what's in our hearts." He let go of Tommy's neck. "Ain't we a pair . . . ?"

Tommy gazed out a kitchen window at morning breaking on the desolate desert. Mourning doves cooed their songs of commiseration.

"Maybe . . . by losing the game last night, maybe I got saved . . . right here in Rio Feo."

"When we're at the bottom is usually when we get saved. We're too damn proud the rest of the time."

Tommy slapped the antenna in Pop's hands to make it go *boing*.

"How'd you like to quit running and head back to Kentucky?" Tommy asked.

Pop relaxed and exhaled as though he were releasing ten tons of worry.

"My bones do ache for the Bluegrass."

"I'll give the dead man his name back and try to find some self-respect."

"Life can make you feel like a yard bird pecking willy-nilly for seed without the right person beside you. Call Lori and make things right."

"I don't know what to say."

"Words don't matter much when you're in love."

Tommy flipped the unappetizing-looking pancakes. "How about those yahoos out front?"

"They showed up right after Maria and Tony and me got home from the game. Been there ever since."

Tommy poured thick coffee into a cup. "You change the oil?"

"It'll keep you from choking to death on them flapjacks. Eat up and go give 'em their interview."

Unobserved by either Pop or Tommy, a huge face peered in through a kitchen window. The man's West Virginia birthmark had turned red in the desert sun. Puff had donned safety glasses for protection against flying glass fragments. When Puff was certain he had identified his target, he aimed his pistol at Tommy. A second later, he felt an uncomfortable nudge at the rear of his crotch. Maria braced the barrel of her shotgun between his legs.

"Now, drop that gun, Fatso, or I'll relieve you of your castanets."

Puff dropped his gun onto the sand. Maria prodded him to point him west.

"Now, start running toward that hill and don't stop."

"My car . . . ," Puff said.

"I don't care about your wheels, *Gordo*. I never want to see your ugly mug again. Now . . . run!"

Puff jogged away from the back of Pop's house into the desert. Mounds of flesh shook and shimmied as he made tracks westward. He shouted over his shoulder.

"There are snakes out here! I could die!"

Maria fired a bird shot load, and a few hot pellets stung Puff. He accelerated down-range with new urgency.

"Keep it moving, Tubby!"

Pop and Tommy appeared through the kitchen doorway into the sparse back yard where all the action was.

"Big game," Maria said. She fired a second round at the fleeing mobster. Puff skipped and yelped when the pellets hit him in the rear.

"You know that slicker?"

"I believe I do," Tommy said.

"That your Eye-talian?" Pop asked.

"Yep. That there's Puff."

"He ain't accustomed to stepping out so smart-like," Pop observed.

Maria fired a third cartridge into the air in the general direction of Puff. The big man skipped a step and yelped again.

"That'll focus his attention," Maria said.

"He's doin' fine, now," Pop said, "he's got him some

momentum."

———✦((●))✦———

Moments later, Tommy left Maria cleaning her shotgun in the kitchen beside Pop who was washing up the breakfast dishes. Tommy ventured out through the front doorway. The first rays of the sun illuminated objects too brightly, too harshly. He kicked a tumbleweed from the foot path. The TV newswoman and her cameraman had bounded out of the Channel 17 News van in response to the shooting. Rachel Cisneros had endured a rough night. She didn't look like a woman overflowing with compassion. Rachel spun on a dime and started jawing into a mike while the cameraman – all stubble and puffy eyes — aimed his camera at her.

"This is Rachel Cisneros for Channel 17 News Live bringing you this exclusive interview with the former coach of the Rio Feo Weevils."

Rachel crowded Tommy's space.

"I'm here live with Coach B.J. Bates from Rio Feo, New Mexico."

She shoved the microphone under Tommy's nose, prompting him to speak.

"Fact is, this is Tommy Gunn from Toxic Lick, Kentucky. I've got a lot of explaining to do."

"Tommy Gunn?" Tommy nodded while Rachel scrambled to back-and-fill. "What about this scandal?"

"I've learned that a fifty-inch vertical doesn't get you very far if your character is stuck to the ground."

Rachel gave Tommy free rein. He looked directly into the camera as if he knew what he was doing.

"I'm the guy who let down Kentucky Barber in the basketball final against Brut. I lost the game, but, instead of being accountable, I ran like a coward. I lecture about morality to my players, but I got mixed up with some shady characters . . . and I'm sorry for that."

The cameraman shifted angles to get Tommy's face in full sunlight.

"I preached about integrity to my players, but I stole another man's name and credentials. I apologize to the late Bobby Joe Bates and his family up in Oklahoma. I never meant to dishonor him. I'm sorry. I've been looking for a second chance ever since that night in Lexington when I blew the game, but I was bound to fail, because I never came clean. That's why I'm apologizing as sincerely as I know how. I want to say something to Lori Tolliver, the finest girl in the world, down in Polo, Texas: I'll always regret letting you down. Please forgive me."

Rachel yielded to her instincts and remained silent, a rare moment in her career.

"All my life I wanted to *be* somebody. Lori came along and tried to show me that I already *am* somebody. You've been right all along, Lori. I love you."

⟾ ((•)) ⟽

Lori was still wearing her robe after a short nap in her El Paso hotel room. She was watching Tommy on TV, her eyes brimming with tears. She had waited a long time to hear those words from the mouth of Tommy Gunn.

———◄◄◄◉►►►———

FBI Agent Bogart turned the television volume up, a cue for quiet in the command center. The partition walls around them were covered with mug shots of Igor, Puff, The Smelt, and a dozen college basketball players. Banjo's mug shot was crossed out. One of the pictures was a close-up of Tommy Gunn, pre-facial surgery.

"Get me a still shot of this new image of Tommy Gunn," Agent Bogart said. "We're going to have a chat with Mr. Gunn, see what kind of story he's got to tell."

One of Bogart's agents said, "Gunn just admitted he was involved with bad elements."

"This is dirty stuff, see?" Agent Bogart said. "Dirty, I tell you. We're gonna bust it wide open."

———◄◄◄◉►►►———

Principal Bradley, his wife, and his son Chip suspended eating cereal at their breakfast table to watch Tommy on TV. Principal Bradley coughed and grunted during Tommy's monologue.

"Pathetic," he growled.

Mrs. Bradley clucked sympathetically.

"*Portwait* of a loser," Principal Bradley grumbled.

"I don't think we see eye-to-eye on this one, Dad." Chip got up from the table.

———————⟫◉⟪———————

Two cable TV sports announcers spread sarcasm on their news report like mayo on a sandwich.

"The KBC guard who blew the championship game — Tommy Gunn — is back in the news."

His tag-team partner jumped into the ring.

"The man with the fifty-inch vertical changed his name, forged a diploma, had cosmetic surgery, and stole a dead man's identity to land a high school coaching job."

Tag.

"Gunn, also known as Bobby Joe Bates, took the Rio Feo Weevils to a nineteen-win season in New Mexico. After the deception was discovered, the school board fired Gunn and forfeited all nineteen wins for the season."

Final tag.

"So, if you're looking for a zero-and-twenty coach who can jump really high but has trouble telling the truth, call Tommy Gunn in Rio Feo, New Mexico."

Chapter 49

DEPARTURE

TWO DAYS LATER, Tommy and Pop were packing their few possessions into Tommy's clunker. In the distance, Tommy could see cars lining the shoulders of the highway to Texas. The Lopez boys came from their trailer behind Maria Hernandez's house. Tommy met them halfway to shake their hands.

"Goodbye, Alberto," Tommy said.

"I'm Carlos, Coach."

"Good luck, Carlos."

Tommy shook the hand of the next triplet.

"Goodbye, Alberto."

"I'm Ernesto, Coach."

"Keep mellowing out, Ernesto."

The third triplet grasped Tommy's hand.

"You must be Alberto," Tommy said. "Good luck in everything you do."

"Stay cool, Coach."

Tommy hugged Maria, his emergency fortune-teller, peeping neighbor, gunslinger, and friend. Then he hugged

Tony, still as wiry and jovial as the day he had met him at the Mundo Circus.

"Thank y'all. Pop and me . . . we'll never forget you."

Maria put her arms around Tony and nudged his face with hers.

"Thanks for keeping Rio alive for a day or two longer," she said.

Tommy slid behind the wheel. Pop rode shotgun. Tommy drove past Raul Santos and his posse of wrestlers attired in their letter jackets. He drove past Rocky High leaning on crutches beside his father and Sandi Ramirez.

The three ball boys were standing in the back of a pickup truck. Felipe had lost his baby fat. Rondo had muscled up and filled out. River had a stethoscope hung over his *serape* and he wore a Nazi helmet on his head. Sure enough, River was waving like a pansy.

"There's a young lad who's traveled a fair distance off the reservation." Pop offered a commentary on everything he saw.

"I predict he'll go far," Tommy said.

Tommy drove past cheerleaders and more boys in letter jackets. A few teachers were scattered among the crowd. Even the loony chemistry teacher was there, standing next to Z. Anna posed regally on a secluded knoll. She was dressed in pearls and a low-cut evening gown. Tears were streaming down her cosmetic-laden cheeks. She stoically rendered a Queen Elizabeth wave as Tommy drove by.

"There's a young lady with a sense of occasion," Pop said.

"Go slam your pecker in the door, Old Man."

"I ain't no threat," Pop said. "But I can see how she could make a man backslide."

The clunker reached the front of the high school. Principal Bradley had just finished raising the flag, and he watched with contempt on his face as the Gunns drove by. Chip moved closer to the curb. He waved and forced a smile as the car drove by just twenty feet away. The car passed by the two Weevil metallic blue travel buses. The chrome hubcaps were missing. One tire was flat. A thick layer of dust covered both buses. A dust devil swirled around the icons of Weevil fame.

"Glory's a fickle wind," Pop said.

Tommy drove the car onto the highway leading toward Lubbock.

"How about a detour to Polo?"

"I could tolerate it."

Tommy dialed up Lori's cell phone number.

In her El Paso hotel room, Lori was dressed in her blue business suit, ready to go to work. She recognized the caller on her cell phone display.

"You're world-famous again," Lori said. "The news says you're the worst *bandido* since Billy the Kid."

"I'm only about half as bad as the Kid."

"And you're probably only about half as good as I remember. I saw your interview on the news . . . ."

"Did you hear the last part?" he asked.

"What was that?"

"The part at the end."

"What did you say . . . exactly?"

Tommy cleared his throat and looked out at the desert hurtling by the car window.

"The part there at the end . . . where I said . . . uh, *I love you*." Tommy waited for her response.

Lori smiled through her tears. "First time you ever said it."

"It's easier on TV than in person."

"That doesn't make any sense."

"There you go again, looking for sense in a windfall."

Lori's voice softened. She was past sniffing.

"Any chance of you coming to Polo?" she asked.

Pop was looking cross-car for clues. He had heard enough to believe that the future was looking bright.

"I 'spect you got admirers down there."

"Hundreds of 'em."

"Are you willing to get to know me again . . . to give me a shot against all those other . . . the competition?"

"It won't take long. I already know you on the inside."

Tommy nodded to Pop. *All systems — go.*

"And every mile marker you pass," she said, "can remind you, that, at the end of the road is a girl who loves you. You are loved, Tommy Gunn."

———— ◆ ————

Tommy pulled off the highway near San Angelo to fill up the clunker's fuel tank at a gas station attached to a curio shop. Tommy bought Pop a strawberry popsicle. The elderly Native-American man who ran the shop told Tommy he couldn't fill his order for Pop's favorite — an RC Cola with peanuts poured into the bottle.

"How about a Coke or a Pepsi?" the old man asked.

"No, it's gotta be an RC."

"I don't want to be any part of giving you second best," the old man said. His worn jeans were held up by a belt with an ornate rodeo buckle.

"That belt's special. You musta rode."

"I rode until I was forty-four . . . up in Oklahoma mostly, but Colorado and Nevada, too."

"You ever get to Winnemucca?"

"I rode there once," the old Indian said, his eyes squinting pleasurably at the memory. "A mean old critter stomped the livin' shit outta me. A rodeo clown passed out in his barrel, so some cowboys had to get that bull off me."

"That's a memory you might want to forget."

"At my age, you hang on to all of 'em. How about you? Ever been through Winnemucca?"

"Never have." Painful truth made lying easy.

The man took a long look at the ring at the end of the chain around Tommy's neck.

"Got yourself some *Golde* there," he said.

"It's not much."

"Yeah, it is. I said *Golde*, not *gold*. *Golde's* got a *e* on the end. It's real malleable. You can beat an ounce of *Golde* into a thread fifty miles long."

"Never knew that."

"Yeah. *Golde* is a special deal. It's only been found in one place in the world. The atoms have an extra electron in the outer ring. They say that *Golde* brings lovers good luck."

"How can you tell it's *Golde* and not *gold*?"

"I just know. I know bulls and *Golde* pretty good. All the *Golde* played out a while ago, so they shut down the mine. I'd take good care of that ring if I was you."

"Where's that mine located?"

"Little town in New Mexico, name a' Rio Feo. They turned to potash, but now that's gone, too. Ever been through there?"

"Never have," Tommy lied.

He didn't have time to explain.

Chapter 50
BUSTED

TOMMY'S STOMACH CHURNED as Agent Bogart interrogated him. Agent Bogart's tie was loose and his sleeves were rolled up, displaying forearms hairier than anything Tommy had ever seen outside a zoo. When Agent Bogart crossed his arms, Tommy saw two mink in coitus, like a three-dimensional Rorschach Test. Agent Bogart led off by frightening Tommy with stories of long prison sentences given to cheating athletes.

"What if I told you that Bumbo Turner got thirty years in San Quentin for throwing the Stanford-Cal game?"

It didn't matter that Bumbo Turner was non-existant, Cal had played Stanford, and that was enough for Agent Bogart's purposes. "Your parents will be senile by the time you get out, see," Bogart said. "Maybe dead."

Tommy didn't explain about his parents and Detroit. Things were complicated enough already.

"You kids today think you're smart. So, Wise Guy, tell me one great idea . . . not some scheme to make you rich, but an idea to make the world a better place."

The first thing that popped into Tommy's mind was the Toxic Lick town hall clock stuck for decades at five-fifty-five. How many times since the age of eight had Tommy asked Pop about the broken clock? The clock was not only the *first* thought in Tommy's mind, it was the *only* thought in his mind. He spoke up. He had nothing to lose.

"Synchronize every clock in the world."

Agent Bogart stared at Tommy incredulously.

"Put every clock and watch in the world on the same time," Tommy said. "I don't care which time zone you choose. It could be Greenwich or Tokyo or Rome or Newfoundland, but . . . ."

Tears flooded Agent Bogart's eyes. He leaped up and pressed Tommy's cheeks together with his hair-free palms. The mink were on the move.

"Yes! You understand! You brilliant son-of-a-bitch-no-offense! You're not going to jail. You're going to tell me everything you know about the Russians and the Italians in exchange for infinite immunity. I don't care what you do the rest of your life, you're not going to jail."

Tommy recognized that for the good deal it was. He agreed immediately. Agent Bogart had turned out to be a nice guy. You just had to know how to talk to him.

Several weeks had passed since Tommy and Pop had moved to Polo. Lori had helped Tommy land a night-watchman job at Polo Arena. During his nocturnal rounds, Tommy checked for breaches of security, leaks of water, threats of fire, and any other form of peril within the confines of the most beautiful arena on earth.

Tommy always paused reverently to view Polo's NCAA Basketball Tournament Championship trophy on display in its bullet-proof case. The black sneakers that were part of his night-watchman uniform didn't harm the Yang Dong hardwood playing surface, so he often walked out to the center of the court, looked up into the unlit Nottyhyde seats, and dreamed of playing before thousands of adoring fans in such a venue.

An important part of Tommy's pay package was a free Polo-spa token per shift. He didn't take the perk lightly. He was no hoarder, so, every morning at about two, Tommy inserted his token and perched on a luxurious Polo-spa toilet to enjoy the ride of his life. On this morning, he sat in sterile comfort listening in stereo to a cheerless, high-definition TV broadcast about death — floods in Bangladesh, earthquakes in Indonesia, and bombings in Syria. The redundant carnage that flashed across the screen didn't alter Tommy's heartbeat in the slightest. The image that *did* spike Tommy's heartbeat was the ugly, obese, pockmarked face of Puff.

"This evening in Chicago, John 'Puff' Conducci and Francis 'The Smelt' Frantupo were arraigned in a Federal Courtroom on five counts of racketeering stemming from a basketball point-fixing scheme," Edwina Yonk said in a frantic, muffled voice as though she and the microphone had a secret to be shared only reluctantly.

The mug shot of Puff's pock-marked face went from bad to worse when the camera did a close-up of the West Virginia birthmark showing a boil where Charleston ought to be. The left profile shot of The Smelt was even more alarming. The Smelt's angry scar would make a tough guy puke. The front shot wasn't much better. The Smelt's hate-filled eyes bored into the camera lens.

"An FBI sting netted the Frantupo Syndicate using evidence supplied by college basketball players paid to shave points in a plea deal that turned them to state witnesses," Edwina said. "Three similar counts . . . ."

Igor's image flashed onto the screen. Igor's New Mexico trip had taken a toll on him. Most of the stitched cuts on his face were as straight as an arrow, on account of the edges of the metal folding chair used by Raul to batter him. His nose pointed in a new direction, and his swollen eyes were six shades of purple. He stared straight ahead with the same Vladimir Putin eyes, but with more reason for their absence of humanity.

The men who wanted Tommy dead were going to prison. The Polo-spa rinse cycle was complete and Tommy was well into the warm air drying phase when his picture appeared on the TV screen along with eight other plea-deal witnesses. It was a moment to remember, a cushion of hot air swirling around his lower parts at the same time his upmost part was being broadcast to the nation.

Tommy's running days were over. He committed to staying in Polo to earn Lori's trust by working at the best job he could get. He promised to shun shortcuts in return for the restoration of his optimism and his respect for virtue, birthrights of his Southern heritage.

Then a letter postmarked in Switzerland arrived.

———— «(●)» ————

Dear Tommy,

I am writing as a friend, because your lawyer has been unable to reach you. I got your address in care of Polo University through the efforts of the *Police Cantonale Vaudoise, Départment des ressources humaines.*

Mssr. Roux, the lawyer of your friend Rance, represented you in an action against the insurance company of the driver in the car crash that caused your injuries. A settlement has been reached and net proceeds of 104,000 CHF (about 111,000 USD) awarded to you have been placed in a *compte sèquestre* at the *Banque Cantonale de Vaudoise Sur* in Mies.

I have enclosed the card of Mssr. Roux at the firm of Laurent Müller, LLP in *Genève.* You may call Mssr. Roux to transfer the moneys.

I am sure you have very little memories of your times here in hospital. You and I worked together for many weeks to restore your normal functions. You often talked of being guilty and, in your words, "dicking up". I assure you that you are one of the kindest patients I have ever worked with. You could not hide your goodness from me, and you have no reason for feeling guilt.

Bien sincèrement, Docteur Sophia Arnaud

———— «(●)» ————

Tommy decided to say nothing about the money to Pop or Lori. His past encounters with large sums of money had brought him only momentary joy followed by long-term misery. He intended to tuck the money away in an account, perhaps for years. He didn't want money to pollute his fresh start with Lori. Perhaps, at some time in the future, the money would be a pleasant surprise for Mr. and Mrs. Tommy Gunn.

He said a prayer for the deceased Swiss girl. He had never faulted her for crashing the car. It was the work of chance. He had been kinder to her than he had been to himself. As for Sophie, he was more grateful for her kind words than he was for the money.

Chapter 51

SOMEBODY

TOMMY WAS AFRAID to open the envelope embossed with the imprimatur of the NCAA Division One Championships and Sports Management Cabinet, so he laid it on the kitchen table in quarantine as though it were hazardous material. Its bulk made it all the more intimidating. He reopened negotiations with God. He made extravagant offers to the Lord if He would spare Tommy from the bitter fruit of his misdeeds. How could God resist? His openers were to stop drinking hard liquor and beer, to stop using the Lord's name in vain, and to stop being bigger than his britches. Surely God would jump at the chance to extract these concessions. He asked the Lord for a sign. Almost immediately, Tommy's eyes fell on the envelope he had intended to drop in the offering plate with two-hundred dollars months ago. The empty envelope on the kitchen counter wasn't the sign he was hoping for.

Then Tommy pondered the situation from the Lord's

point of view. Thousands of victims had just died in Bangladeshi flooding. Two thousand lives had been snuffed out by Indonesian quakes. Millions of poor souls were suffering from hunger in China, Sudan, Pakistan, and Syria: why would God give a diddly about Tommy Gunn? From God's omnipotent, omniscient point of view, Tommy was an insignificant speck of plasma doomed to live in shame, dishonor, and regret. The pain in Tommy's heart was the sum of every hurt he had ever endured.

Lori burst into the kitchen and hugged Tommy.

"What's wrong?" she asked breathlessly.

Pop arrived seconds later, surprised to find Lori there and Tommy awake from his nightshift nap.

"What's wrong?" Pop asked.

Tommy pointed at the NCAA envelope. "I'm really done this time," he said.

"Before you go running in front of a bus," Pop said, "d'you think you ought to open it?"

Lori gave Tommy a table knife, which he used to slit the envelope rather than his throat. He gave the opened envelope to Lori.

"I can't bear to read it," he said.

Lori opened the envelope and began reading. Lori was a good soldier. She didn't break down into tears and she didn't wail a primeval lament. Just the opposite: she controlled her emotions with amazing composure. Then, Lori smiled. She grabbed Tommy with both arms and squeezed him tighter than she ever had before. Pop squirmed as the inexplicable kissing session intensified because he didn't covet the role of voyeur.

"I take it you ain't gonna fry in the 'lectric chair."

Lori and Tommy rocked in one another's arms.

"What's that letter say?" Pop asked.

"What *does* the letter say?" Tommy asked Lori.

Lori caught her breath. "It says the NCAA has overturned the championship game. Brut has to forfeit the game because of a cheating scandal."

Tommy staggered toward a kitchen chair to lean on. Pop's mouth fell open.

"Kentucky Barber is the national champion!"

Tommy grabbed onto Pop who was ready to career around the kitchen with joy.

"Hala-friggin'-louya!" Pop exclaimed.

Tommy's mind was racing. Was the deal with God legally binding? The letter had already been written when he had made the deal to be a teetotaler. It was a legal and theological quagmire.

———◄(◦)►———

The room was dark except for light from an open door. Tommy started awake, jerking as if he were falling. Pop was standing over him, gently shaking his shoulder.

"Wake up for your shift, Tommy."

Pleasure faded from Tommy's face as he realized the letter was a fantasy, a concoction invented by regret and the universal human appetite for do-overs.

"I dreamed that the Cutters won the championship,

that they overturned . . . ."

"Big difference between dreaming and living," Pop said. "Come on, Lori's got dinner waitin'."

Tommy slipped out of bed and followed Pop to the kitchen. On Lori's finger was the *golde* ring that once had belonged to Tommy's mother.

"Hungry?" Lori asked.

"Always," Tommy said. "I was dreaming that they overturned the Brut game and we won the championship and I was really somebody."

"Winning a game doesn't make you somebody," Lori said. "I've told you that before."

Pop tossed in his opinion: "All this time you been shortcuttin' and name-changin' and bustin' your ass to be somebody. Me and Lori *knowed* a long time ago, you been somebody all along."

"And. Pop," Tommy said, "all this time you've been tormenting yourself about not telling your son that you loved him. You didn't have to tell him, Pop, he already knew."

"How do you know?" Pop asked.

"Because I've always known you love me and you never told me diddly-squat."

Lori wrapped her arms around Tommy and Pop. "Give me a kiss," she said. Tommy kissed her. "You too, Pop." Pop pecked Lori on the cheek.

"When it comes to lovin' your grandson, I reckon I do," Pop said. "And I love you, too, Lori Tolliver. Reckon we got ourselves a breakthrough."

Lori wasn't married to Tommy and Pop wasn't in

Kentucky and Tommy wasn't a famous coach, either, but none of them wanted to be anywhere else at that moment. Despite all the ups, downs, false starts, bad ideas, setbacks, and failures, Tommy's convoluted journey had gotten him pretty close to where he needed to be.

Tommy Gunn had been saved.

DEDICATION

Coach Ralph Tasker, 1919 - 1999, Hobbs High School, Hobbs, New Mexico, Won 1,122 – Lost 291. Coach Tasker won twelve New Mexico State Championships, eleven of them at Hobbs High School. One of his Hobbs teams averaged 114.6 points per game. Coach Russ Gilmore succeeded Coach Tasker at Hobbs and went on to win five additional state championships.

Coach Robert Hughes, 1928 – present, Dunbar High School, Fort Worth, Texas, Won 1,333 – Lost 264. Coach Hughes won five Texas State Championships, two of them at Dunbar High School. His son, Robert Hughes Jr. followed in his footsteps at Dunbar.

Coach Morgan Wootten, 1931 – present, DeMatha Catholic High School, Hyattsville, Maryland, 1,271 Wins – 192 Losses. Coach Wootten won twenty-two District of Columbia Championships and five Catholic High School National Championships. His son Joe is a successful high school coach in Virginia.

CPSIA information can be obtained at www.ICGtesting.com
Printed in the USA
BVOW11s0935250915

419634BV00002B/3/P